BT starts 15 May.
My stat 23 May.

SEAHURST

SALLY HARRIS writes as S. A. Harris, and her first
novel, *Haverscroft*, was published by Salt Publishing
in 2019. *Haverscroft* was a *Den of Geek* Top Ten Read
2019 and a *Prima Magazine* Halloween read 2020.

She was runner-up in the Brixton Bookjam Debut Novelist
Competition and won the Retreat West Crime Writer
Competition 2018. She was shortlisted for The Fresher
Prize First 500 Words of a Novel Competition and
published in their anthology, *Monsters*, in November 2018.

Sally was born in Suffolk and lives with her
husband and children in Norwich, Norfolk,
where she works as a family law solicitor.

ALSO BY S. A. HARRIS

NOVELS
Haverscroft

S. A. HARRIS

SEAHURST

CROMER

PUBLISHED BY SALT PUBLISHING 2023

2 4 6 8 10 9 7 5 3 1

Copyright © S. A. Harris 2023

S. A. Harris has asserted her right under the Copyright, Designs and
Patents Act 1988 to be identified as the author of this work.

First published in Great Britain in 2023 by
Salt Publishing Ltd
12 Norwich Road, Cromer, Norfolk NR27 0AX United Kingdom

www.saltpublishing.com

Salt Publishing Limited Reg. No. 5293401

A CIP catalogue record for this book is available from the British Library

ISBN 978 1 78463 271 7 (Paperback edition)
ISBN 978 1 78463 272 4 (Electronic edition)

Typeset in Neacademia by Salt Publishing

Printed and bound in Great Britain by Clays Ltd, Elcograf S.p.A

SEAHURST

THE SUFFOLK COAST,
JANUARY, 1286

THEY ARE COMING as she knew they would. Their voices slip beneath the heavy wooden door, spreading across the brick floor on frigid air to where she sits. Her body aches huddled about the sleeping child. No light from outside. No window to let her know if the dawn has come.

She had put the candle on the floor hours ago, now little more than pooling wax solidifying about a guttering flame. Her brother starts from fitful sleep, his narrow back pressed against the opposite wall. He stares at her through the smoking candlelight. Shadows scatter across the low vaulted ceiling, shifting along the walls to crowd all around them. He has heard them too; boots ringing in the corridor, raised voices calling to one another. Coming closer. Growing louder

The draught grows stronger, rushing at her between wood and brick. The flame flickers. Dies. And for a moment, there is absolute darkness. A blackness so pure she thinks she might let go of the infant, reach out and touch it. More voices; three, maybe four.

Light glimmers beneath the door. She looks at her brother, his tunic folds about long skinny limbs like those of the newborn lambs they raised last spring. His pale face seems to float towards her, his eyes great glazed moons above hollow cheeks. His stare is fixed. Vacant.

Please, God. Not now.

'Eli?' He cannot hear her fear. Cannot hear her at all. Boots scuff to a halt beyond the door. Too late. Nothing she can do. The light beneath the door is fractured by the feet of the men outside. A low voice. The rasp and snap of a bolt drawn back. A key, grinding. The bundle in her arms shifts and squirms.

'Billa?' The child's voice is slurred, soft with sleep.

'Hush now,' she says, pulling her sister closer.

The door swings open, and she raises her hand before her eyes, squinting. Three men step into the room. One has great chain loops hanging from his shoulder; another holds a lantern high above his head. They look at her, then at Eli laying on the floor, limbs twitching, his eyes open, unseeing. She struggles to her feet beneath the weight of the child. Her legs are numb from sitting for too long. The infant cries out, the bone rattle falling from folds of linen to the floor. Two of the men step towards her brother.

'Please!' They turn to her, startled by the shrillness of her tone. 'Don't hurt him,' she says, hating the pleading tone in her voice.

They grab the boy under both arms and drag him to his feet. His head lolls forward, his thin body convulses. She hastens towards them. The third man steps before her and grips her elbow. No need to be rough, she will not resist him. They all know how this plays out.

'Come quietly, for their sakes,' the man says, his words slow and calm. He looks her full in the face as the men drag her brother into the corridor. She scoops up the rattle and pushes it into the pudgy hand of her sister.

'Come,' he says, turning towards the door. He waits while she gathers herself. Her feet have grown dirty and cold. Where did she lose her shoes? They hadn't let her snatch up anything other than the linen to wrap around the child. He holds the lantern high as she hobbles into the passage, the cramp in her joints easing as she moves.

The cool air smells of damp stone, and she thinks of the Abbey, limestone arches curving to tall ceilings. If she had fled there . . . But there is no sanctuary, not for them. She tries to quicken her pace, but he holds her back.

'My brother needs me.'

He does not acknowledge her words, and she can contain herself no longer. The taut band beneath her ribs rises to her chest and into her throat. Fear wets her underarms and prickles her upper lip. She tries again to hasten, to reach the stone steps and the gash of cold daylight spilling down them. The roar of voices, shrill and angry, rises and falls, and she is thankful Eli will be lost to these people. They cannot harm him.

'Why in such a hurry?' he says as she strains against his hand. He is close enough for her to see the golden flecks in his grey eyes, smell his sour breath.

'You gave me your word,' she says. His gaze falls to the up-turned face of her sister as they reach the first step. He drops his hand, indicating for her to move ahead of him. 'When I am gone. You will help them? They have done nothing,' she says, her voice so low she wonders if he hears her.

The roar of the mob rises above them. He jerks his head towards the top of the flight. She hitches the child higher onto her hip; there are ten, maybe a dozen narrow stairs. Her courage dissolves, acid burning inside her empty belly like poison. The rhythm of her heart quickens with the crescendo of the crowd. His hand cups her elbow, urges her on. She puts out her foot, feels cold stone beneath the soles of her feet as she climbs.

She stops at the top of the flight in the arched stone entrance to the yard. All of them turn towards her, faces of neighbours and friends. The roar of the crowd dies as they see her. She searches their faces; friends she ran with, played with, learned to gut fish and skin rabbits with. The people who fed and clothed her, shared their hearth with her and a pew on Sunday. She raises her gaze beyond them to the Abbey soaring at their backs. The square hulk of the bell tower, black against a cold sky, streaked red. He has not come then, her accuser.

The crowd murmur as metal clinks. Her brother lays on the ground in front of the low round wall of a well. He is still now, face pale and dazed as the men wrap chains around his waist.

'No!' she screams, running forwards. The man at her back takes her arm roughly, jerking her backwards. They cross the chains over his chest, turn the boy on his side and coil them about his neck.

'You swore!' she spits her words into the face of the man gripping her arms. His eyes are dead things, no emotion, nothing at all. She twists and kicks out, but cannot free herself from him. The child cries and puts up small arms, flinging the rattle that rolls across the cobbled ground towards the feet of the crowd. *Click-clack, click-clack.* People draw back hissing, 'Witch!'

She holds her sister towards the man as the other two men approach, chain swinging between them. The man is motionless, his arms crossed over his chest. *How did I let myself believe you?* She turns to the crowd, the familiar faces.

'Will you not help?' She holds the infant out before her,

4

arms aching. 'She is not yet two summers.' She holds the gaze of the midwife. The woman ducks her head and turns away, weaving between the onlookers packed into the yard.

The men are beside her, the chain about her waist and ribs now. They wrap it about her skirts and ankles. Her mind goes numb, all of her shaking. She pulls the child close, rocks her. Strokes her silken hair. *Mama, how did you bear this?* She closes her eyes. *Help me do this for Issy and Eli.*

The weight of the chains presses down on her body. The crowd grows silent. She hears only the heavy breathing of the men as they work and the *caw caw* of the crows high up in the tower.

The men leave her, she hears their boots crossing the yard. They pant with effort, the crowd stirring, voices calling out. Words she cannot make out. She must see him, one last time. *Eli.*

The three men hold her brother upturned by his feet and ankles, his head just visible above the lip of the wall. The clear blue gaze of her younger brother, whose body would curl into hers in the dark of a cold winter's night, finds her across the filth of the yard. She tries to curve her lips, but cannot make herself smile this last time.

The crowd roar as the men release their burden and step back from the well. A silent scream goes off inside her. She shakes violently, her teeth chattering. They turn to her; she is ready. Anger flares inside her. She pulls herself to her full height, lets her gaze linger across the faces of the crowd.

'As God is my oath, I curse you. May you perish by water, and this town fall prey to the mighty North Sea.'

CHAPTER ONE

TORONTO AIRPORT, 26TH
DECEMBER, PRESENT DAY.

I PULL TO a halt beneath the departure board, drop the suitcase at my feet and scan the list of international flights.

'That's ours, Mom. The gate's up already!' Alfie stands just in front of me, jabbing his forefinger at the list of destinations. His dark hair is a mess. No time to sort it before we left, not that he's bothered anyway.

On-Time. Boarding, Gate 11.

'Let's get the bags checked in.' I shift my rucksack higher onto my shoulder as we wait for a gap to open up in the busy flow of passengers. I glance back past the floor-to-ceiling Christmas tree to the entrance doors, jammed open by the constant crush of travellers. Shoulders and hats sparkle with snow, the light flurries when we left the apartment turning to something steady. I scan the pale faces of people hurrying back and forth beneath the glare of fluorescent lighting – no sign of Seth.

I nudge Alfie forwards. 'Let's go.'

We merge into line behind a rowdy family of five, their trolley piled with enough luggage for a dozen people. The toes of my suede ankle boots are darkened and wet. Stupid to wear them; they're killing already. No chance I'll find my old scuffed black leather ones amongst all the stuff we jammed into the suitcase.

'I'll try and get hold of Uncle Luke again,' I say, struggling to drag the case behind me while hitting redial on my mobile. I should call Mum as well, but what's the point? There'll be hell to pay either way, and she'll be asleep by now.

'Come on, Mom!' Alfie bolts off, weaving between people milling about the concourse.

'Hey! Wait up, Alfie. We must stick together!' This suitcase is way too heavy to do anything but trundle along with the travellers massing towards the check-in desks. 'Alfie!' I crane my neck to see through the crowd. 'Alfie, wait!'

The man in front half-turns his head and looks back at me. I ignore his irritated frown and glance down at my mobile, the call connecting. I put the phone to my ear and try to cut out the background jingle-jangle of Christmas carols. An unfamiliar, distant dialling tone drones through several rings. *Pick up, Luke, pick up!*

What time is it in the UK – maybe he's out someplace or at his mother's – what does he do over Christmas and New Year? A family dash past me, shouting to each other, jostling agitated people out of their way. I jam the mobile to my ear and pull the case out of the stream of traffic. I must catch Luke before we board.

Across the sea of knitted bobble and ski hats, Alfie is stuck behind a dawdling party of school children. The tannoy trawls through half-a-dozen delayed flights to the US; I can hardly hear the ringtone through the blare of it – if only we could have left earlier, given ourselves more time. The ringtone stops, the line crackles to an automated voicemail – leave a name and number, he'll call right back.

'Luke, it's me. I've tried . . .'

8

'Evie?'

'Luke? Thank God! I've been trying to call you for over an hour. Did you get my email?'

'It's the early hours of the morning here! You're lucky I didn't have my mobile on silent. I'm reading it now. What made you change your mind?'

'Long story,' I grab hold of the case, give it a sharp tug and rejoin the flow of people. I need to catch up with Alfie. 'Is it okay if we still come over? Just me and Alfie.' The blare of carols drowns out the call as I pass under a speaker. 'Luke?'

'Still here – said I can't wait to meet Alfie.' Luke's voice and something else, jazz playing in the background cutting to the mellow tones of a late-night radio show host.

Flight number *** 4:07 to Heathrow now boarding at Gate 11.

'Say that again, Luke.'

'I'm so glad you're finally coming over.' I dodge between piles of ski and boot bags scattered across the walkway, surrounded by groups of milling, chattering teenagers. I catch a glimpse of Alfie up ahead. 'How long are you over for?'

'A week. Alfie's back to school on the 6th, so home before then, if that's okay?'

Luke's laugh is a deep undulating sound, so like Dad that, for an instant, I'm running up the cliff path to the Abbey ruins to meet him, my kite bobbing behind me on a scorching July evening.

'Stay as long as you want, both of you. Lou and the crowd can't wait to see you. No Seth?'

'The restaurant's busy until after New Year.' I jerk the suitcase behind me as I try to keep Alfie in sight. 'We can't both be away, not just now.' The case catches a crack in the floor. It twists my wrist, the rucksack slipping off my shoulder and down my arm. 'Jesus Christ!' I say as a woman swerves to one side and heads around me.

'You okay?' says Luke.

'Half of Toronto's travelling today, and Alfie's run ahead.'

'It'll be good just the two of you. It's pretty quiet here at this time of year. Not too much going on. I'll have to wait to meet Seth another time. Besides, there's stuff we need to sort out.'

'Stuff?' I say, picking up the case. Alfie's getting too far ahead.

'About the house . . . and Dad.'

'How do you mean?' A man steps sideways into my path, his broad back right in front of me. I jolt the case to a halt; he's oblivious to my presence. There's no way past him, bags and people everywhere. I can't concentrate on Luke's conversation and keep Alfie in sight at the same time.

'Things aren't as we thought. I'll let you go, Evie. We can talk once you're both here.'

'Great idea, it's manic right now, and we're short on time to check-in. You've got all the flight details?'

'I'll be at arrivals, big board with your name on it. You won't be able to miss me.'

'Don't forget,' I say, laughing.

'Very funny! See you in a few hours.'

The walkway opens out to a broader space lined with check-in desks. I weave between passengers, craning my neck for a glimpse of Alfie. Air Canada's stretch of red and white fill the wall along the left-hand side. Alfie will have gone to our desk to get in the queue. I pat the side pocket of my parka, feel the bulk of our passports as I hurry down the line scanning the destination boards. My mobile vibrates in my hand. I look at the screen, Seth's number again. I let it go to voicemail as I find our desk. Alfie's halfway down the queue, his dark hair falling in his eyes as he jumps up and down, waving madly.

'Mom!'

I ignore the muttering from the guy behind Alfie and lower the case to the floor. 'Don't rush off like that again, Alfie. We have to stick together until we board, all right?'

Alfie nods, watching the passenger in front of us boarding his bags. We should make the gate no problem if there's no delay at security.

'I'll call Maxwells,' I say, pressing the restaurant's number on my mobile.

'Call them after check-in!' Alfie's reaching for my mobile. I turn away and hear the call go through to voicemail. I leave a message about tomorrow's order. Let them know I'll call about next week's menus once we land in London and apologise twice for the lack of notice.

The man in front is done, Alfie's at the desk, putting the suitcase on the conveyor. He turns back, his eyes holding mine. I'll make things right for him once we get to Suffolk, have a proper Christmas and New Year. I pull the passports from my parka as Alfie loads the rest of our bags.

Within less than a minute, we're running across the concourse towards passport control. The queue presses between taped barriers, zig-zagging towards the overhead scanners. Boxing Day is far busier than I thought it would be.

'Do we have to wait in line?' Alfie's looking past passengers shuffling between the tape to the rows of conveyors.

'If we get the last call for the flight, I'll ask the security woman if we can go ahead.' Alfie sways one foot to the other, looking past people, assessing the speed of the queue.

'Stop stressing, Alfie. We're moving quickly. We might even have time to grab some food if you're hungry.'

Alfie came through to the kitchen this evening straight after Seth left for Maxwells, his first words, as ever, asking what was there to eat. Once he saw my laptop screen, the flight booking whirling and confirmed, he'd got dressed, packed and into the car in under fifteen minutes. Other than a stale bottle of water he found on the backseat, he'd had nothing since lunchtime. My mobile buzzes in my hand, a text on the screen:

Hurry up, you'll miss your flight.

I stare at the message; my stomach does the weird thing like I'm in an elevator dropping too fast. I glance about the concourse, scan the faces of the passengers hurrying past us. Seth can't be here?

'Can I have a burger then?'

'What?' I say, looking into Alfie's grinning face.

'A burger? Just this once, if there's time?' he's looking at me, his grin faltering. 'Is it Dad?' he says, looking down at the mobile.

'How?' I say. 'How can he know we're here and so fast?'

'Did you change your password like I said?' Alfie's eyes are wide as he stares into my face. I nod and look back at the message. I haven't used our joint account to pay for our flights or the car parking. I've used my credit card for everything.

'You have to be right. He hacks my emails, Alfie. It's the only way he could know.'

I look at my son as the line shuffles forward. 'Alfie?' I follow his gaze between the shoulders of passengers in front of us to the head of the queue. A guard checks boarding tickets and feeds passengers through to the security area. Beside her, just outside the taped barrier, stands Seth. His black puffer jacket is unzipped, the red cashmere scarf he bought himself for Christmas hanging loose at his neck. In his right hand, he's holding his mobile. My eyes meet his as my cheeks flood with heat. My phone buzzes in my hand. I don't bother to check the screen.

'What do we do?' Alfie is tugging my coat like he did when he was five years old, his focus still on Seth. I glance at my mobile, a second message on the screen.

You didn't say goodbye.

There are four missed calls from Seth's number; I can't have heard the last one in the commotion of checking the bags in. Alfie sees the screen.

'What do we do, Mom? We're still going, right?'

I'm nodding on autopilot. My mobile chimes – an incoming text.

Your mom's worried. Says you didn't say goodbye to her either.

Shit! I knew he'd speak to her, but he's onto all this so fast. I glance up, although I know I shouldn't catch his eye. Seth raises his right hand in a small wave, smiles again as he leans across the barrier, says something to the security guard as he points in our direction. Another text.

Are you okay? I'm worried about you, so's your mom.

I read the message, hardly register what he's saying.

'Mom?'

'Let me think, Alfie.' The line moves forward.

'We're going, right?'

I don't answer, just pull my scarf up over my chin and catch a glimpse of myself in the polished dark glass of the drug store we're filing past. I look like Alfie, eyes wide and glassy. I've piled on too much foundation. It gives my skin a ghostly pallor but thank God it's covered the bruise. There had been no time to shower; my hair, in dire need of a wash, is pulled back into a scrunchie. I smooth back a stray strand of blond hair, see it slink back across my forehead.

'I bet he put the tracker back on your phone. I'm checking mine for sure,' Alfie scrolls through the settings on his mobile.

My phone rings - Mum's number. I let it go to voicemail. There's nothing she'll say that'll help right now.

'He can't stop us going, can he, Mom?' The queue shuffles again, the woman behind us close at our backs. Alfie steps forward, looking back at me. I move to stand beside him. 'Mom?'

'I don't think so, Alfie.'

'You don't think so?' Alfie opens Google on his mobile, and I let him search. I did the same thing last night after everything calmed down. The engagement ring is still on my ring finger - why couldn't I take it off and leave it at the apartment? My mobile buzzes again.

We need to talk about Alfie.

There are two groups of travellers between Seth and us. The stout security guard is waving the first forward at the head of the queue. Seth's having a conversation with her. What the hell am I dealing with now? Alfie waves his mobile at me and hisses under his breath.

'He can stop me going, Mom, can't he?'

If I had Alfie's rage, his fierce temper, this would be a whole lot easier to handle.

'I checked out the regulations last night,' I say, keeping my eyes lowered, watching the heels of the woman's snow boots in front. If I look up now, Seth will be just a couple of metres beyond her. 'Dad probably doesn't know he can stop you.'

'What? Are you crazy, Mom? He'll know for sure!'

'We both go. I won't leave you behind.'

'You totally promise, right?'

I nod and squeeze his hand. 'I would never leave you behind.'

The couple in front follow the guard's directions, and we move to the head of the queue. Seth dives forwards, ruffles Alfie's hair, my son ducking, jerking his head to one side. Alfie hates that, he's been too old for it for years. Seth persists just to irritate the hell out of him.

Seth's gaze is on my face. He'll see my cheeks burning. I pull my scarf up over my chin and to my mouth. Seth's smile is smooth and confident. It must look like a romantic farewell in the sort of Hollywood movies I hate watching. He pulls me into a tight hug, his lips brushing hot against my face. I feel like a piece of rag, unable to find any strength to pull back. His grip tightens, his warm, damp breath whispering into my ear.

'Leave, and you'll be begging to come back before you know it.' He releases me and brushes my cheekbone with the back of his hand, my skin crawling beneath his touch.

'Excuse me, Ma'am?'

The guard indicates for us to move forward with a beckon of her fingers. Alfie rushes to the nearest empty scanner slinging his rucksack into a blue plastic tray.

'Got engaged yesterday,' Seth explains. The guard's smile is uninterested as she continues to wave me forward. 'Trying to persuade her to stay for New Year's.' Seth presses his lips into a flat smile.

The guard looks at Seth, then at me. 'What's it to be?' she says, glancing to where Alfie stands in front of the scanner. His coat and boots are thrown on top of his rucksack, the plastic tray moving along the conveyor. 'Do I call your kid back?'

'He can't go, Evie. Alfie stays here.'

'You can't look after him and Maxwells.'

'Your mom's helping out.' Seth's hand holds my elbow, steering me away from the queue.

The guard is calling Alfie back. She's not interested in us, only the long line of people she has to feed through to the departure lounge. Alfie's looking back at me, his face white and full of uncertainty. I've U-turned so many times . . .

'Let's go back to the apartment and talk this through sensibly. You can rebook the flights, and we can fly over together like we planned.'

'Luke's picking us up,' I say, my voice so quiet I barely hear myself over the hum of the airport. The guard ushers Alfie back from the security area. His eyes find mine, the deflated expression tears at my chest. I look away. The electronic ripple runs across the departure board. The information updates. The flight to Heathrow – Boarding. Last call to passengers.

'Our bags are all loaded,' says Alfie, a red flush now across his cheeks as he drops his rucksack at his feet.

'What's it to be, Evie? Your decision.' Seth smiles as we move further away from the queue. His grip on my elbow tightens.

'It's not Mom's call.'

Seth turns back to where Alfie stands. He's hugging his coat and boots to his chest, his socked feet either side of his rucksack.

'What did you say?' Seth smiles at Alfie, but the expression in his eyes makes me shudder.

'It's not Mom's call.' Alfie's eyes flick to me and back to Seth. 'It's mine.'

CHAPTER TWO

L OU HUNCHES OVER the steering wheel, focusing on the pothole-riddled track. I can't get over how great it is to see her after almost fifteen years. Rough grass scrapes the underbelly of the Beetle, wheels rocking into puddles spraying mud along the length of the car. I roll down the window and draw in a deep breath.

'What the hell are you doing?'

'I want to smell the sea,' I say, laughing at her outrage.

The woods are silent, black trunks twisting upwards into a dense, pressing mist; a sharp green scent beneath a soft shifting canopy. I've never seen them this way before. Earthy dampness threads through the cold air rushing across my face as I close my eyes, and I hear them, ever so faintly – waves crashing on shingle.

'Close the damned thing. You're freezing me half to death!'

I roll up the window. 'I don't remember you being such a wimp,' I say, laughing. I look at my mobile. 'Still nothing from Luke. I can't think where on earth he's got to.'

'No worries.' Lou throws a glance my way, smiling. 'Betty and me were so excited to pick you up.' She taps the flat of her hand on the steering wheel as I glance back at my phone. 'She actually started first time.'

I smile at her and stare out at the trees. There's nothing from Seth either, which is so weird it's starting to worry me. No way is he letting me come over here this easily. I look into the back of the car at the top of Alfie's head. Still on his phone. What the hell was he talking about at the airport? I turn back in my seat. Three missed calls from Mum. I should call her as soon as we get to Seahurst, but Seth will be grilling her for info for sure. Lou stamps on the brakes, my seatbelt snapping across my chest as rubbish from our petrol station takeaway shoots off the dash and into my lap.

'This track is worse than ever!' she says.

'I'm so sorry to drag you all the way out here, Lou!'

Despite what she says, I know my frantic call earlier caused a degree of chaos up here as arrangements were hurriedly made to meet up at Saxmundham station. I should have thought to grab a cab. The Beetle hits a rut and jolts sideways.

'Shit!'

'Alfie!' I twist in my seat to glare at my son crushed between shopping bags and our suitcase on the narrow back seat.

'That messed up the level!' Alfie doesn't look up from his mobile, his thumbs working furiously against the screen.

'Come off your phone. We're almost there.' I watch the top of my son's head, but there's no response. 'We'll see the sea any second.'

He's hardly said two words since we made it onto the plane. He's never been like this. Has Seth been messaging him instead of me? It would make sense – I need to ask him again what the hell is going on once Lou's dropped us at the house. I turn back in my seat and gaze out of the passenger window. I remember the track dropped down here; gnarled tree roots writhing like ancient limbs through banks as high as the window, ivy smothering everything it touches. Mum's three voicemails are increasingly short-tempered, but what's Seth up to? It's totally unlike him not to spam-call and text.

'I can't get over you still driving this old thing,' I say, aware I'm all but ignoring Lou when she's gone to so much trouble to pick us up.

'We usually leave her tucked up in her garage, lovely as she is; reliability isn't her thing.' Lou's knuckles are white. The dark red lipstick, eyeliner and black mascara had taken me straight back to the last few summers here as we hugged outside the train station earlier. 'I'm a bit worried I won't get her back up here once I've dropped you two off.'

'She'll be happier going uphill so long as you take it steady.' The track sinks lower, bullied on either side by bracken and bramble. It narrows to a single-vehicle width; Lou constantly on the brakes. 'Do you want me to drive?'

'In those smart boots? What the hell happened to dog-eared sneakers and bare feet?'

'I guess we all grew up,' I say, as the lane turns left then right, the trees thinning as the track widens out to undulating heathland dotted with rabbit holes. 'Can you believe we're thirty-two? Luke will be forty next year.'

'He's practically a fossil,' she says, laughing. 'Maybe he's had to dash off to Essex.'

'Surely he doesn't still dance to his mother's tune?'

He had seemed so clear on the phone about meeting us at the airport. I feel edgy about it; the radio silence seems so strange. I've called him a dozen times since we landed. Maybe I'm just tired; Lou seems chilled about it.

'At least she won't be visiting here. Wouldn't that be difficult, you and Nicola Symonds in the same room?'

Lou winks at me and grins just as she used to when she
had mischief in mind – I'm so relieved she hasn't changed, but
I can't blame Nicola. Mum and Dad's affair must have hit her
like a shit-storm.

'I'll drop you and run, if that's okay. I've got this top chef
coming over for dinner later and need to get sorted.'

'Who would that be then?' I say, returning her grin. 'You
know an omelette is just fine? Seriously, I see far too much
fine dining.'

The bracken and gorse are sparse now. Course tufted grass
clinging to rough sandy ground, and the sea: choppy water
flecked with white horses as far as the blurred horizon.

'Alfie, look!' I sit forward in my seat, the belt tight across
my chest. I glance into the back of the car, into the angry, red
face of my son.

'I've only got one bar, Mom!'

If Lou weren't here, I suspect he'd tell me how much time
he's lost on his damned game – inevitably, it'll somehow be
all my fault.

'Come off the phone!' I snap.

I turn back to the front of the car as Lou gathers a little
more speed. 'Sorry, he's not usually so rude.'

'The signal is patchy around here. It might be better once
we're away from the trees.' Lou glances at me, her eyebrows
raised. 'Don't worry about it. It's been raining for days – the
mist is lifting a bit, the weather knackers the signal.'

'We're both tired and hungry; a bad combination.' I lean
towards the narrow windscreen. 'I'd forgotten how massive
the skies are here.'

The wipers smear the glass as I watch the sweeping bend

uncurling in front of the car. My heart quickens, and I realise I'm holding my breath. We round the bend, and the fern and gorse peter out to an open, flat landscape sloping to the cliff edge.

Seahurst has its back to the woods, sky and clouds reflecting off the face of the rectangular glass and steel building as it stares out across the sea to the horizon. Luke must be home; the kitchen and sitting areas are lit. Way up above Seahurst's flat roof, the Abbey ruins are wreathed in thinning white mist on top of the rise.

'Luke told me about the tower,' I say, staring up at the ruins as they fade in and out of view.

'Still can't get used to it. I always knew from the beach where your dad's place was when we saw the tower, just the arch left now.'

'Where did the tower go?' says Alfie.

'There was a huge storm about eight or nine years ago. The tower was a ruin, right on the cliffs' edge, it got washed into the sea,' I say.

'No way!' I glance back at Alfie. His mobile lies dead in his lap. Hopefully, we can forget about that for a while.

'It land-slipped onto the beach, the council had to bulldoze it away, but your mum's version sounds so much better.'

'We can go for a walk on the beach once we're unpacked, if you like,' I say. 'We'll need to do something to keep ourselves awake until dinnertime.'

'Mum can show you where the skeletons from the graveyard hang out of the cliff face.'

'Is she for real?'

I laugh at the enthusiasm in Alfie's voice and pull a horrified face at Lou. 'There's nothing there now – at least, I hope not.'

'The papers were full of it at the time, but they reburied the bones in St James' church.' Lou glances at Alfie in the rearview mirror. 'We passed the church before we drove through the village.'

'Can we go there?'

'The church?' I stare straight ahead at the brightly lit building. 'If you want to, but there'll be nothing much to see.'

Luke had mentioned his concerns about the eroding cliffs. One of his pet subjects, along with nagging me to visit. It's hard to judge, but there must still be at least thirty feet between the house and the cliffs. Hardly an imminent threat, surely?

'Where does the archway go?' Alfie's voice is loud in my ear as he leans forward between the front seats. I look up and see it clearly as the mist retreats inland.

'Nowhere, not any more,' says Lou. 'Just fresh air and saltwater if you take a walk through there now.'

A black 4×4 is parked at an angle to the slate path leading to Seahurst's glazed front door. The Beetle crunches across the gravel apron as Lou parks alongside it.

'Luke must be home. This is his Jeep,' she says.

Freezing damp air floods into the car as Lou throws open the driver's door and jumps out of the vehicle. Alfie pushes her seat forward and is outside in an instant.

'Hey! Take your . . .'

The door slams and Alfie runs past the car holding his mobile out in front of him, the camera presumably still working. I pull my beanie hat over my ears and zip my parka to my throat. Wind yanks the door lever from my fingers, flinging it back on its hinges as I step out of the car.

'He's keen all of a sudden then,' says Lou raising her eyebrows. 'Let's go and find out what's been keeping your brother all this time.'

'I'll grab the rucksacks,' I say.

Lou dashes between puddles heading for the slate front path, her long dark hair swirling about her head. Alfie waits for her, his arms wrapped about his waist, his hoody pulled low against the mizzling rain. He's looking up at the glass box of a building. Dad's last big project, never quite finished. He would have been so excited to show his grandson around.

The stiff offshore wind snatches my breath from me, and I clutch my scarf tight at my throat. Some summer days here could be chilly, but this is something else. I drag my parka hood over my beanie, slam the car door and walk to the post-and-wire fence that skirts the cliff edge. I've dreamt of standing here so many times. Now here it is, the North Sea beneath the weight of a vast December sky. The land slopes steeply away, tilting towards the sea, the cliff edge a jagged line dissolving into the ozone. I press my knees against the soft, rotting stump of the fence and dig my hands deeper into my pockets. Sea spray feathers my face as I suck in a lungful of damp, salt air. The beach is hidden beneath the overhanging cliffs. The tide must be in; the roar of the waves ebbs and flows to the rhythm of the wind. The thought of the drop makes me dizzy. I take a step back. It was so right to come here - we should have come sooner, much, much sooner than this.

I'm shivering after roasting in the dry air of the Beetle's rattling old heater, and my parka is far from windproof. I can stand here as long as I like tomorrow and for the next few days. I head back to the car, open the boot and drag out our rucksacks. The suitcase was a nightmare to get onto the back seat and needs two of us to haul it free. I shift my backpack onto my shoulder and carry Alfie's under my arm.

Seahurst glows as the day fades. Luke has every light on in the place, bright slats cutting across the dark ground. I can make out the square units of the kitchen, but the reflection of the clouds drifting like ghosts across the face of the glass makes it difficult to see much else. I put my head down against the wind and pick my way along the slippery slate path. The security lights that winked on as Alfie and Lou ran up the path blaze at me, rain tumbling through the white beams like shards of shattering glass.

The front door is open, water driving across the threshold and pale wood floor. The rubber-boot mat is awash, the black and white woven runner beyond it looks soaked. Alfie dashes to the door and stops just in front of me. He glances back over his shoulder to where Lou stands beside one of the oversized sofas.

'What's up?' I say.

My son looks at me, his expression uncertain.

'Evie?' Lou looks back at me, an urgency in her tone.

I step past Alfie, the door sliding shut behind me with a soft thunk. I drop his rucksack on the floor and walk to where Lou stands. The room is so familiar but different in a way I can't immediately put my finger on. There's a mustiness, an old, closed-off smell.

'The door was wide open,' Lou says. 'Rain has to have been coming in for hours.' I stare dumbly back at her. 'I nipped downstairs, the place is empty. No one's home.'

CHAPTER THREE

THE GREY GRANITE countertops gleam beneath halogen spots at Lou's back as she stares at me.

'It's bloody weird he's not here, Lou. Should I be concerned or pissed off?'

After all these months of nagging us to come over, promising to pick us up at Heathrow . . .

I drop my rucksack onto the brown leather seat of the nearest of the two sofas. Dad's coffee table is in the space between them. On its glass top is a half-drunk mug of tea, a plate scattered with crumbs and a laptop.

Beyond the sofas is an open area. There is a wood burner and its tall metal flue rises to the ceiling set opposite the spiral stairs; chrome and leather loungers face the rise to the cliffs.

'There's a lot of square furniture,' Alfie says.

'Don't you like it?' I'm suddenly aware of how much it matters that Dad's grandson approves of this place.

'What's down there?' Alfie walks towards the metal banister that curves down to the lower ground floor.

'The bathroom, bedrooms, we'll go and find where we're sleeping in a minute.' I cross the space to stand beside him, hold onto the rail and look down the spiral stairs.

'Hello? Luke?' My voice echoes into the brightly lit corridor below. Silence. Alfie moves away, taking in the oversized TV opposite the sofas. A Luke addition. It's fixed to the metal girder rising above the old flint and brick wall jutting just above ground level. He glances back to where I stand beside Lou and grins.

'There's an Xbox.'

'Thank goodness for small blessings,' I say, feeling more grateful than I should that my brother wastes his time on such stuff. 'I'm sure Uncle Luke won't mind you taking a look.'

Lou glances about the room. Dusk gathers outside, light rebounding off the glass, the restless, crowding trees lining up along the back wall. I look up at the slab of stone recycled from the Abby ruins. Sunk into the chimney breast above the wood burner, the crude daisy wheel carving cut into the stone was Dad's pride and joy. Lou walks away from me, passing the sofas, and points out the ruins at the top of the steep rise to Alfie.

I leave them chatting and wander to the kitchen. Wind sweeps rain across the face of the triple-layered glass, the cliffs, sea and sky bleeding into each other. On the floor, a dozen or more carrier bags sag in front of the kitchen cupboards. Another bag is in the sink, the tap dripping water onto the plastic. I turn off the tap, stand in front of the induction hob and stare outside. Dad's sunken garden looks neglected and bare, more gravel and slate than the sea holly and lavender that used to be there. Lou's hand on my shoulder makes me jump.

'I'm sorry, are you okay?'

'Fine,' I say. There's concern in her hazel eyes, so I smile. 'Your dad used to sit in the garden with mine, do you remember?'

'Putting the world to rights over a few beers while we got up to God knows what.'

I smile again, and she turns away. The pull of sadness feels overwhelming. It's almost fifteen years since Dad's suicide, but even so, coming back is harder than I thought it would be.

'Still like the Tardis, isn't it?' Lou's looking across the room to where Alfie stands, pointing the remote at the black TV screen. 'All a bit faded now, though.'

I run my fingers over the cold surface of the hob.

'The kitchen's pretty much the same. The leather on the sofas could do with a stain and polish.'

I pull out my phone and look at the screen. More messages from Mum. Silence from Seth. Nothing from Luke. I press redial on my brother's number, then cut it off as it goes straight to voicemail. I've left enough messages already today.

'Maybe Luke hasn't been gone as long as we think. He's not like your dad, that's for sure.' I look at Lou, I don't get what she's saying. 'He always had the place locked, didn't he?'

'He was a bit hot on security, but no one's been in. That laptop would be the first thing they'd take,' I say.

'There's a hell of a lot of water on the floor, Evie. That didn't happen in five minutes.' She holds my gaze for a moment then continues, 'I've loads to do for dinner tonight, but I can help you find a bucket and mop and get the worst of it cleared up, if you like.'

'You get off, Lou. Like I said, just an omelette would be great.'

I want her to stay, but she's anxious about getting Betty to the main road, and we've already ambushed her day. I've so wanted to come back here, but nothing feels right. I pull off my beanie and run my fingers through my hair. I've never arrived without Dad or Luke being here. Winter is so different from summer. I hadn't given it a thought; how strange it would feel. The light is already grainy, fading as dark clouds throw shadows across the bleached floorboards.

'It feels like a time shift,' I say, as much to myself as to Lou. The TV blares, and I jump again. I need to eat and sleep.

'Sorry!' says Alfie, pressing buttons madly to kill the volume.

'He's got food in at least,' says Lou. 'I guess he's still expecting you.' Lou crouches on the floor with her back to me and starts delving into the nearest bag. 'This stuff needs putting away, Evie. Something's leaking everywhere.' Lou holds up one of the bags, a string of pale liquid dribbles from it. She puts her hand under it and dumps it in the sink. 'The lid has popped off a tub of ice cream,' she says as we look at a gloopy pink lump oozing from beneath the bag. 'This stuff has been here for hours. What the hell's your brother playing at?' Lou piles packets of ham, bread and a sweating block of cheddar onto the counter. 'At least the underfloor heating doesn't seem to have been on, although you might want to look at that, Evie, warm the place up a bit.'

A small metal dish is on the counter beside the sink. Lou follows my gaze to a wallet and bunch of keys.

'No mobile. I guess he has that with him,' I say. 'Just wish he'd bloody well answer my calls!'

Lou is back to emptying bags: eggs, packets of rice and pasta, milk. A packet of peppermint tea. 'Like I said, the signal's crap around here, no point taking it half the time.'

Beneath the metal dish is a long receipt, I pull it free and look past the list of items to the very bottom. 'He picked this lot up this morning,' I say. 'So, where's he gone, Lou, without his wallet and keys?'

'I'd say that's the big question, wouldn't you?'

'Should I call the police?'

'That's a bit of an overreaction, Evie. It isn't like it's the first time he's gone AWOL, is it?' Lou holds a pack of kitchen rolls in her hands as I stare back at her.

'That was years ago!' The arguments with Dad, Luke taking

off without a word. No idea if he planned on coming back.

'He won't have gone far, not in this weather.' She pauses for a moment and starts to rip the plastic off the kitchen rolls. 'He often goes walking for miles, tramps all the way up to Covehithe and back sometimes. You know he's taken up running?'

'Running?'

'Along the clifftops and back along the beach. Dad sees him sometimes when he's heading home after a night fishing.'

'I didn't know Luke ran,' I say, astonished.

'He told Dad he'd give you a run for your money when you got here. He's probably getting in some last-minute training.'

I must have talked about it at some point when we Skyped; how my run to and from the restaurant keeps me sane, clears my head.

Lou holds up a half-empty bag and shakes it.

'Sorry, let me give you a hand.'

'I'll finish unloading. You find a bin-bag and sort that out.' Lou's eyeing the messy carrier bag and sticky ice cream carton in the sink. 'Run the tap for a bit. It might clear the smell.'

'What smell?' I slip off my engagement ring and drop it into the saucer with Luke's wallet. 'All I'm getting is ice cream. We met over a dripping pink ice cream, do you remember?' I say.

'In the beach car park with the boys and the kite.'

There's laughter in her tone as I pick up soggy cardboard. I try the cold tap, but it's stuck. I twist it hard, and water splashes into the sink, spraying up the front of my parka.

'Steady on!' Lou's laughing, shaking her head as she moves things around to make space in the fridge. 'It must need a new washer.'

I turn the flow of water down and watch it pull the pink

sticky mess into the plughole. 'I was just thinking, that boy with the kite you liked worked out pretty well, didn't it?'

She's smiling, her skin pale beneath the halogen lights. 'Can we save the reminiscing until dinner?' She stops suddenly, looks at an egg carton and the large slab of cheddar. 'You're not vegetarian, are you?'

'Alfie is,' I say, keeping my voice level as horror creeps across her face. 'I've been vegan for a while now.'

She stares at me, her eyes searching my face. 'A chef, vegan? Shit!'

My lips tremble, a smile forcing through.

'No, you're not!'

She laughs, snatching up a kitchen roll, and I duck as she swings it at my head.

'No!' Alfie tears towards us, the TV remote held high above his head. He grabs the roll from Lou. 'What are you doing?'

'Hey?' I say. 'It's fine. We're just messing about.'

Lou looks astonished, staring at Alfie as if he's gone insane. Alfie turns to me, his face scrunched into a frown, his eyes bright.

'Really, it's okay.' I reach for the roll and gently pull it from him.

'Have you got the Xbox working?'

Alfie shakes his head. With a side glance at Lou, he heads back across the room, picks up a controller from the low table and sits down in one of the chrome and leather armchairs in front of the screen.

'Let's get this done so you can head off,' I say, moving swiftly between the fridge and cupboards, worried that Lou would somehow know about the bruise, although Alfie would say if anything started to show. I'll have to tell her, but now's not the time. 'There are plenty of logs in the rack below the wood burner. I'll have a go at lighting it once you head home. It'll cheer the place up no end.'

'That's it, I think.' Lou scrunches the last of the orange carrier bags between her hands. 'It's so good you've come back, Evie. Tonight will be perfect, you'll see.'

She's staring at me again, just like she did at the station. I can't quite make out her expression.

'Shall we get the case in then?' I say.

Lou drops the carrier onto the counter, and I follow her to the door. She's right, there is a ridiculous amount of water here. I pull up my hood and run after Lou, security lights popping on as we head for the car. It can't be much after 3:30 pm, and it's getting dark already.

'It's a shame the weather's like this,' Lou shouts above the wind as she pulls the driver's door open. 'We've had three solid days of it now.'

Between us, we wrestle the suitcase off the back seat and out of the car.

'You go, Lou. I can manage it from here.'

She nods, her hand holding her dark hair off her face. The Jeep is behind her. I reach out and pull the driver's door handle. Locked. Something is on the back seat. I peer through the wet glass, Lou right beside me. The brown cardboard placard looks like it's been cut off the side of a large box and is about a metre square. The capital letters are written in black marker pen.

'WELCOME HOME!'

'Maybe he mixed up the days?' Lou says. I think this whole thing might be starting to bother her too.

'He had just woken up when I called him.'

'He'll probably show up any time now,' Lou says as we hug tightly. I wish I was ten years old again and could beg her to stay. She lowers herself into the driver's seat of the Beetle. 'Sure, you'll be okay?' She looks at Seahurst as she speaks, uncertainty in her tone. Lights blaze behind the glass, Alfie standing in front of the TV, the Xbox logo filling the screen. 'We'll be just fine. Drive carefully. We'll see you at dinner.'

CHAPTER FOUR

'I'VE BEEN WORRIED, sick, Evie. Whatever are you playing at?'

I let Mum vent, there's no point even trying to plead my case, she simply isn't capable of hearing it. I hold the mobile a little away from my head, her voice perfectly audible even though Alfie has a game on the console at full blast. I stare past Luke's Jeep as I hitch myself onto one of the kitchen barstools, rain sweeping like grey curtains across the surface of the sea.

'Is that right, Evie?'

I try to concentrate, but the jet lag kicked in as Lou left and now that we're finally here my eyes are heavy, fatigue leaching into my bones. 'What's that, Mum?'

'Are you even listening? Seth says you're engaged.' I bite my lip. I should've known this was coming. 'He says you're getting married, in July, planning on mentioning that, were you?'

'He proposed.'

'Well then, are you – getting married?'

'I'm thinking about it.'

'What's to think about? I thought you'd finally do the right thing. Stop this living together nonsense. Won't do when there's a child involved and you've the restaurant to think of.'

I glance across the room, Alfie is intent upon shooting as many zombies as he can in the shortest possible time. I should say something to Mum now before the moment passes, as it has so many times before.

'Seth's worried about you, worried you've been overdoing it . . .'

'Mum . . .'

'To be honest, so am I, Evie. I've got a great big turkey here that's only half-eaten. Your brother and sister were disappointed beyond belief that you and Alfie didn't come over Boxing Day. You ruined it for them.'

I doubt my step-siblings were in any way bothered that we didn't show up. Darren was likely delighted. I let my eyes follow the shadows rolling across the pale floor, rising up and darkening the sofa where Alfie sits.

'It's not normal to take off like that, Evie. Seth says Maxwells was in an uproar with you dumping your shift and to take Alfie without a word to anyone. He says he can get a court order, did he tell you that?'

My heart is thrumming against my chest, my throat tight. I can see where Seth is taking this, making it look like I snatched my own child.

'Seth was at the airport, Mum, did he say he'd spoken to us?'

I watch Alfie as Mum rattles on. He's wide awake again now and totally absorbed in the same grim game Seth has back home. What the hell did Seth and Alfie speak about at the airport? I was all ready to cave in and go back to the apartment: Alfie's red face as he stood in his socks, holding his boots and coat, was inscrutable, but I could see he was doing all the talking. Seth didn't look back at me once, just turned on his heel and strode away without so much as a word. No way is Alfie's tale of Seth just wanting him to ask 'nicely' to come with me ringing true.

'This obsession with your father, Evie, you need to accept these things happen and move on, stop trying to rationalise it. It's high time you saw him for what he was. I don't like to think of you in that goldfish bowl of a place. Have you seen anything of her?'

'Nicola Symonds?' I let the silence drag out. I can imagine the tendon in Mum's jaw twitching as she waits for a response, any mention of Dad's widow never fails to bug her. 'Why would I? You know as well as I do she doesn't come over to Seahurst. I must go, we need to unpack. I just wanted you to know we got here okay.'

'Seth wants to know when you're coming back – I assume you are coming back?' The sarcasm irritates the hell out of me, why does she insist on taking Seth's side every time?

'Of course, we're coming back, you both know this trip was planned. Seth just cancelled it like he always does. I've got open tickets for the return flights. We'll be back before Alfie's term starts.' For once there is silence at the end of the line. 'I'll let you know when our return dates are fixed.' I end the call and instantly feel bad about being so short with her.

The room is silent, only the rain drumming against the glass. Alfie's game is frozen on the screen, the volume on mute. He's at the top of the spiral stairs, but the way he's standing is all wrong. Too still. That's not right. His head cranes forward to see down the shaft of the stairs, the TV remote still in his hand.

'Alfie?'

He snatches a look my way, flaps his arm at me to be quiet and returns his attention to the stairwell. 'I heard a weird noise down there.' His voice is so low I only just catch what he's saying. I shift off the barstool and join him to look down the stairs. The triangular metal treads fall away to the corridor below, nothing to see but whitewashed stone walls and polished flagstone floor. My head starts to swim, and I take a step back.

'What did it sound like?'

'Shhh!' Alfie frowns, head cocked to one side.

'Just the wind, Alfie. It can sound quite eerie sometimes.' I put my arm around his shoulders. 'You'll get used to it.' He shrugs free and takes a half-step closer to the banister.

'I heard it twice, it's not the wind. I can't hear it now, you're making too much noise.' Alfie is more the grumpy teenager by the day.

'I can't hear anything, Alfie.' I brush past him and grab hold of the polished steel handrail. It curves away from me, curls around the pale wooden steps before descending into the gloom of the lower ground floor. I've snapped at Alfie and wish I hadn't - I shouldn't take the last 48 hours out on him.

'Houses all make weird sounds, like the ticking central heating back home. You just need to settle in.' Alfie doesn't respond and I can see from his expression he's not convinced. 'I'll check around. Then you can unpack while I fix us a snack.' My foot clangs on the first step. I've forgotten how much spring there is in the metal and wood. How loud a footfall rings in the empty corridor beneath here. I hesitate, take a firmer grip on the rail and look straight ahead.

'You okay, Mom?'

'Fine,' I say, irritated with myself. I've used these stairs countless times. I'll be okay if I don't look down.

'You should've checked around when Lou was still here.'

I glare at Alfie. 'Don't be silly, what could she do anyway?' Seahurst was empty as we drove down the track; Mum's not too far off the mark when she calls it 'the goldfish bowl'. We'd have seen anyone in here - unless they had been downstairs.

'Hello?' My voice rebounds back at me. Alfie has a point, it would have been good to scout around while Lou was here. 'Luke?' I move down the spiral, Alfie at my back. 'Stay there, let me take a look first.'

I can just manage to keep the arched opening to the corridor in sight out of the corner of my eye without having to look down. The up-lighters Dad installed where the walls meet a vaulted ceiling glare against the whitewashed stone walls. Why would Luke leave all the lights on if he was going out? Maybe Lou left them on. I hurry down the final few steps and look along the length of the passage. Alfie is a little way up the flight.

'What's in there?' Alfie's voice is a low hiss, his face pale and tired. He's had a long journey and a stressful few days. I muster a smile and hold out my hand. These days he usually ignores it, but he takes it now, his skin cool and soft against mine.

'Your grandfather's old room, I have no idea what's there now.' What has Luke turned the room into? A spare room, an office or, knowing my brother, a junk room? The door is closed, and I'm sure no sound came from inside, but my reluctance to go in there has nothing to do with Alfie's anxieties. The wind whistles, rises in pitch then falls away again.

'Is that it?' I laugh to lighten the mood.

Alfie shakes his head. His shoulder brushes against my arm, and he's gripping my hand a little too hard. I used to lie in bed and listen to the weird sounds at night, slinking beneath the covers and pulling the pillow over my head. Somehow though, it was always worse by day, when there was nothing here but an empty basement.

'It sometimes does that when the wind blows really hard.'

Alfie's looking at the door to Dad's room, all the other

doors down here are open, other than the new one at the far end of the corridor. It's strange to see it there; a blank wall before Luke knocked through to the garage.

'Shall we look in?' Alfie's eyes are round pools of concern. I'm going to have to look inside at some point so I might as well get it done. I step to the door and put my hand onto the metal handle. When Dad was working, when I'd been told not to disturb him, I'd press down gently and open the door soundlessly. Somehow, he always knew I was there, knew I crept beneath his duvet. In the morning, when I was still quite small, I'd find myself tucked up in my own room again with the light spilling through the glass bricks around the top of the wall. I press the handle hard, shove the door away from me.

Dad's desk, the bed, and wingback armchair are all still here. A book about Suffolk myths and legends is on the footstool in front of his chair. Dad's left torn pieces of coloured paper poking out from the top of it where he's marked different pages. It's his glasses, folded closed on top of the book as if he only just finished reading, that stops me breathing. If I run across the room and spin the chair to face me, he might still be sitting there, smiling up at me. The weight in the pit of my stomach is like someone poured a ton of concrete inside me. I'd assumed Luke would have cleared this years back: clothes, books, even the furniture perhaps to a local charity shop or a skip. Maybe he's struggled as much as I have after Dad? Alfie dips under my arm and rushes forward.

'This is crazy!' he says, laughing. He stops at the desk and glances back to where I stand in the doorway.

'State of the art when I was your age,' I say. My voice is thick, and I cough to clear my throat. Alfie's too absorbed looking over Dad's old iMac to notice. 'Don't touch it,' I say, sounding more like myself. And we hear it. A scraping sound as if someone is dragging something along the ground. I turn around and look back along the empty corridor.

'No way's that the wind.' Alfie is beside me in an instant.

I have to agree, definitely not the wind, but I can't place it, it makes me think of cardboard scuffing against concrete. It comes again, one prolonged sound.

'It sounds different now,' Alfie says, staring along the corridor.

Just beyond the stairs is Luke's room, the door is open, but the sound came from further away.

'Whatever it is comes from down there,' I say. The low vaulted ceilings form a tunnel to the stone staircase on the far wall. I look at Alfie. 'Do as I say and stay here while I check it out.'

I make my voice firm and calm, although my heart is racing. Luke told me he recently knocked through to the new garage as Dad had planned to do. The sound wasn't muffled though, so perhaps a bird or something had got in when the front door was left open and is trapped in my room or the bathroom.

I pass Luke's room, my feet sinking into the hollows in the flags. I loved the way the stones have worn with the traffic of people back and forth for hundreds of years. I stop at the bathroom door, push it wide open. On the opposite wall hangs the huge mirror. I had a love-hate relationship with that thing as a teenager, now I look startled as if seeing myself comes as a surprise. Jetlag isn't doing my skin any favours, dark channels beneath my eyes contrast with the rest of my pasty complexion, my jaw-length blond hair a ruffled mess from wearing my beanie hat for so many hours. The mirror reflects all of the room – a dark shape behind the door.

'Oh!' I say, stepping backwards, bumping into Alfie in my haste to move away from the room.

'What?' Alfie's fingers grip my arm, pressing through the fabric of my parka. I laugh and point to the mirror, a bathrobe reflected, hanging on a hook on the back of the door.

'Luke's robe made me jump.'

'For God's sake, Mom!' Alfie shakes his head like he's not nervous at all. 'He's a bit messy, isn't he?' he says, taking in the collection of coloured plastic bottles crowding by the wall of the walk-in shower.

'Thought I said to wait at the stairs?'

The glass shelf above the sink is packed with shaving foam, at least half a dozen old toothbrushes in a blue glass and a partly-eaten apple, the flesh darkly discoloured. Alfie looks at the toilet pan, then at me as he lowers the seat and lid.

'This room used to knock me out.' Alfie stares at me, his face questioning. 'I'd never seen a wet room before, and that shower-head is bigger than a dinner plate.'

'Really?' Alfie's tone is one of utter disbelief.

'It was very modern when your grandfather renovated Seahurst.'

He's taking in the low ceiling, the red brick arches in-filled with grey flint and mortar. He starts taking panoramic shots of the room - no need to send a postcard back home then. There's nothing in here that could explain what we heard - nothing loose to rattle, no window to bang. The extractor fan is a possibility, but it isn't even running right now. I look into the mirror, run my hand over my hair, my fingertips lightly skimming my cheekbone. Alfie watches me.

'You'll be all right now, yeh?'

'Just fine,' I say. Goodness knows what it'll look like when the make-up comes off, but it doesn't feel so tender now. I step towards the shower and stare at a thin orange stain crawling down the wall to the drain beneath the shower-head. The whole floor needs a thorough scrub.

'It smells funny.' Alfie is looking around as he speaks. 'Like someone's peed on the floor but worse.'

He's right, the musty smell is rank. Would it be coming from the grille beneath the washbasin? I hated that brick air-vent, and as I look at it now, nothing has changed. Anything could lurk behind those tiny black holes. Alfie wrinkles his nose, the smell seeming to get stronger the longer we stand here.

'I'll run the shower, maybe it's stagnant water trapped in the drain.' I leave the water running. Luke was coming up here after Christmas, if he hasn't been here for a while, it makes sense. 'Come on, let's finish checking around and get sorted before we go out tonight.'

'Do we have to go?' Alfie whines.

'Yes, we do!' I head back into the corridor, no way do I want a battle about going over to Lou's for dinner tonight. I don't have the energy for Alfie's antics right now. I'd like to find out what the hell this noise is though. The last thing I want is it happening tonight when we're trying to sleep.

'Why's the lock on the outside?'

I turn back. Alfie stands in the passage outside the bath-room looking up at the heavy wooden door.

'Who knows, Alfie. It's not been a bathroom that long though. That's the only original door left. Probably eight or nine hundred years old.'

'No way!' Out comes his phone again. More shots flash white light against the door and ceiling.

'That bolt hasn't budged in centuries and Dad certainly never had a key for the lock.' I leave Alfie taking photos. The garage door is next to my room, set in the end wall at the top of a flight of a dozen or so steps. 'If Uncle Luke's left the garage open, maybe a squirrel's got in or something? They can make a right racket,' I say, nipping up the steps and trying the door. Locked, no key here either.

I hurry down the steps and follow Alfie into my old room. The futon is still in the corner, pushed against the wall beneath the run of glass bricks. A camp bed Lou used for the occasional sleepover beside it. Both beds are freshly made up - mine has the old monochrome patterned duvet set I thought was so cool. Luke is clearly expecting us.

'Hey, look at this!' Alfie sounds excited, holding something towards me as he stands beside the dressing table.

I take the tiny camera from him and pop open the black leather case. 'My Dad gave me this for my eighteenth birthday.' I turn the Leica over in my hands; a beautiful thing and so typical of Dad.

'Does it still work then?'

'It'll work fine, but it takes 35mm film.' I point to the counter. 'I've taken thirteen shots out of thirty-six.'

'Take one now!'

I laugh. 'I doubt the film will be okay after all this time – probably can't get these developed either now.'

'Try it!'

'Stand beside the dressing table then. I'll do an arty shot and catch you in the mirror.'

Alfie takes up a pose, a big silly grin on his face, and I'm surprised how pleased I am that he's interested in this old stuff.

'The light's not great - but let's give it a go.'

Alfie leans his hip against the glass-topped table and folds his arms. I concentrate on focusing the shot - the snap of the shutter is a sharp sound in the quiet room.

'Stay there, I'll take a second one.' I wind the film on and refocus the shot. As I press the shutter, Alfie drops his silly grin to his usual broad smile, and I catch my breath. I lower the camera.

'You all right, Mom?'

'You looked the spit of your Uncle Luke for a second there.'

Alfie rolls his eyes and reaches for the camera.

'Smartphones were becoming all the rage. I'd wanted one to photograph my cooking, but Dad didn't get it – he thought a camera would be better,' I say. 'I wasn't great about it, to be honest.'

Dad's astonishment at my rant turned to anger. We bickered the whole of that last summer; the teenage me unknotting apron strings, but Dad had seemed stressed, snapping at the slightest thing.

The wind moans about the corner of the building, Alfie's head jerking around towards the sound. His eyes scan the length of the glass bricks as if something will burst through them at any second. Trees bend beneath the wind, black branches grazing the skin of the building.

'You don't notice it after a while,' I say. 'The wind is an everyday thing this close to the coast – it's probably what we heard earlier as there's nothing down here.'

Alfie looks at me as if I'm a crazy woman and doesn't return my smile. He moves away, looking about the room, pulling open the wardrobe door and heads towards the books stacked in the nook in the wall at the foot of the futon.

I put the camera back into its case. This film must be of my birthday party. The campfire on the beach just below Seahurst had glowed late into the night. I'd thought the shots would be good, red sparks riding on air currents, soaring beyond the clifftop as we climbed the narrow steps cut into the cliff face. Voices of partygoers loosened by alcohol and the end of the school term and exams had risen up around us, drifting past on salt air laced with the warm scent of gorse. We held hands when we reached the top and turned back on ourselves, walking towards the Abbey ruins. I remember laughing, warm lips on mine for an instant as we melted into the shadows and made our way to the arch.

'You've got so much stuff, Mom.'

I leave the camera on the table and slide the wardrobe door shut on clothes I'll neither look at nor wear again. Maybe now is a good time to ask him, no distractions to let him wriggle off the hook with excuses.

'What did you say to Dad at the airport?'

Alfie freezes for a moment, he knows we have to have a proper conversation about this. 'Why do you keep asking?'

'Because Nanna is furious and says Dad's getting a court order.'

Alfie's head snaps up, his wide eyes blink at me. 'You won't get into trouble, will you?'

I shrug. 'I don't know. I've not heard anything from Dad, which is totally weird.' Alfie continues to stare at me, and I see how scared he is. 'Has Dad contacted you?' He shakes his head. 'This "asking nicely" doesn't stack up, does it? What really happened?'

'I said I'd tell security about him if he didn't let us both go.' I stare at my son – wait for him to continue. 'He messed up this time, didn't he, you know . . .'

Alfie is looking at the side of my face, the bruise across my cheekbone under a layer of concealer. Usually, there's nothing to show, no evidence to make anyone believe a word I say. Seth had been drinking all day on the back of a heavy Christmas Eve. I guess it made him careless.

'Did I do the right thing, Mom? No way would he let me

come otherwise and then you'd have stayed home too.'

I pull Alfie into a hug. He's still for a movement then wriggles free.

'Come on, let's get unpacked and chill for a while,' I say.

We'll probably find out what that noise is while we get sorted. And maybe Luke will decide to finally turn up.

CHAPTER FIVE

I OPEN THE rear door of the cab, and the tang of the
salt marsh sucks in. It's so cold, the air damp and heavy.
I rummage in my rucksack, find my purse and hand a note
to the driver.

I nudge Alfie with my elbow. 'Come on, out you get.' I
smile for the driver's benefit, but my clipped tone isn't lost
on my son. He shuffles along the back seat and makes a slow
effort of getting out of the vehicle. Half a dozen streetlights
cast circles of yellow light across potholed tarmac to the end
of the stretch of low cottages. Beyond them, the road sinks
into darkness. The Black Dog Inn is brightly lit at the beach
end of the road. One property has a Christmas tree in its
window, coloured lights pooling through the wet glass. The
cab pulls away, tyres hissing as the taillights bleed into the
night.

'I won't know anyone.'

'That's the point in coming over to meet people, Alfie.
Please behave tonight. We won't be late, then we'll do something you want tomorrow.'

'Such as?'

'You let me know what you want to do.'

The street is silent except for the ring of our footsteps
as we cross the road. Lou and Adam's two-up, two-down is
tucked between similar properties. Wind rushes through the
salt marsh rattling the reeds at our backs, and for a moment

I doubt myself, unsure which cottage is Lou's, the darkness confusing me.

'What are we hanging about for?'

I ignore Alfie's grumbling and push open the low wooden gate. The front door opens, bright light blinding me for a second.

'How the hell are you?' Adam strides towards us and pulls me into a tight hug. 'It's so good to see you, Evie.'

We step apart, and I'm grinning so hard I'm practically laughing. I haven't realised how much I missed this guy.

'Adam Goodrum, fancy meeting you here!'

He hasn't changed a bit: tall, broad and smiling, his sandy hair tumbles into his eyes exactly like the boy with the kite twenty years ago. He looks past me along the path.

'And this is Alfie?' Adam extends his hand. For an instant, my son looks confused. He glances at me and shoots out his hand. 'Good to meet you. How are you liking England?'

Alfie's eyes flick between Adam and me. 'It's quite dark.'

Adam laughs. 'It's stopped raining and no more's forecast tomorrow. A bit brighter if we're lucky. Come in, both of you.'

Adam waves us inside.

'Let's take your coats and sort out some drinks. No word from Luke yet?'

The last bit comes out casually; a comment of no consequence, a polite enquiry, but Adam never made small talk.

'Nothing. I've left a note tucked into the letterbox at Seahurst to say we're here. I didn't want to leave the place unlocked, not that Luke seems bothered by that.'

Adam is taking Alfie's coat, watching me as I speak. Is he thinking this is so like what happened with Dad, or am I making something out of nothing? Adam stays silent. I look away along the narrow hall that has gone from yellow to soft

47

cream since I was last here. A pale laminate floor instead of the worn brown carpet. Dozens of sparkling fairy lights surround a tall mirror beside the front door, and the rack bulges with coats.

'This is different,' I say, glancing along the hall and up the steep, narrow stairs. 'Very cosy and bright.'

'We've only recently decorated. Kind of difficult, you know, don't want to upset Jack.'

I nod, not quite able to remember what Luke had said about Lou and Adam taking on her father's property.

'Go through to the sitting room Alfie, there's a fire blazing.'

Adam points along the hall; the door to the kitchen at the far end is closed, the door off to the right, though, is open. Alfie looks at me, and I nod. He'd rather wait, and we go together, but I want to hear what Adam has to say about Luke. I unzip my parka and unwind my scarf as Alfie, with a last glare back at me, disappears into the sitting room. I pull off my hat and shove it into my coat pocket.

'Bloody hell, Evie. Lou said you'd gone blond!'

I laugh at his astonishment. 'Years ago, shortly after I went back to Canada the last time. I'd forgotten you guys were expecting something else.'

Lou's startled stare at Saxmundham Station makes more sense now. I'd worried she'd spotted the bruise, then assumed I just looked older, more than expected, perhaps. It was only as I caught her looking a couple of times as she was driving Betty that I guessed it might be my lack of auburn curls.

Adam hangs my coat over Alfie's on the newel post at the bottom of the stairs.

'You all right at Seahurst?'

'Settling in. Lou told you it's all a bit weird?'

Adam nods. 'At least nothing was taken, right?'

'It seems fine. I think we just need to get past tonight, see some proper daylight, but I am worried about Luke. I've called him a dozen times. Where the hell can he be?'

'He's not the most reliable guy I've known, but not being here right now doesn't feel right. He was dead chuffed you'd changed your mind about coming over.'

'You've spoken to him?'

'No, Jack did this morning.'

The rap on the front door makes me jump. Adam grins. 'Steady on.'

I squeeze into the bulging pile of coats as Adam reaches past me for the door. A woman stands on the step, a man just behind her. Adam ushers them in with his usual enthusiasm.

'This is Jenna,' he says, as we all jostle further into the small space so he can close the door. I exchange smiles with a woman who moves with the precision of a well-practised wearer of high heels. Her knee-high black suede boots meet thick wine-coloured leggings. A clinging, knitted roll-neck dress is revealed as she shrugs off her coat and hands it to Adam. I feel underdressed.

'Evie, right?' she says, extending her hand. Her grip is firm, her skin as warm as toast. I nod as she looks past me. 'William's been telling me all about you.'

Will stands on the doormat pulling his scarf from around his neck. He's broader across the shoulders, his thick hair shorter, all the wave cut out; it makes him look more serious than ever. I make myself look straight into his face and hold his gaze for a split second. I'm relieved as I return his smile mine feels warm and relaxed.

'He says you're an amazing chef; he showed me your res-taurant on Google!' Jenna says.

'Did he?' I'm thankful for an excuse to look back at her. She has a small, immaculately made-up round face framed with a shiny chin-length dark bob. Her smile is friendly, a pretty woman. I rather like her and can see why Will would too.

'I don't envy Louisa cooking for a famous chef,' she laughs. The stones in her ring wink in the light as she tucks hair behind her ear. Lou hasn't said these two are engaged.

'I'm not famous, and she knows an omelette is great.'

'Bit of stress going on right now in our kitchen,' says Adam, looking down at a small girl who's wheedled her way beneath his arm.

'Mummy dropped a bag of peas on the floor, and they rolled everywhere. We can't get them out from under the fridge.' She looks up at Adam. 'She shouted for us to get out, didn't she, Daddy?'

The girl raises her hand in front of her face as she speaks, hiding the smile curving across her lips. For a moment, I'm speechless, she's the image of Lou; the likeness is uncanny.

'Grandpops told her to get a grip,' she giggles. I find I can't help but grin back at her.

'I think that's more than anyone needed to hear!' Adam looks slightly flushed. 'Any chance you might smooth things over in there while I read to Mol, Evie?'

'Sure, if I can help out.'

'Will knows where the drinks are. Jack's in the sitting room.' As Adam speaks, Alfie stops in the sitting room doorway. At his back is Jack Maynard. His hair is thinner, whiter than I remember, his skin more lined, but the bright blue eyes twinkle at me as he smiles. I step past Jenna and Adam, register the astonishment fleetingly on Alfie's face as I put my arms about Jack's neck and hug him for a long moment. The last time I saw Jack springs unbidden into my mind. Dad's funeral, the blazing hot sun, grass the colour of straw after weeks of incessant burning sunshine. A semi-circle of people dressed in black huddled at the open graveside. Jack Maynard weeping as I numbly threw a bunch of sea holly into the dark pit.

'Young lady, can I say you've grown?' His words rumble in my ear, and I hold on tight as he speaks, aware my eyes are burning. I blink furiously and swallow hard before I release him and step back.

'You may not!' My laugh is a brittle thing. 'You've met Alfie?' It's clear he has, but words tumble out of me.

'Made plans, haven't we, lad?'

'Already?' I say.

'Jack's taking me fishing at night on the beach.'

I look into Jack's smiling face. 'Come with us, girl, if you're not too soft these days?'

'Definitely! As soon as you like.'

'Do grown-ups still grow?' Molly's voice is reedy and thin, her eyes huge in her tiny round face.

Jack laughs as Molly slips her hand into Adam's huge paw. Her dark hair hangs in damp tangles about her face, her pink PJs sprigged with teddies and purple hearts. Alfie had Spider Man ones just like it at this age.

'Evie was only a slip of a girl last time I saw her, she's done a lot of growing up since then.'

Molly studies my face, her eyes roaming over my ruffled hair, sliding down in that open way children have to my thick jumper, woollen skirt and stained suede boots.

'You're Mummy's friend, aren't you?'

I smile in reply. 'And you're Molly.'

She nods. 'Can I come?'

'Fishing?'

She nods again. 'Santa gave me new pink wellies. I can wear them.'

'You're very small.' I don't like Alfie's tone; I hope these two are going to get on.

'So what? I go day times, and I fix the bait,' she says.

'Just about as good as you once were,' Jack says, winking at me.

The crash from beyond the kitchen door is followed by absolute silence. Adam looks towards the kitchen then back to me.

'Let me go and see what that was,' I say and head down the hall.

⁂

'I wanted it to be perfect.'

'It's just old friends having a meal together, Lou. No one minds if things go a bit off-piste.'

'It's incinerated, for fuck's sake!'

I flap a tea towel at the smoke detector on the ceiling. 'Can you get the batteries out before we're deafened?'

Lou turns towards the sink, her back to me. I give up flapping and wrench open the back door. There's a knock on the door to the hall. It opens a fraction.

'Can I help?' Will hesitates, still standing in the corridor, his hand on the door handle.

'Any chance you can get the batteries out of there?' I ask, nodding towards the ceiling. 'It feels like my eardrums are bleeding!'

He looks relieved and steps into the room, closing the door behind him.

'Watch out for the china!' I point to what must have been a teapot; a handle and spout lie amongst the smashed pieces scattered across the limestone floor.

Will pulls up a kitchen chair as he eyes the black, bubbling casserole dish on the countertop. He looks at me and I shrug. Lou has her back to us, her shoulders hunched, hands spread flat on the worktop staring into the sink. She was right about it being incinerated.

Will clambers onto the chair, and I turn the extractor fan on full. The shepherd's pie must have spilt inside the oven, judging by the amount of smoke belching from it. I grab the heat-mittens hanging from the stove rail, shove my hands into them and pick up the casserole. Smoke blows back into my face, stinging my eyes as I head outside. I dump the dish on the wet concrete path beside the wheelie bins and leave it hissing. I head back into the kitchen as the alarm stops shrieking.

'That's a relief,' says Will, climbing from the chair. We both look at Lou, but there's no response. 'I'll put the battery here and let Adam know to put it back later.'

Will drops a square battery on the kitchen windowsill and looks at me. There's a wine glass on the counter and an open bottle of Chardonnay. I top up the glass and take it to where Lou stands staring into the sink.

'Hey,' I say, putting the glass beside her. 'What have you got hanging about, Lou?' There's a huge bunch of fresh basil in a cup on the windowsill in front of us. 'Any pasta? I'm sure we can throw something together.'

I wait for a response, but there's none. Will watches me and shrugs; the fridge is behind him. He follows my gaze, turns and pulls open the door. I squeeze Lou's hand and walk to stand beside Will.

'Can you sort anything?' Will's voice is low, but Lou must hear him now the kitchen is so silent. The fridge is packed with so much stuff I can't make sense of what's here – random festive food shopping at its worst, by the looks of things.

'Give me half an hour.'

'I could nip to the pub, see if they have any availability.'

I raise my eyebrows. 'For seven of us?' I pull my mobile from my pocket: 19:27. 'Molly will need a sitter. Let me see what I can do. We'll be fine.'

Will nods and looks so serious I can't help but break into a smile. He looks startled, smiles and shakes his head. 'Still got your weird sense of humour then, Evie.'

'No one's died, we'll have a good time. I'm gasping for a drink; get us all drunk, and no one will be any the wiser!'

He nods and heads for the door. 'Coming right up, but shout just as soon as you need any help.' He glances back at Lou and leaves the room.

I root in cupboards, find enough dried pasta to feed the five thousand, and a huge pan that I fill with salted water, a glug of olive oil, and put onto boil.

'Did you have anything planned for dessert, Lou?'

She's finished the wine and is dribbling the last dregs from the bottle into her glass.

'I haven't made it yet.'

'So it was going to be . . . ?'

'Tiramisu.'

'Okay, we can do that.' I rub her shoulders, she flinches at my touch. 'It'll be fine, Lou. We'll have a good evening.'

'You don't understand, Evie . . .'

I can see Lou's trembling. This can't just be a burnt meal.

'What then?' I say. 'What's going on?'

I wait, start to wonder if I should say something else, but what. I've no idea where this is going.

'I thought . . . We've been trying for a baby. IVF. Same as Molly. I was so sure this time . . .'

'Hey,' I say and put my hand over hers. She turns to face

me and I put my arms around her. She folds into me like a child, tears soaking into the crook of my neck. I can't think of a thing to say that won't sound completely inadequate. I hold her for a long time until the shaking stops.

'We only found out this morning,' Her words gulp out as she steps back and scrubs her face with the back of her hand.

'Why the hell didn't you say something earlier?' I tear a piece of kitchen roll off and hand it to her.

'When you'd only just got here?'

'Yes! Why wouldn't you? I could've sorted this out for you tonight or we could've done it another time, Lou. What are best mates for?' Her smile is a wobbly thing. 'Tomorrow would've been just fine.'

She shakes her head as I'm speaking. 'No way, not now you're finally here, Evie. I said to Will, you'd always find a reason not to come back.'

I stare at her. How did I not know any of this was going on in her life? I've been a shit friend to her since our last summer. I ran away from everything and was too ashamed to come back.

CHAPTER SIX

JENNA HOLDS OUT her hand and wiggles her fingers. Small, polished, red nails and a three-stone diamond ring flash in the candlelight.

'So, who's going first?' Jenna catches my eye and smiles as she speaks. I'm more than happy for her to take the lead on this. I've been dreading the inevitable topic of conversation coming up all evening. I sip my coffee and nod for her to go ahead. Alfie is exhausted, watching me with a blank expression. We should go home.

'Will chose it – it's perfect!' she says, and her face lights up her neat features.

'We had talked about it . . .'

The ring is beautiful, similar to my own, and the irony isn't lost on me for a second.

'We've set a date already.' If a person can sparkle, Jenna is doing it right now. She's breathless as she speaks, her smile wide and warm. She looks at Will. 'After taking so long to pop the question, there's no time to waste!'

'It is about bloody time!' Lou's speaking too loudly as she tops up her wine glass. Given what she's put away, I'm surprised she's still conscious. Do Will and Jenna know Lou's had terrible news?

'Alfie?' I reach across and rub my son's hand as it rests between dirty plates and glasses. His head is on his arm, his eyes closed. 'We should think about heading back, we slept on the flight, but it's been a long day.'

'Come with me, mate,' says Adam, pushing back his chair. He gently shakes Alfie by the shoulder. 'Come upstairs for a bit while Mum finishes her dinner.'

I'm surprised Alfie does as Adam suggests; he's so tired he moves like a robot. Usually, he's anxious about where he's sleeping. I push back my chair and stand, but I'm trapped between the wall, Jack and Lou.

'I'll call a cab and get moving, Adam. Get us both to bed.'

Jack pats the seat of my chair. Alfie is almost at the door. 'This isn't Toronto, Evie. No taxi is coming out this way at this time of night. Sit yourself down; we'll get you both home in a bit, don't you worry,' says Jack.

I sit down. I'm tired and this is not a conversation I want to have, but I still need to ask about Luke. Easier if Alfie's upstairs.

'So, this date, when is it?' Lou is determined as ever. She looks like she should have been in bed hours ago.

'Christmas Eve next year – if it's free at St James's,' says Jenna.

'You'll get married here, in the village?' Lou looks between her brother and Jenna. 'Not in Norwich?' Jenna really has got a move on, or did she know Will would finally be proposing? Lou blinks at Jenna for a moment. 'Well done, Will. After Evie, I didn't honestly think you'd ever get there,' says Lou.

The silence is so sudden and absolute; it feels like a tangible thing. Lou is smiling at me, her eyes glazed and unfocused. I stare back at her, willing some witty banter to spring into my head, but there's nothing. I can't catch Will's eye, only glimpse his stunned expression. Why doesn't he say something?

'I've no idea where you get these notions from, Louisa!'

Jack laughs as he finishes speaking, but the look he gives his daughter is one of pure irritation.

'Are you having a traditional dress?' I say, abruptly. I babble on about menus and canapés and matching wine to courses.

'So, you got engaged too, on Christmas Day?' Jenna says.

Lou hands me a plate of mince pies. I shake my head, we've eaten so much.

'Similar thing, just after we opened the presents.'

Jenna is looking at my hand. 'No ring?'

'I took it off when we were unpacking the groceries.' Everyone's attention is turned onto me as I knew it would be. I can't fizz with excitement like Jenna. 'I completely forgot it in the battle to get Alfie ready and out of the house in time for our taxi.' I manage to raise a smile which fails to satisfy Jenna, judging by her puzzled expression. 'We don't have any plans yet. Seth surprised me, a bit like you two. It came as something of a shock, to be honest, so I'm taking a few days to reflect on it.'

'Reflect on it?' Lou's voice is loud and slurred. 'What's that supposed to mean?'

'Louisa!' Jack looks annoyed, catching Adam's eye as he comes back into the room. 'What's got into you tonight?'

'What have I missed then, people?'

'Nothing much,' says Will. 'Jenna's briefed everyone about our news and Evie's reflecting on hers.' Will's voice sounds even enough, but I can't help feeling he's taking the piss.

'Big decision, getting hitched,' says Adam. 'We were all looking forward to meeting Seth, checking out he's good enough for our Evie.' Adam's teasing I can happily deal with. He brings the cafetière with him to the table and sits beside Lou. Her head lolls against his shoulder, her eyes heavy. I pick up her wine glass and hand it to Adam, she's had more than enough. He puts it onto the side table at his elbow.

'When did you get together with Seth?' says Jenna. Will looks up from his coffee cup. Jenna continues when I don't immediately reply: 'Have you known him long?'

'He managed a restaurant in Toronto, the first place I ever worked. The usual part-time job through high school. We started dating when I returned to Canada after Dad died. Mum wasn't so keen early on, he's ten years older than me. A little bit older than Luke.' I feel Will staring at me, but I don't look at him. 'We moved in together a few months before Alfie was born.'

'You must have been very young when you had Alfie,' says Jenna. 'You've done so well to have a career as well.'

'I guess,' I say. 'I was nearly nineteen.' I rattle on about Maxwells, our apartment, and an apparently idyllic life. Maybe if it were just Adam, or Lou, I could explain how it really is?

'Will says you emigrated when you were very young.' Jenna is looking at me as she speaks, her expression so earnest I can't help glancing at Will. They must have had quite a conversation.

'Mum was offered a job in Toronto when I was around six years old. We never came back to live in the UK as she met my Canadian stepfather, Darren.'

'You came over each summer though?' says Jenna.

'Every year to stay with Dad,' I say. I look past her, determined to change the subject. 'Lou says you've been hanging out with Luke. Do you have any idea where he might be, Will?' My question sounds like an accusation. I have no idea why. Will's head jerks up from the cracker joke he's been studying.

'I've been working up here the last few months, we've had a couple of drinks. He's not around that often, he's usually in

Essex. We've only seen each other on an occasional weekend.'

'Would you have any idea where he'd go?'

'We were supposed to meet at The Black Dog last month, but he never showed up.' Will holds my gaze for a second before continuing. 'Dad saw him on the beach this morning, though.'

'He didn't stop and talk,' says Jack. 'He just said that you'd told him you were coming over after all and he was dashing back to Seahurst. Typical Luke, he'd forgotten to put his food shop away before going for a run. He was dead chuffed you were coming over, Evie.'

'What time was that?' I ask.

'Somewhere after 9.30 a.m., I'd say.' Jack glances at Will. I can't make out his expression. Is Will annoyed for some reason? 'He often goes running about then,' says Jack.

'Are the cliffs safe? Does he run up there?' I ask.

Will keeps his head down, brushing party-popper streamers from his dark trousers.

'If you stay behind the fence it's perfectly safe,' says Jack. I stare at him. *If you stay behind the fence.* Jack knows how Dad died. What is he getting at?

'He'll have been summoned by his mother if she's got wind of your arrival, Evie,' says Lou. 'I said about it earlier.'

We watch Lou as she slops coffee into her saucer. She sips a little and clatters the cup back down. Adam puts his arm around her, and she leans into him, puts her head on his shoulder and closes her eyes. She did say something about Luke going to Essex.

'What's she on about?' I say, keeping my voice low.

'You'll have to call her, Evie.' Lou's eyes flicker but don't open.

I look between Adam, Jack and Will. I would be reluctant

to contact Nicola Symonds, but if he doesn't turn up soon . . .

'I don't have contact details for her, do any of you?' I ask.

'She never had anything to do with us folks up here, you know that.' Jack raises his eyebrows as he looks at me.

'I just don't think he'd go off like that. Why would he need to let his mother know we were coming over?' I look around the table at slightly startled faces. I've spoken sharply, my voice too shrill. I try to lower my tone. 'Have any of you tried calling Luke?'

Will and Adam exchange a swift glance. 'We tried a couple of times after Lou got back from dropping you off,' says Will. I hold his gaze for a long moment. 'Luke comes and goes, you know what he's like. He'll probably be at Seahurst when you get back.'

Jenna is looking utterly bemused, staring up at Will as he pushes his chair back and gets to his feet. I realise she doesn't know any of us very well. How long has she been with Will? Luke hadn't mentioned Will, let alone anyone he's been seeing. Our increasingly regular Skype chats over the last eighteen months have moved on from awkward to a relaxed catch-up, but it was me who did most of the talking, the escalating problems with Seth and my worries for Alfie stuck in the middle of it all. In hindsight, Luke gave little away about his life here or in Essex.

'We should make a move, Dad, if we're still going fishing,' says Will.

Jenna pushes back her chair and stands, smoothing the knitted dress down over her hips. 'Nothing would get me sitting on the beach for hours at this time of night,' she says to me rolling her eyes.

'Where are you staying?' I say.

'We're at the pub until New Year. The rooms are really cosy there, aren't they Will?'

Will nods as he puts his hand behind the small of her back and they move towards the hall door.

'Let me sort out the coats,' Jack says. I realise he's probably been waiting to head off most of the evening.

'We should be going as well,' I say. 'I'll nip up and see how Alfie's doing, if that's okay? Do you need a hand?' I ask, looking at Lou and then the sea of dirty dishes and pans on the table and kitchen countertop.

'We'll be just fine.'

'You're sure?'

Adam nods. I know he'll look after Lou. I head for the hall.

Will, Jenna and Jack are all standing next to the front door. Will has his back to me, speaking to Jack as he holds Jenna's coat for her to shrug into. I can't hear what Will's saying, but Jack looks up as I approach them. Will and Jenna turn to look at me, their faces a little surprised. I can't help thinking I might have been the subject of their conversation. I look between them.

'Everything all right?'

'I'll drop Jenna back to the pub, then Dad and I will ride back to Seahurst with you. Lou has Betty insured for you, did she say?'

I nod as I look past Will to where Jack stands with his hands deep in his trouser pockets. He looks annoyed.

'I'll be fine. I don't want to put you out, Jack.'

'Don't be daft, Evie. We'll see you home safe and sound. Besides, you'll save me the walk.' He looks at his son. 'And Will here can make sure I don't go wandering off and get myself lost.'

CHAPTER SEVEN

JACK CLOSES THE boot of the Beetle, the thunk deadened by the dank air. Alfie climbs into the rear of the car as Will strides towards us from the direction of the pub. His wellingtons splash through puddles pooling across the broken pavement as he pulls the zip of a dark wax jacket up to his chin.

'Are we off then, time's getting on? The tide will turn before we get started at this rate.' There's irritation in Will's tone. Is it me he's annoyed with? Jack? Or is he just an angry guy these days?

I dump the bag and my rucksack in the back of the car as Will gets in the opposite side. I climb into the driver's seat. It smells like pear drops and dust in here, and the vinyl seat is freezing. I wiggle the key into the ignition and fiddle with the choke, trying to remember just how this thing works.

'You all right to drive?' says Jack as he settles in the passenger seat.

'I've only had a glass, I'd be dead on my feet after that flight otherwise.' I turn the ignition. The car shudders into life, the engine roaring.

'Take it easy, Evie, we'll be halfway across the Channel at this rate!' says Will. 'Alfie's trying to sleep in the back here.'

'It's so long since I've driven her!' I say, glancing in the rearview mirror, but Will and Alfie are lost in the darkness.

'She's a bit different from my automatic back home.' I find first gear and slowly pull away from the kerb.

'Can't have you driving around on your own in this weather, whatever would your dad have said about that?' says Jack. The car coughs and judders as I change into second. The steering is so weird I'm relieved the road is clear of parked cars. 'I miss him, Evie, even after all these years.' Jack's voice is low, his comment catches me off guard, and I can't find a reply. The Beetle's fog lights barely cut more than a car's length into the mist. I'm relieved to have an excuse to concentrate on driving. I thought I was solid talking about Dad now, but the tightening in my chest suggests otherwise. 'You've got on, Evie, made a life for yourself. He'd be proud of his girl.'

The road narrows as it straightens out and runs adjacent to the coast. The headlights pick out the grass verge. My hands grip the steering wheel too hard as I follow the curve in the road.

'The questions about Dad don't ever go away, do they?' I say, wiping the fogged-up screen with the back of my mitten. Betty's headlights are too weak to pick out potholes before her wheels jolt into them. Lou won't be happy if I knacker the suspension.

'I don't reckon they ever do. No good keep dwelling on it though.' I wait for more, but Jack only turns the heater up to try and clear the screen.

'Luke said what happened . . .' I glance at Jack, try to gauge if I can go on with this line of conversation. Speaking of Dad's suicide never gets any easier. 'There's stuff I should know. Things weren't as we understood them to be.'

The car crunches into a rut as I take the turn along the narrow coastal track towards Seahurst. I glance in the rear-view mirror, but there's nothing from Will. I don't trust the ancient brakes on the sandy, sloping surface and drop down a gear.

'I can understand Luke would want things to be different, we all would, but it is what it is. No sense driving yourself silly chasing down what might-have-beens, it won't change a thing.'

'Luke hasn't said anything to you, then?' I glance in the rearview mirror as Jack replies, not sure if Will is even listening to our conversation.

'Nothing that I recall. He's worried about the cliffs eroding. He mentioned that a couple of times.'

'He's forever banging on about it. I can't see why it's such an issue for him all of a sudden – feels more like an excuse to get us to come over, to be honest.'

'Maybe. Several properties have been lost up and down the coast over the last few years. Your dad was philosophical about it, he knew when he built Seahurst it wasn't forever. Luke's had a bee in his bonnet about the Abbey ruins. Says they need recording before they're completely lost.'

The trees thin, and I sense the sea in front of us. The wind is picking up, the mist low and patchy. I turn the car sharp left to bump along the track with the woods to our left. The scraggy hedge beyond the driver's window taps against the side of the car.

'Luke must struggle to get his Jeep down here without ruining the paintwork. I don't want to upset Lou.'

'Don't you worry about Louisa. How's your mother these days?'

'Busy being a mother: two children under nine years old doesn't leave room for much else. You knew she got married a while back?'

'Bit difficult for you, is it?'

I glance at Jack; he always had a talent for hitting the nail on the head.

'Darren's okay, he makes me welcome enough, but there's always a feeling I'm a bit in the way.' I shrug. 'Perhaps it's me being over-sensitive.'

'Your dad was sure she'd move to Canada to stop him seeing you when he refused to leave Nicola. To be fair though, she let you come over regular as clockwork.'

Light splinters through the thin hedges as they peter out, and Seahurst is before us.

'Did you leave the lights on?' Will leans forward in his seat staring out at the brightly-lit house.

'I thought it would just be Alfie and me coming back here. Unless Luke's finally showed up. I've felt a little uneasy about the place.'

I park Betty beside Luke's Jeep. We unload the fishing tackle and Lou's bag of emergency supplies with a biting wind at our backs. Alfie hunches into himself as he runs towards the house.

'You're both crazy going fishing in this,' I shout to stop my voice dissolving into swirling salt air. I bunch my hair into my hand as it whips across my face. 'It's utterly freezing.'

'You don't know what you're missing – you've gone soft since you've been in Canada,' Will laughs as he nods towards Seahurst. 'Want me to have a quick check around before we head off?'

I don't want to delay him, but those weird noises...

'You go ahead, Dad. I'll catch you up.' Will strides towards the house as Jack chuckles and shifts the rod bag onto his shoulder. I'm so relieved and hurry after Will, rummaging in my rucksack for the door keys. 'Your note's still here.' Will eases the damp limp paper from the letterbox as Alfie shivers on the doorstep beside him. 'Guess we can assume Luke's not back yet.'

I unlock the door and we hurry into the silent house. It's so still after the buffeting wind outside. Will paces around the sitting room, boots squeaking on the polished surface. He glances across to the kitchen and stops at the top of the stairs. Harsh white light from the security lights invades the kitchen casting shivery shadows towards the back of the nearest sofa. The far end of the room is pitch-black, impossible to make out the rise or the ruins. Seahurst has never felt as much like a box as it does right now. I hurry to switch on the rest of the lights, the floor up-lighters and the kitchen spots.

'Alfie heard a noise after we arrived. We didn't find out what it was.' Will watches me without moving a muscle. I should have kept quiet. He must think I'm paranoid, perhaps I am? 'A sort of scuffing, scraping at the far end of the corridor.'

'Come and check around with me, Alfie.' Will heads downstairs without another word. I nod at Alfie and he scampers after him.

I peel off my coat, take off my scarf and boots. The suede will dry overnight though I have no idea if the water stains will brush out in the morning. I lay my beanie and mittens to dry on the shelf beneath the mirror beside the front door. My hair looks a fright. A stripe of dark roots is widening along my parting. A bit different from Jenna's immaculate dark bob. I pray the box of hair dye got thrown into the case, but I don't recall seeing it when we unpacked earlier. Will's moving about downstairs; doors open and close, light switches click, his footsteps shuffling on the flagstones. It makes such a difference having someone else here. Everything would be just great if Luke would bloody well show up. The stairs clang again.

'Nothing and no one down there.' Will pauses, his hand on

the steel banister. 'A bit different from the last time we were here. Place needs a little TLC, doesn't it?'

'I can't really see Luke's done much, to be honest, other than the TV, which impressed Alfie.'

'I've switched the shower off. It was dripping like crazy.'

'That'll be Alfie, he showered before we went out.'

'He's getting into bed. Don't think you'll hear much out of him tonight.' Will doesn't move, keeps his hand on the banister as he looks around. The glass reflects the room back at us: the glint of the spots on the kitchen countertops, white light from the uplighter, the trees and scrub along the back of the house, faint, black shapes shifting, almost invisible in the darkness outside. I can't bring myself to look at the sofa. Does Will think about us sitting there? Making out when Dad and Jack were off fishing or out on the boat. My face is suddenly hot and I'm glad of the low light and shadows in here.

'A very different place in the winter. Lou would find room for you both if you wanted to stay over.' A camp bed in the sitting room, Alfie on the sofa. I'm sure they would find space. 'Or the pub might have rooms free.'

'I think I should call the police, Will.' He holds my gaze. 'Tell them about Luke – it feels too much like Dad.' My voice is a whisper. I've been scared to say it out loud before now, it makes it seem too real. I babble on before Will has a chance to say anything. 'I'm just tired; I seem to do nothing but worry at the moment about Luke, Alfie, this place. I'll be more rational in the morning – promise.' I send him a smile which probably isn't very convincing right now.

'Your dad never bothered with a landline, did he?' he says, pulling his mobile from the back pocket of his jeans. 'Do you get a phone signal up here?'

'I spoke to Mum earlier okay.'

'Call them while I relight the wood burner. If you keep it going over night it'll get rid of the God awful smell. The place needs warming right through.'

Will heads for the front door. I watch him outside, see the dark shape of him walking along the back of the house, his head down against the wind. I need to get my act together, get sorted and settle down. But Luke is another thing altogether.

I sink onto a sofa, my bones suddenly throbbing with fatigue, my fingers slow and clumsy as I search for the number to call. There's still nothing from Seth but he's the least of my worries right now, I just hope he isn't bugging Alfie instead of me. I dial the local station as Will comes back in, his arms laden with logs.

A woman answers. I explain why I'm calling, give all the detail I can and answer her questions. Will's on his knees, his dark hair wind-ruffled, falling over his forehead like it used to. I watch him busy with logs, paper and kindling as the woman's voice comes back on the line. I put my hand over the phone as he holds a match at the base of the pile, yellow flames catching, spreading along the layer of scrunched paper.

'Can you give them any information about when he's usually here?'

Will stands, brushes down his jeans and walks towards me. I hold out the mobile and lay my head back against the sofa as he speaks. His voice is low and calm, and I try to concentrate on his words - Nicola Symonds - the last details they had for her - her business in Essex. Luke's laptop is still on the coffee table in front of me. I sit up as Will starts explaining about Jack's conversation with Luke on the beach. I open the laptop. It's a small, slim thing, the screen stays dark so I press a couple of keys. A battery symbol briefly lights up - no charge. Should I be nosing through Luke's stuff? Anything could be on here.

I glance up at Will, but he stands near the stove with his back to me, the phone still pressed to his ear.

The coffee table has a shelf beneath its glass top. I rummage between headphones, Xbox games and handsets. I find a cable that's clearly nothing to do with the laptop underneath some of Dad's old notebooks. I rummage a bit more, stand and look about the room. I haven't seen a charger here, but Luke must have one. The Jeep or his bedroom would be the most likely places to look. Will finishes the call to the police.

'What did they say?'

Will hands my mobile back to me. 'They've taken the details and say they'll check if he's down in Essex with his mother.'

I continue to look at Will, waiting for more. 'So what will they do, other than contact Nicola?' I'm relieved that isn't down to me now if I'm honest, but it still seems like an outside chance Luke is with his mother, unless he did somehow manage to mess up the dates.

'That's all they said. The woman I spoke to didn't seem so concerned; she says he's only been gone a few hours.'

'I get that, but it all feels wrong to me.'

'She said people go AWOL for a few hours all the time and usually turn up safe and sound.' Will looks about as convinced as I feel.

I nod towards the laptop. 'I thought there might be something on there that would tell us what he's been up to, but the battery is flat. I'll check his room for a charger.'

'He'll have a password, no way to guess that. Could be anything.'

'It was open like that when we got here, as if Luke had been using it.'

'Maybe he's been following up your father's research on

the Abbey like Dad was saying,' Will says. I pick up one of the notebooks lying beside the laptop on the table as Will continues. 'From an archaeological point of view, Luke said it's fascinating as the ground plan of the buildings pretty much survives intact. There's supposed to be a large medieval cemetery.' Will grins. 'Sort of thing we'd have loved when we were kids.'

'Who says it stopped there?' I say, handing the notebook to Will. 'Alfie will be thrilled to hear that.'

Will flicks through the notebook, the pages filled with Dad's scrawled writing, sketches and floor plans here and there. 'Luke was more interested in the folklore side of things, he's wanting to record what he could before all of it's lost.'

'Church bells tolling beneath the waves?' I say, raising my eyebrows in surprise.

'More to do with the Abbey itself,' he says, grinning. 'Old wives' tales of moaning monks and curses whipping up a storm to drown the town.' Will scans page after page of the notebook. 'It's a while since I spoke to Luke about it now. Mind if I take a look at this while we're fishing tonight?'

'Help yourself. It's just not my thing.'

'Like Dad and fishing – I could do without it tonight, if I'm honest.' Will tucks the notebook inside his jacket and pulls the zip up to his chin. A wave of panic washes over me at the thought of him leaving, at being here, just Alfie and me. I squash it down as I push myself up from the sofa. We're standing so close I expect him to step back but he doesn't.

'Why are you going then? I got the impression Jack likes fishing solo most of the time.'

Will looks me, his dark eyes hold mine. 'Dad's been much better lately, but he's pretty closed about things. Sitting on the beach fishing is a good time to find out how things really are with him. Lou and Adam have been tied up with all the IVF thing.' He's silent for a moment. 'Sure you don't want to go back to Lou's?' He's watching my face intently. 'She'd be chuffed to have you stay over.'

'I've wanted to come back for a long time; I'm not bottling it now and I want to be here to scream at Luke when he shows up.' I smile as the crinkles at the corner of his eyes deepen. I wish I could confide in him. Tell him it all. 'I'll be fine, dead to the world as soon as my head hits the pillow.'

'If you're sure.'

'I'm glad we made the call,' I say. 'It feels better to have actually done something.'

CHAPTER EIGHT

A DRAUGHT NIPS at my ankles as I leave Luke's room and hurry down the passage, switching lights off as I go. Alfie has left the bathroom door open and the light on. Better than total darkness on our first night. Hopefully, he's already asleep.

Shadows leap about my room as I stop in the doorway. Alfie's in his PJs, his duvet wrapped around him, crouched on the floor at the foot of my futon. In front of him is the huge china bowl I picked up in a junk shop decades ago, his phone torch trained on the contents of the dish.

'You should be asleep,' I say.

'You've found the laptop charger then,' he says glancing up at me.

'Found it in Uncle Luke's room just now.'

'You think something's happened to him, don't you?' He watches to see my reaction. I switch on the bedside lamp, put the laptop beneath it and plug in the charger.

'Let's hope I'm wrong about that. I'll go for a run before breakfast,' I say changing the subject. 'Come with me?' I pull on my PJ bottoms. Alfie has his back to me shaking his head. There was a time when he crazed to run with me, now he rarely does. 'The floor is bloody freezing,' I say, crawling into bed. 'Lou's right about the heating. God knows why Luke hasn't got it running 24:7.' I set the alarm on my mobile and look across at Alfie. There are only a few inches between our two beds.

'What's this?' He's weighing a stone from the bowl in his hand.

'A hag stone. I picked up loads of them on the beach over the years. They're supposed to bring you luck, keep you safe from evil spirits, all that stuff. They say you can see your future if you look through the hole.' Alfie looks towards the door. 'That's the biggest stone I ever found. Luke helped me carry it back here. I was younger than you then. Always made a great doorstop.'

'Can I have this one?' he asks, turning the mottled grey stone in his hand.

'Sure, but the magic only works if you find the stone yourself,' I reply, grinning.

'You're weird sometimes, Mom.'

'Get some sleep,' I say, turning off the bedside lamp.

The room falls into gloom, the light from the bathroom only just creeping to this end of the passage. Alfie wriggles about, the camp bed squeaking until eventually he's still. The sheets are freezing, it's hard to tell if they're cold or damp.

'Thank you for saying what you did to Dad at the airport.' Alfie doesn't respond. Is he already asleep?

'Did you hear the noise again?' Alfie's voice is sleep-slurred as the wind whistles around the corner of the building. 'It was coming from inside the walls.'

'I doubt that, they're solid flint and brick. It was probably nothing. We'll have all day tomorrow to check it out.'

I listen to Alfie's slow, rhythmic breathing and wish I could fall into sleep so quickly. The run of glass bricks glistens, bright patches on the walls and dressing table, the camera in its leather case. Something has triggered the security lights, perhaps the swirling air currents coming off the sea. There's nothing more than weather and rabbits out there. Will and Jack are on the beach and will probably call in on their way home.

I sit up with a start, heart pounding, breathing hard. It takes a second to realise where I am. My room, grey outlines of a suitcase and door, open to the dimly lit corridor. A nightmare? Hardly surprising with everything that had gone on lately. I try to stop my heart from racing. In the back of my mind, I sense I heard something. A fuzzy recollection of a sound. Some movement stirred me from sleep. I lean across to the camp bed, put out my hand and find an empty pillow.

'Alfie?' My voice is thin and uncertain in the silence. He must have nipped to the bathroom. Perhaps that's what disturbed me, Alfie crashing about. It's black as pitch outside; the security lights off again. My eyes adjust, light scattering along the corridor from the bathroom. Was that Alfie, or did I hear the scraping sounds again? My breathing is shallow, my heart too fast as I look around the room. There's nothing now, only the wind. This place has not altered since I was eighteen years old, but everything has changed. I wrap my arms around myself. Dad isn't here to chase away bad dreams, to lead me back to bed.

I snuggle beneath the duvet and wait for Alfie. He must be in the bathroom. The heavy feeling in my chest has been growing ever since we left Heathrow. It would have been easier if Luke had been here to fill the space, make me laugh, and talk about old times. It was never straightforward coming back, but his absence makes it all so much worse. The moon comes out, a soft white light pushing through the grimy glass bricks. A shadow is in the doorway, tall, as if a person stands there.

'Alfie?' It's just how the light falls against the frame, but my eyes fix on the space where a face should be. On the edges of my vision, smaller shadows crawl along the walls, the trees outside spreading spindly fingers all over the room. The scratching sound is loud; the whole of me instantly still. Listening. It comes again -- like something scraping along the floor. Something heavy being dragged. I sit up in bed and try to pinpoint where it's coming from. Where the hell is Alfie? How long does it take to use the bathroom? Scuffling. Scraping. More now, as if whatever it is grows more confident.

'Alfie?' The scratching stops abruptly. Does it hear me? I fling back the covers and walk silently to the door. I peep into the corridor, not sure if the noise is in my room or out there. The garage steps on my left are in deep shadow. The door, closed. To my right, the brickwork ribs along the corridor run to the stairs. Only the bathroom door is open. Alfie stands outside it staring into the room.

'Alfie, you okay?'

No response. He doesn't move at all, and the way he's standing . . . so still. Something isn't right. I hurry towards him.

'Hey?' It's as if he doesn't see or hear me. He doesn't move at all. I stop beside him and follow his unblinking gaze into the bathroom. We gape into the mirror. Alfie's vacant stare is terrifying. He looks ill.

'What's wrong, Alfie?' I say, studying my son's face. His skin is ashen, so pale his lips are blue. I put out my hand to touch his arm - let it fall to my side, unsure what to do.

'Was there something in the bathroom?' I say, stepping towards the door. I move into the empty room. The rank smell lingers, but there's nothing else. I see myself in the mirror, my brown eyes confused, fearful. I pull on a smile as I turn around to face my son.

'Were you worried about something? There's nothing here.' I step back to where Alfie stands and put my hand on his arm. He doesn't move or pull away. 'Were you worried about the lock?'

Alfie starts to shiver. My feet feel like blocks of ice. He has to be frozen standing here. I take his hand. Usually so much warmer than mine, but it's cold. Alfie looks at me, and relief floods through me.

'Are you okay?' Alfie doesn't answer, just stares up at me. 'How long have you been here? Did you need the bathroom?' I rub my son's hand between mine, not sure how to take it from here. The house is weirdly still. No noises, not even the wind.

'Dun . . . know.' His voice is small and stuttering, like when he was a toddler, scared after a night terror.

'I can wait right here if you want to pee?' Alfie shakes his head and moves closer to me. 'Let's get back to bed before we both freeze to death.' I put my arm about his shoulders and he lets me lead him along the passage.

We reach my room, and I glance back along the corridor. It's so silent, like the house is listening. No bizarre noises, no whistling wind. Nothing. The lights I left on upstairs filter down the flight, the metal handrail glinting. Light blazes from the bathroom across the flagstones to the whitewashed wall opposite. A patch of darkness is beyond it, before the stairs, seeping from the wall as though someone stands there in the shadows. I blink, and it's gone. A trick of the light, my tired brain seeing things that are not here. The passage is empty, only the wind howling again around the corner of the house.

'I'm cold, Mom.' Alfie is crawling onto the camp bed. I snatch the duvet from the floor and tuck it around him. He's shivering so much, his teeth chatter. I hop back into bed.

77

'We'll soon warm up, Alfie. What happened? Why were you out there?' The wind buffets against the glass bricks. 'Alfie?'

'Can I come into your bed, Mom?' Alfie doesn't wait for a reply. I let him clamber in. We squash into the narrow space, and he settles with his back to me. I pull him close. All of him is so cold I feel it through my PJs. His feet on mine are freezing.

'I don't get what happened,' he says, as wind gusts off the sea, and pummels the dark glass. 'How did I get out there, Mom?'

I have no answer for him, morning can't come fast enough.

CHAPTER NINE

I STOP TO catch my breath at the crumbling wooden stile.
I've run too hard up the rise, but it feels so good to be out
of the house. First light had taken a lifetime to brighten the
horizon. Sleep had been fitful curled up beside Alfie, trying
to keep still so as not to waken him while worrying about
Luke. At least I don't recall hearing any more weird noises,
but my brain is sludgy, my nerves jangled. What was wrong
with Alfie last night? He's never been a sleepwalker? So much
stress lately. Maybe it was a one off, confused by jet lag and
a strange house.

Fog hangs over the marsh, the low winter sun blurry and
yellow above the silent reed beds. I lean against the slimy,
wooden stile. Everything is wet, but at least the rain has
stopped for now. Up ahead, the broken bones of the Abbey
drift into view, the onshore wind picking up, pattering my
face with misty, cold air. Its stark beauty is enchanting. I pull
my hood over my beanie and climb over the stile.

The ground is rough, slippery with mud and tufted grass,
rabbit holes waiting to turn my ankle if I pick up too much
speed. I drop my pace and wander between the stones, the
ghosts of rooms laid out here and there, an occasional wall, a
half-arched window. I can see now why Luke might find this
interesting. A great block of grey looms suddenly before me,
the fog dissolving as the wind strengthens. I'd forgotten the old
pillbox. We rarely played inside its dank interior stinking of

piss and fox. It looked out of place between the broken-down Abbey walls, like it had been left here by mistake and forgotten about. I make my way past it to the first few uneven flagstones we used to run along on our way to the clifftop.

The arch up ahead has a trace of mist about its square stone feet, the rest of its flint and brick soaring skywards. The low moan of the wind, rising, falling, makes me shiver as I step into its shadow. Dad's tall tales that the strange tone was a siren luring innocents to a watery death made me press my hands to my ears for years. I don't remember it being so loud though, but the wind is stronger now, coming from a different direction. I sit in one of the stone nooks at the base of the four massive columns and hear the murmuring ebb and flow of the waves beneath here. The cliff edge is much closer than I remember; the post and wire fence intersected with warning signs. It's hard to judge how much land has vanished, it looks so different with the tower gone. The flagstones cut beneath the fence, running across no man's land, the final jagged stone jutting out into salt air.

Cold seeps through the fabric of my jacket as I lean back against the stone and stare out across flat grey water to the horizon. I haven't had such a bad night's sleep in a while. The weird noises, Seahurst feeling so strange and Alfie's behaviour last night are unsettling. I expected us to be relaxing by now with time to think about the problems back home. Things with Seth have been miserable for too long, the restaurant busy and stressful for months. Until I know what's happening with Luke, though, no way can I think straight.

It's a mile or two to the car park café. I can run back along the beach then, follow the tideline, be back to Seahurst before the crowd roll up for breakfast. I push myself to my feet. I'm getting chilly sitting here. I walk to the fence but can't see the beach. The overhang must be deep, waves thunder below, salt spray on my lips. Luke is right to be concerned for the Abbey.

I walk away from the arch, weave between the footprints of rooms, pick up the coastal path and start to run. The track is soft and springy underfoot; earthy scent mingles with the sharp smell of fox. Gorse gathers more thickly, the track sinking down, bramble and skinny hedges rising to head height. Not a sound other than my muffled footfall and breathing. I let my mind go blank, concentrate on the rough, winding path and the rhythm of my feet.

The hedges peter out as the black bulk of the café comes into view. The sandy track twists inland, my old running shoes slipping as I come alongside the tarred-timber building, boarded up against the weather until spring. I pass it and continue across the rough ground of the car park. Small boats, shrouded beneath tarpaulins, line up where the car park meets the marshes. I sprint past them and head for the steep bank of the dunes.

The wind snatches back my hood as I reach the summit. I pull off my beanie and let the salt wind stream through my hair. The tide is high, only a thin ribbon of the beach running around the bay, the water at the foot of the cliffs in places. The tide will have turned by the time we've done with breakfast, so Alfie can go and find his hag stone. The cold makes my eyes water, but there's nowhere I'd rather be right now. I head down the beach and turn into the wind towards the pale doom of the power station and Seahurst.

I run for a while, my body sinking into the rhythm of each pounding step. The cliffs are shrouded in shadow, mounds of earth fenced off, warning notices with skull and crossbones nailed to posts. There had been the odd landslip; parents repeated warnings not to go near, not to climb the cliffs, be aware of the overhang. We'd ignored them once or twice in our teens and dug about in the crumbling orange sand. We hadn't found dinosaurs or fossils, not even any old monks' bones.

Stoney firm sand gives way to deep shingle. If Luke can run here he's fitter than me, for sure. The Abbey comes into view above the headland jutting into the foam. Below it on the beach is a black fisherman's brolly, a soft thread of light spreading out in front of it. A figure stands, knee-deep in the sea winding in a line.

'Hey!' I wave as I shout, the wind tugging the sound from me, scattering it out across the water. I head down to where the shingle flattens out, the waves lapping over the stones. I can run a little here. Jack raises his hand as I skip away from foaming edges of the waves as they rush at me.

'What are you doing about at this time?' Jack's voice has an ethereal quality as it carries towards me on stiff, salt air. 'I thought you'd be dead to the world, or I'd have been knocking on your door for a coffee by now.'

'Jet-lag, my body thinks it's 7:30pm.'

I pull up where the foam fizzes on the shingle and put my hands on my knees, my chest, heaving.

'Any sign of that brother of yours?'

I shake my head, taken by surprise as my throat closes up. I can't find any words to answer him. My eyes are burning as I look away from Jack and peer into his large, black bucket.

'Caught anything?' I say.

'Not a damned twitch. I'm thinking of calling it a night.'

'Where's Will?'

'Went back a couple of hours ago.' I'm disappointed to miss Will, I wanted to thank him for his patience last night. Jack looks further along the beach. 'That's some of what's been getting your brother all worked up.'

I follow Jack's gaze to where the arch soars above the clifftop. I don't immediately see anything but sea and cliffs and lightning sky in the grainy dawn light. A wave rolls up the beach, hesitating, spreading thinly, drawing back, leaving white lacy froth spread across stony sand. As my eyes focus, I see the water licking at the edges of a dark mound. It takes shape, a great pile of soft, crumbling sand slowly being dissolved and pulled back into the sea.

'We've had so much rain lately, it weakens the cliffs. It must've come down last night. Too dark to notice when I came down here. Tide's carried some of it away already.'

'Luke told me it's happening a lot.'

Jack turns back to the sea and begins reeling in his line again. I duck beneath the umbrella and sink into his canvas chair. I pull a chequered blanket across my knees and look out at the breakers hitting the shingle. It's quiet out of the wind, warmer too. Jack comes prepared: a camping stove putters beneath a tiny pan of water, yesterday's newspaper weighted beneath a large, flat, grey stone.

'Help yourself to a brew if you're cold, Evie.'

Jack's leaning back as he reels in the line, the water swirling about the calves of his boots. I settle back and watch him. Dad sat out here and talked through the night. I'd listen to them, tucked up against the weather, sand scouring the little camp. The last couple of years, I'd run down with bacon rolls, coffee and lardy cake, and we'd eaten it watching the sunrise. Jack walks towards me.

'Does Lou ever come down here?'

'Not at night, not since Molly came along.' He starts to pack the rod into its case. 'I don't always sleep so good in my bed. Never have a problem with that down here.' He turns off the small stove, empties a mug onto the sand. 'Will reckons. I should get myself a job of some kind. He's probably right, but it would put an end to sitting out here of a night-time.'

'Are you okay then?'

'Mostly, more good days than bad now for a while. I get under Lou's feet. It's only right they have the cottage to themselves. It's been a bit tight all of us there.'

'Surely it's your home first, though?'

'Not since Juliet passed.'

I hadn't expected that. I should have. The cottage was their home together, not just Jack's. He carries on packing his rucksack, collecting everything together. I stand and start to collapse the camping seat.

'Everything kind of happened at once, didn't it,' I say.

Jack pulls the brolly from the sand and turns it to face the wind. He lets it down and begins to wind the flapping cloth beneath his hand. I'm thinking he's not going to reply, maybe change the subject, when he looks at me. His woolly hat is pulled low over his ears and brow, silver stubble grazes his jaw and neck.

'We lost Juliet, your dad, and then Will left for university a couple of weeks after you went back to Canada. He hardly ever came home, always a friends' place to go to, some holiday job or other. It was hard on Lou.'

I stare back at him, unsure if the sudden aggression in his tone is directed at me. I push my hair from my face as the wind flaps the black fabric of the brolly. I can't think of what to say. Jack continues catching the flaying material. His smile, a flat thing.

'You know how it is at that age, and there's not much to keep anyone here,' he says.

How old is Jack? Dad would have been sixty-one next

birthday; he must be close to that. I watch as he secures the brolly, picks up the bucket and rods.

'You could've kept in touch with Lou more than you did.' He doesn't look at me as he speaks, just heads up the beach taking long, swift strides. I watch him for a moment, but he doesn't look back. Jack's right. Lou's letters and cards piled up, tucked inside a box at the bottom of my wardrobe in Canada. I should have kept in touch, but those first few raw weeks after I left here become months then years. Lou's letters stopped coming. The longer I left it, the harder it became to break the silence. Maybe we never would have, if it hadn't been for Luke coming up here again.

I pick up the camping chair. Jack is splashing through the surf, water spraying all about him. I head further up the beach, skipping just beyond each curling wave as it surges forward. I break into a run, surprised how much ground is opening up between Jack and me.

'Jack! Slow down a bit.'

No way does he hear me, his head down, walking into the wind. A wave sweeps across the shingle, foam popping on the rough orange sand at the foot of the cliff. I jump back to keep it from washing across my running shoes as it turns, sliding back into the sea.

A light pattering on my shoulder, down the back of my jacket and in my hair. I look up thinking it's raining again. I fling my hands up in front of my face but too late, it's in my eyes, my mouth, and I am screaming. I cover my head with my hands, duck to make myself as small as I can. I blink madly, my eyes scratchy, full of sand, the world a blur of shapes and colours. I blindly try to run forwards, feel my legs staggering, my shoe catching, stumbling.

'Jack!'

I fall forwards, crashing to my knees, landing face down and on top of the camping stool. Water and sand swirl all about me. I try to push myself up, look back over my shoulder. Someone is up there, on the very edge where the earth meets the sky. I try to shout, my mouth and eyes full of sand. I blink, can't see them. Only the cliff face moving, sliding; a great sluice of earth and debris mixing with foaming white water. All of it coming down on my head.

CHAPTER TEN

LOU DROPS HER scarf across the back of the kitchen bar stool as she hurries towards me. 'Things happen when you're here, Evie Meyer.' She pulls me into a tight hug, her dark hair damp and smelling of shampoo. 'And the police here too! Tell me you're all right.'

'Just fine, all a bit of a drama over nothing.'

'Hardly that, girl. It could have been quite a different outcome,' says Jack.

We move apart and look towards Jack, who is draining the dregs from his third mug of coffee as he sits at the kitchen counter.

'What happened, Dad?'

'Just a small shower of dirt, but it could have been a lot more than that after the weather we've had.'

'Why were you right up against the cliffs, Evie? What were you thinking?' Lou stares into my face as she speaks, her expression full of concern.

'Just trying not to get my feet wet, and the tide was right in . . .' I shrug. 'I'm fine now – a bit shocked at the time.'

Adam takes off Molly's coat, and Alfie pulls himself onto the kitchen barstool next to Jack. My son looks so serious; his eyes hold mine. I smile, but he doesn't send anything back. I guess he was worried.

Beyond where they sit, I watch the police liaison officer walking back to her car through the glass at the end of the house. She stops beside Luke's Jeep and peers through the rear passenger window, shielding her eyes with her hand, her bright red scarf flapping at her neck. It was hard to tell what she made of the whole situation with Luke. I got the impression she was here to say all the right things: *Don't worry, Every effort is being made, Most people turn up safe and well.* The lights on her black hatchback bleep. As she opens the driver's door, she looks back at Seahurst, sees me watching and raises her hand. I do the same.

'She seemed very nice.' Lou stands at my elbow, and I think she says something more, but I can't focus on her chatter.

'Let's hope they managed to get hold of Nicola Symonds,' I say. 'I don't hold out much hope that she'll return my call.' Jack and I debated who should leave the voicemail after I hung up on the company answer machine. Eventually, I redialled and left a message.

'I'm starving, Mom.'

I pull open the fridge door, relieved that Alfie's ravenous as usual. I move around the kitchen, finding a frying pan and oil as Jack regales the morning's events yet again. Nothing had been injured other than my pride. Jack had scared the hell out of me, dragging me along the beach. I realise now he'd been shouting at me with the shock of it all. When I'd asked if he saw anyone up on the cliffs, he'd said no, he'd have seen anyone up there. Even so, I can't shake off the feeling someone was watching us. I try to put it out of my mind and listen to Alfie. He's following me about the kitchen. I hand him a hunk of bread, thickly buttered.

'Has Dad called?' His voice is low, his eyes focused on mine. I shake my head as he bites into the bread.

'We'll have a good day today, chill a bit and call him later, okay?' Alfie nods, his mouth too full to speak. 'Sit down while you're eating. Crumbs are going everywhere.'

'How long until food's ready?'

'You know how long it takes me to cook pancakes. The batter is already made, now shoo!'

Alfie heads for the sofa where Molly is pointing the remote at a blank TV screen. It's good to be cooking. I want today to be fun, for Alfie to have a good time.

Adam has gone outside, his back to the cottage, thick brown hair flapping in the wind streaming off the sea. Beyond him, just visible in the bright milky sky, a search and rescue helicopter hovers in pretty much the same place it's been in for the last half hour.

'Can I help?' Lou smiles. 'After last night, I feel I should redeem myself.'

I shake my head and laugh with her. 'I'm impressed you're so perky today. Just keep the coffee coming and I'll look after the rest of it.'

'Paracetamol and a gallon of water in the early hours worked wonders,' she says, rinsing out the empty coffee pot.

'Stop it!' Alfie shouts, his face pale and angry as he wrestles something from Molly's grasp. He hurls it towards the sofas at the far end of the room. A loud crack makes me wince as it hits the floor and skids to a halt at the base of the glass wall. Molly looks astonished.

'Hey!' I say, hurrying towards the children. 'What's going on?'

'I found it!' Molly says, charging across the room towards the sofas. I grab Alfie's arm to stop him chasing after her. He jerks away from me so violently I lose my grip, but Lou is already beside Molly. The little girl snatches something off the floor and holds it behind her back as she stares furiously into

Alfie's face. A sharp, *clickety-clack* comes from behind her as she pokes her tongue out at Alfie.

'Give that to me, Mols,' says Lou reaching towards her daughter. Molly shakes her head as she backs towards the glass.

Clack, clack, clickety-clack. The sound puts my teeth on edge, like fingernails down a blackboard, although it's a totally different noise.

Alfie has his hands over his ears. 'Stop it!' Molly looks startled. I realise Alfie is on the verge of tears. 'Make her stop it, Mom!' He turns towards me and buries his face in the crook of my neck. I register the astonishment on Lou's face as a frightened-looking Molly drops something into her mother's open hand.

'What is it?' Lou says, looking at me. She turns the creamy coloured object over in her palm. It *clack-clacks* as she turns it. One end looks to be broken as if a section of a handle snapped off. Lou shoves it towards me. 'Take it, Evie.'

I don't want to touch the dirty old thing, but take it from Lou as she pushes it towards me. Molly watches, her eyes huge now in her solemn face. Alfie is trembling against my chest, and I can't understand why he's reacted so badly. It is a horrible, grimy thing. An intricately carved dome about the size of a tomato, with a small stone trapped inside it. I guess the slim section running off it was once a slightly longer handle.

'It's not pretty,' says Lou, pulling a face.

Jack stands beside me. I haven't heard him in all the commotion. 'Luke showed me that last year. He found it when the digger was clearing the ground for the garage build.' He looks between Lou and me. 'We thought it was made of ivory or some sort of animal bone. He was going to try and find out what it was. No idea if he ever did, though.'

'Where did you find it?' asks Lou.

Molly points to the shelf above the wood burner. 'It was next to the TV remote,' she says.

Lou takes it from me and puts it back on the shelf. I'm not sure what to say to Alfie, although he has stopped shaking.

'We thought it might have been a child's rattle,' says Jack, patting Alfie on the shoulder and giving him a grin.

'That disgusting thing?' says Lou. 'You'd certainly hope not.'

'We'll walk across the marshes after we've eaten, Alfie,' Jack says, looking at my son. Alfie pulls away from me. 'We can walk home along the beach.'

'You might find a hag stone,' I add, smiling at Alfie. He won't catch my eye. Better to speak to him later about what's wrong.

'I don't want to go for a walk, not right now.' Alfie looks ill. His face is ashen, a sheen of sweat across his skin. Whatever that thing is, it isn't nice, but Alfie's reaction seems a bit over the top.

'You don't want to go crabbing? See where Jack will take you fishing?' I raise my eyebrows in mock surprise. Alfie hesitates and glances at Jack.

The banging is so sudden and so loud we all jolt around towards the stairs.

Alfie jerks towards me. 'What the fuck's that?'

'Alfie, that's enough!'

The hammering grows louder, getting faster, vibrations running through the floorboards, shivering into the soles of my feet.

'It did that earlier when your mum was in the shower,' Jack says, laughing. 'A whole lot of shouting and wailing there was, just as that policewoman turned up.'

I dash to the sink and turn off the hot water. The noise

gradually slows, quietens and stops. Jack's right; it had totally freaked me out. I'd told Jack about the scraping noises last night, but there were no weird sounds when we got back earlier. I risked a shower, but even so, I'm sure Jack thought my screaming fit was a total overreaction to some dodgy plumbing.

'Not often I see a young woman in only a bath towel these days,' Jack chuckles.

'It's the hot water. Hopefully, Adam can sort something out.'

'I'll need to shower. It's working, right?' Alfie sounds more grumpy now than upset, and I suspect he's still tired like me.

'If there's a problem here, you can use the shower at ours,' says Lou.

The front door sucks open. Adam is laughing as he pulls off his scarf and unzips his gilet. 'I could hear that on the path outside, you've probably got air trapped in the pipes. I'll take a look while you're cooking. Do you know where the stopcock is?'

'It used to be in the old outhouse. I guess it's in the garage now?'

'You cook, I'll look around.' Adam heads towards the stairs. 'Come on, Alfie, you're plumber's mate today.'

I'm amazed as Alfie follows Adam, but I guess he might be embarrassed about his behaviour. 'There's a stink in the washroom – it's rancid,' Alfie says.

Adam grabs the banister and stares at my son, then looks across the room at me. 'Let's go take a look then. That breakfast better be good!' Adam winks as he starts down the stairs with Alfie and Molly hot on his heels.

I throw him a grateful smile. 'Ten minutes.'

'I'll go and see if the worker wants a coffee,' says Jack.

Lou leans back against the worktop. 'What was wrong with Alfie?'

I shrug. 'No idea. He was unsettled last night. I guess we're both tired after so much travelling yesterday.' My phone pings with an incoming text. I snatch the mobile from the counter.

'Any news?' Lou says.

'Will asking if I'm okay,' I say, glancing up at her. I send a reply letting him know I'm fine.

'How many are we cooking for?'

'Just the six of us. Will and Jenna are completing on a place together in the New Year. Jenna wanted to go bargain hunting in the sales for house stuff.'

'Oh? Jack didn't say anything.'

'I don't think Dad knew. A sudden change of plan this morning, according to Will.'

I don't know why I feel disappointed they are not coming over. I liked Jenna, but it's awkward with Will. Better off just us, easier to relax today.

'Dad'll miss Will when he moves out again. He's been working up here a lot of the time since the October gales,' says Lou as I drop a ladle of batter into the pan. 'You're sure you're okay, Evie? You gave Dad such a fright. He was in a right old panic when he called earlier.'

'I'm fine.' I'm snapping at Lou, which is the last thing I want to be doing, but I'm concerned about Alfie. She's silent for a few moments, and I'm about to apologise when she speaks again.

'Did the police say they would do anything about Luke? Follow it up, I mean?'

'They're getting in touch with Nicola Symonds – if he's in Essex or been in touch with her, we'll at least know he's okay.'

The groaning noise starts again, quietly, building, getting louder.

'That does sound freaky,' I say as the knocking kicks in. 'Poor Alfie hasn't had a great time here so far.' I tell Lou about the scraping sounds last night as she clatters cutlery onto the countertop, and his wandering off in the middle of the night. 'Hopefully that's not happening again.' I pull out my mobile, the screen lights as I look at the phone. I'd called Luke again after I showered, but the call failed to connect. There's nothing from him. Nothing from Seth. Nothing from anyone. Lou's watching me.

'It was early when I called Nicola this morning. Shall I try again, or is that too much?'

'How can she complain if you're just concerned about her son?'

I hit the last number redial and walk to the far end of the room as I wait for the call to connect. I stop at the wall of glass and stare up at the Abbey. Birds ride the air currents, gulls judging by their size, swooping behind the jagged old walls, diving beyond the cliffs to the beach. The phone rings and rings at the other end as I watch the blurry outline of my pale reflection in the glass. The call goes to voicemail. The shock of hearing her voice earlier had left me speechless, and I'd hung up, had to redial to leave a message. My heart has quickened now, and I'm gripping the mobile hard. I've only ever had half a dozen exchanges with Dad's widow. Never anything long enough to be called a conversation, but I know her voice, an undercurrent of Essex accent behind the clipped business-like tone. She reels off the opening dates and times over the festive period I heard earlier. The line beeps.

'Mrs Symonds, it's Evie Meyer again, just to say the police

sent a liaison officer over earlier. There's still no sign of Luke here. It would be good if you'd call just to let me know he's with you and okay.'

CHAPTER ELEVEN

A DAM AND JACK follow me along the narrow side-path running the length of Seahurst. Unlike the weather-bleached slate and shingle out front, this area is dank and slimy from lack of sunlight and air. White trainers are not a great choice of footwear.

'I'm kind of glad to have you guys with me.'

'Don't know why you'd be feeling like that, Evie,' Adam says, laughing.

'These need cleaning to get a bit of light in downstairs,' I say, tapping the toe of my trainer against the run of glass bricks as we pass Luke's room. 'Five minutes with a cloth and some soapy water would make the rooms a lot brighter.'

'The building work won't have helped,' says Jack. 'The workmen left at the beginning of last summer, Luke's not been about much to clean up.'

Adam and Jack both have their hands deep in their coat pockets. Jack's navy wool hat is pulled low about his ears, his scarf wrapped over his chin. This path was cold and shady in summer. With the wind rattling down it, it's a freezing wind-tunnel today. I continue towards the garage.

'Luke can't bring his Jeep down here,' Adam says. 'This lot hasn't been cut back for a while.'

I turn sideways to slip past a clump of brambles. Broken fern fronds reach from the woodland floor like long brown fingers, their earthy scent strong as we crush them underfoot.

'What am I going to do about Betty, will it be okay to leave her out front?'

'You'd better speak to Lou, she's a bit crazy when it comes to that car,' says Adam.

We reach the end of the building where the house used to fall away to a square patch of soft ground, all sand and pine needles and a ramshackle brick and flint outbuilding. We played here when the tide was in. Our basketball hoop on the back wall is gone, the space filled with the new garage.

Dark green wooden doors are closed, a padlock hanging by an open clasp from a metal eyelet. Luke's not spared the budget here so why not cut back the woods and sort the house out? Adam begins opening the doors, which run smoothly on a track and runner sunk into the ground. I gag and press my hand over my nose and mouth.

'What in God's name is that stench?' Adam pushes the door as wide as it will go as he speaks.

I step back from the threshold as the acrid, sweet odour makes me gag.

'Will said there was something last night when he picked up logs for the burner,' says Jack.

'He didn't mention anything to me,' I say as Adam and Jack walk into the garage.

'Didn't want to spook you. Said you were strung out from the flight as it was,' Jack says, glancing back at me over his shoulder. I can't disagree with that. I must have seemed as jumpy as hell.

'Smells like something's died,' says Adam, looking around the long narrow space. There would be room for the Jeep, but not much more than that in here. Adam walks further inside, his lower face pressed into the crook of his arm. I follow and stop beside him.

'The smell is dreadful.' Adam looks across at the far wall as he speaks: washer-dryer, chest freezer and Dad's old fishing gear. 'He's got a fancy new condensing boiler there.' Adam sounds impressed. Despite the smell, I laugh. He steps towards a white unit on the wall beside the steps, which lead down to the internal door into the house. 'This is powerful enough to keep a place twice this size cozy.' Adam glances across to where Jack and I stand. 'And I reckon this is the garage key?'

I feel my eyes widening as I look at the door to the house. A key is in the lock, a yellow plastic fob dangling from the eyelet. 'Anyone could have let themselves in at any time,' I say, hearing the horror in my voice.

Adam nips down the stone steps and turns the key. Very faintly the mechanism clicks in the lock. 'I don't think there's much risk of you being murdered in your sleep, Evie. Mardle Lane only goes to Seahurst, no one would come this way on the off-chance.'

Adam winks as he glances back at me and pulls the door open, the hinges grinding. The empty corridor is brightly lit, the vaulted ceiling running away towards the spiral stairs. Faint sounds of china clattering and the Xbox come from the upper floor.

'It could do with a bit of oil, it can't have been used much.'

Surely the weird noises we heard couldn't be anything to do with this? They're clearly coming from inside the house. As Adam says, this door hasn't been used regularly – I'd have heard anyone who tried to get in. I turn away from the door, trying to hide how unsettled I'm feeling. There's something about the garage that makes me shiver, something much more than just the cold and the dreadful smell.

Jack stacks a few stray logs back onto the pile just inside

98

the garage door. Beyond him the trees stand like sentinels, shifting beneath the salt wind gusting off the sea. To my right, propped up against the wall, is my old blue bike. The tyres are flat, and the front light droops down at an angle. On a hook above it are a couple of hula hoops and hanging limply next to them is my old red kite, its long tattered tail twisted and spread across the concrete floor. Why did Luke keep all this old junk?

I walk towards the bike, trying and failing to recall what happened to the front light. The seat and paintwork are dusty, the tyres cracked and crusty.

'Jesus Christ!' I stumble forwards, my foot twisting, pain shooting through my ankle. I throw out my hand towards the wall to stop myself falling.

'Are you all right, Evie?' Jack rushes towards me, hand outstretched, he grabs my elbow and steadies me.

'What the hell is that?' I say, looking back at the floor. I feel the blood rush to my cheeks. I bend down and rub my ankle.

'A drain cover, girl,' says Jack. 'That's what that is.'

We both laugh as we look at a smooth, round stone, a thick iron ring set at its centre. The rim where it meets the brickwork is rough and chipped, green with algae. I stand and stare at it for a moment.

'Are you okay, you're trembling?' There's concern in Jack's tone, and he's frowning as he looks at me. My ankle is throbbing.

'Just a bit cold. I should've worn my hoody as well as this coat.'

I rub my ankle, trying to hold back tears that are stinging my eyes. What the hell else can happen? After the beach earlier and with no sign of Luke...

Jack goes back to stacking logs as I rub my ankle and

get myself under control. I stare at the flattened bike tyres – there's something on the floor in the gap between the rubber and the wall.

'Oh!' I say, hobbling a step forward and clasping my hand again over my nose and mouth. Jack comes to stand just behind me, peering past my shoulder.

'I'd say there'll be more of them traps judging by the stink.'

'I knew I should've recognised the smell,' I say, stepping backwards. 'The alley behind the restaurant sometimes reeks like the bathroom here, not quite as strong though.'

Adam steps past me and stands shoulder to shoulder with Jack.

'Shit!' Adam turns away looking horrified. 'I'll fix the plumbing, but that's my limit, Evie.'

I laugh as he heads back to the boiler, its cover hanging open.

'There's a spade over here, Jack,' I say, trying to move without putting too much weight on my ankle.

'There's a run down this wall, Evie, it goes behind the logs, and there are two more traps here, it looks like they sprung a couple of days ago at least.'

I don't reply as Jack moves about the garage behind me. On the shelf above the washer-dryer, bottles of fabric conditioner and washing powder stand beside car stuff; screen-wash and wax – a roll of black bin-liners. A couple of screwdrivers are on top of a socket set, and beside them, a large pair of gardening gloves is beside two rat traps and a battered box of bait.

'Luke must have had a bit of a problem,' I say, glancing over my shoulder at Jack. He looks at the shelf as I point to the bait, then back at the trap he's pulled out from behind the log pile with a hiking stick, a decomposing rat caught by its neck beneath the metal spring, its body splayed flat.

'Traps'll need resetting.' Jack looks across at me, stares into my face, and I can't help but grin back. He shrugs.

'For goodness sake, boys – really?'

I hobble to where Jack stands and nudge the rat with the tip of the spade – one front paw is missing, its eyes, open and dull.

'Grab those gloves and a bin bag, Jack.'

I squat beside the rat, pull on the gloves Jack hands to me and gather myself. Once or twice, when no one else has been about, I have had to put a dead rodent from the alley into the industrial metal bins behind the restaurant. I've never had to remove one from a trap before.

'How do these work?'

Jack is bending from the hips, hands on his knees a couple of feet away. Adam has stopped fiddling with the boiler and looks over to where I am kneeling on the concrete garage floor.

'Just press that metal bar back a bit.' Jack points with the stick. A gust of wind scatters dead leaves across the floor, raising the fur on the tiny corpse for a fraction of a second. I know it's dead, but I can't help jerking backwards. The wind dies away, and I take hold of the edge of the trap. The weight of the thing surprises me, makes me shudder in spite of myself. Jack holds out an open black bin bag.

'You could drop the lot in there, Evie. Pick up some new traps, there's a decent hardware store in town.'

I push down with my forefinger on the metal bar. It raises a fraction. I shake the trap, and the body falls away, rustling against the plastic.

'One down then,' I say. 'Can you reset these things?'

Jack nods as I hobble across towards the bike. 'Watch that damned drain cover,' says Jack.

'For sure, I've collected enough bruises this morning to last me the rest of the trip.'

We find four traps in all, three have stiff fury bodies in them in various stages of decomposition.

'My guess is your brother's okay setting these things, but not so keen on dealing with the results.' I nod at Jack as I peel off the gloves. He ties a knot in the top of the bag. 'Reckon you've found out what your weird noises are though.'

'Thank goodness for that. I never thought I'd be pleased to find we have rats. I need to wash my hands,' I say. 'Probably best if we don't mention this to Alfie.'

'I'm nearly done here if you two can stop larking about.' Adam has his back to us, the cover of the boiler still open. 'I've turned down the water temperature, it was on full blast for some reason. The boiler's a good one though, practically brand new.'

'The shower I had was lukewarm, I couldn't get any heat out of it before that noise set off. The underfloor heating hasn't been great either.'

'The system probably just needs resetting. That's easily sorted,' says Adam, closing the boiler cover.

'Will that take much time? I don't want to mess up your whole day.'

'You want that racket then every time you use some hot water?' Adam grins at me as I gingerly put some weight on my foot – sore, but not too bad.

'Got my heel caught on the metal ring,' I say.

Adam looks at the round stone cover, his forehead crinkling. 'I don't remember it being here, do you?'

'It must have got uncovered during the building work,' I say, hobbling towards the open garage doors. 'It looks ancient.'

'Walk normally on it, Evie.' Jack has his arms full of logs. 'It'll ease faster that way.'

Adam slides the garage door closed.

'I've no key for this,' I say.

'The internal door to the house is locked, you should be fine.' Adam holds up the key, the yellow fob between his fingers. I wish I had his confidence.

'How is that smell getting into the bathroom?' I say. 'Maybe through the air brick beneath the sink?'

'Probably. It must vent to something,' says Adam as we set off back along the side of the house. Alfie hurries towards us, and I can see from his expression there's trouble. My son stops well before he reaches us.

'Betty's passenger door's been left open all night. Louisa's furious – the inside's all wet. It's ruined the carpets, she said.'

We follow Alfie to the front of the house. Lou has a bucket and cloth and is bailing water out of the passenger footwell of the Beetle. She throws a swift glance in my direction. I can tell she's majorly pissed off but trying to keep a lid on it. The rubber foot mat lies on the gravel beside the front wheel.

'I don't mind you using the car, Evie, really I don't, but we look after her.'

'I'm sorry, Lou. I could've sworn I locked it.'

'Let me have a go with it, Louisa.' Jack dumps the logs in a pile and beckons his daughter to move aside. Lou stands, her gaze still on the car, not looking at me.

'I can't understand it,' Jack says. 'We locked up once we got all my fishing stuff out.'

'When you say it was open, do you mean wide open?' I say. 'Surely we'd have seen it?'

'Not properly closed, but the rain's been driving against the car, so it's leaked really badly.'

Lou's voice is flat, her words clipped. Better not to pursue the details just now.

'What about my coat?' says Alfie.

'What about your coat?' I hear the exasperation in my voice.

'It was in here, the Superdry one Dad bought me,' says Alfie. 'Someone's nicked it.'

'It's probably indoors, Alfie. Have you looked for it?' I ask.

'It's not indoors, it's been nicked like I said.'

'No one's nicked your sodding coat! No one comes down here!' I stride up the front path, my eyes are hot, and I feel totally rattled. My ankle still hurts, and no way do I want anyone to see my overreaction to something so stupid. How did I leave the door open?

'It was expensive, Dad said so!' Alfie's right behind me. I stop abruptly and turn to face him. He looks astonished.

'You should look after it then, shouldn't you? How many times have I asked you to wear it? At the airport, at the railway station? Hang it up? Not throw it on the floor or leave it in the back of cars.'

Alfie stares at me. I turn back to the house and head indoors. Molly sits on the nearest sofa watching *Peppa Pig*. She doesn't move as my wet trainers squelch across the floor. I head into the kitchen, gather the remaining plates and start to fill the dishwasher.

'Jack asked if you have a bucket and more cloths?'

I glance up at Adam and open the under-sink cupboard doors. I pull out a new pack of kitchen sponges and a couple of tea towels. Luke is more domesticated than I've given him credit for. I hand them to Adam.

'I saw a bucket in the garage,' I say.

Alfie is hovering where the kitchen meets the sitting area,

with *Peppa Pig* in full swing he's without purpose. His face scowls.

'Run these out to Jack for me, Alfie? I'll help out here so your mum can search for that coat of yours.'

Alfie doesn't respond. I follow his gaze across the room to the carved stone above the mantel and realise he's looking at the weird rattle the children were fighting over earlier.

'Alfie?' He's gone pale again. Surely he's not still bothered by that thing? I cross the room to where he stands. 'What's this all about, Alfie?' He shrugs and looks down at his feet. I glance back at Adam, who's still clutching the cloths. I look at my son, put my hand on his arm. 'Alfie?'

'I don't like it. It makes the noise that leaks out of the walls.'

'Hey, mate,' says Adam. 'That's nothing to do with anything. It's the boiler or the pipes vibrating through the building. We'll get it sorted, okay?' Adam holds out the cloths. Alfie snatches them from him and heads back outside.

'I'm sorry about Alfie and the car, Adam. I just don't understand how we managed to leave it open.'

'It'll dry out. The soft top leaks at the best of times anyway. I told Lou if you used the car, the roof would leak. She was happy enough about that, just said we'd dry it out after you go back to Canada.'

'I did lock it, once we unloaded everything. Do you think someone's broken into it? The lock is so basic anyone could pick it if they wanted to.'

'Evie, forget about it, it's a bit of water, not the end of the world. That door lock's been an issue for a while and Lou knows it.'

'You're not just saying that, are you?' Adam's such a good guy I wouldn't put it past him.

'Defiantly not. The garage need to look at it next time it MOTs.'

We stand looking at each other. I'm relieved to see he's not annoyed, but I can't quite get his expression. 'I think we all need to get out, go for that walk,' I say.'

Adam smiles. 'Let me help you finish up here while they sort out the car.'

I nod and pick up the last two mugs from the breakfast bar.

'Lou spoke to you then, about the IVF?' Adam takes the mugs from me and finds space for them on the crowded top shelf of the dishwasher.

'She was too upset to say much, to be honest.'

'We tried for a couple of years to have Molly.' His voice is low, and he glances across the space to where his daughter sits glued to the TV screen. 'Spent a fortune, but we got lucky in the end. This time around though we're getting nowhere.'

'How long have you been trying?'

'Since Molly was two. Yesterday's result came as a shock. She was convinced the last round had worked. She was dying to welcome you with the good news.'

'Oh my God, I'm so sorry Adam.'

'Nothing to be done, in my opinion. We have Mols - she's good - move on, you know? Enjoy what we have rather than this endless cycle of hope and misery.'

'But Lou's like a dog with a bone?'

'Just can't give up and accept we're great just the three of us.' Adam folds his arms across his chest and stares at the floor.

'Adoption?'

'Don't even go there.'

I don't know what to say, I had no idea. If I'd given it any thought I'd have assumed, given Molly's age now, they'd decided to stop at one after all the IVF the first time around.

'I make good money, and don't take it the wrong way, but we spend all our spare cash on these endless cycles. I'd rather be taking Molly to Disneyland or getting ourselves a bigger place, somewhere with a bit more going on for Mols.'

'I'd no idea, Adam.'

'If you get a chance, talk to her? I really just wanted you to know, Lou's moods – they're all over the place, what with the drugs and hormones she's on. She won't listen to me half the time, like getting pissed last night. None of it helps. So, if she's a bit short, it isn't you. Just so you know.'

'Mom!' Alfie runs into the kitchen.

'What now?' I try to soften my tone. He's a thirteen-year-old boy, they lose things, it's what they do, or what this one does, at least.

'There's a car, coming down the track, coming this way.'

CHAPTER TWELVE

ADAM STANDS AT the glass, looking out at a mid-
night-blue car with a cream soft-top splashing through
potholes, mud spraying high up behind the front wheel arches
as it trundles down the track. It pulls up and parks just
beyond Betty. 'It's an Audi sports,' he says.

Jack and Lou have their backs to us and watch the car. Lou
holds a Chamois leather in one hand. Jack, his sleeves rolled
up, leans his hand against the Beetle's roof.

'Luke?' I say, hearing the upward inflexion in my voice.

'He just has the Jeep, as far as I know, unless he's gone to
buy something fancy to use while you're here.' Adam nudges
my elbow with his own and grins.

'Idiot,' I say.

I jump as Alfie's cold fingers curl around my wrist. 'I can't
see who's driving, can you?'

My son watches the car. The sun glowers behind clouds
pregnant with rain, glinting off the windscreen so I can't make
out the driver. Has Seth followed us, is that why there's been
nothing from him? But this is the wrong sort of car, no one
hires this from an airport desk.

The driver's door opens, jerking wide, bouncing on its
hinges. The wind has caught our visitor unawares. A flat,
brown, ankle boot tests the muddy gravel, a woman pulling
herself from the low-slung seat. She looks over at Luke's Jeep,
tucking shoulder-length blond hair behind her ear. The tails of

a checkered wool scarf flutter at the neck of an upturned collar of a closely-fitting wool jacket. At this distance, she could be a well-groomed woman, slightly older than me, but there's no mistaking her as she turns to Seahurst and looks through the glass and into my face.

'Do you know her?' Alfie's voice is full of relief. This woman is no threat to us, in my son's opinion.

'Nicola Symonds, your uncle's mum.'

Is Luke in the car too, perhaps taken ill and couldn't contact us? Nicola strides around to the passenger side of the Audi and opens the car door. She leans in for a moment, then stands, pulling out a brown leather bag and slams the door shut. The indicators blink as she walks towards the slate path. No Luke, then.

'She's coming in, Mom.'

'She might have news of Luke,' I say heading for the door. A tight little knot balls in the pit of my stomach as much from fear of her as of any bad news she might be bringing. But things are different now. No Dad. Mum married, living in Canada. Me all grown up. In the mirror beside the front door is a presentable woman, hair washed, neatly tied back. Shame about the roots, but you can't have everything. Usually, I'd have a bare face at this time of day, but with Jack here, I needed foundation to cover the bruise, so put some mascara on too. But I shouldn't give a damn what Nicola Symonds thinks. She's nothing to do with me and never was.

She stands a little back from the step, looking at me through glass streaked with salt spray. The bag hangs from her shoulder, her hand holding her hair off her face.

I open the door and take a step forward to stand with my trainer toes butting against the metal weather shield. I make no move to suggest she comes in. Beyond her, at the end of the path, Jack and Lou stand watching. Lou pulls a face which I ignore to focus on the woman who was married to my dad for thirty years. Why it strikes me now, I've no idea. Nicola is attractive, a very pretty woman. She has to be late fifties or early sixties, but her skin is clear and smooth, a touch of mascara and coral-pink lip gloss and well-cut honey-blond hair.

She looks past me into Seahurst. Alfie hovers beside the sofa, watching from the sitting area, Molly still glued to *Peppa Pig*. Adam leans with his back to the stove.

'Is Luke home?'

'No.'

She rushes on before I can say any more. 'Do you have any idea when he's expected back?' We stare at each other, neither of us smiling, but I recognise the concern in her blue eyes as my heart sinks. She has no news . . .

'I left a couple of messages on your business number. It's the only contact details for you I could find,' I say.

'I picked them up a few minutes ago.' She stares at me silently – her scarf ripples in the wind.

'I've been trying to contact Luke ever since we landed at Heathrow yesterday.' She says nothing, just continues to look into my face. 'You'd better come in.' I step back from the door and cross my arms against the wind. She looks reluctant to move, continues to study me for a long moment.

'I won't, thank you, Evangeline.' It's the first time I recall her ever using my name. 'It's unlike him . . .' Her lips press into a thin line. 'He always answers his phone. Texts, you know?'

I explain about the place being open and my last call with Luke. I can't remember how much detail I rattled onto her voicemail. She watches me silently, her eyes on my face as I speak. 'I'm really quite worried,' I say, aware I am shivering, the wind pouring across the threshold is damp and cold.

'May I see his mobile?'

'It's not here, just his wallet and house keys. I assume he has it with him.'

'Have you checked the Jeep?'

'It's locked and I haven't seen any keys for it here.'

The wind is rattling along the side of the building, freezing air gushing at me. She must feel it on her back.

'Come in for a second.'

'I won't, if you don't mind.' She steps away from the door and opens the front flap of her bag. 'I have his spare set with me,' she says, rummaging in a side pocket. She glances up at me as she turns away and heads back the way she came. I watch her back for a second. Should I follow her? Lou and Jack turn their attention back to mopping out the Beetle.

I hurry after her along the path to the car. She has the Jeep unlocked and sits in the driver's seat, leaning across to the glove box. She pulls it open as I stop alongside the car. She reaches in and pulls out a mobile phone and charging cable. She snaps the glovebox closed and sits back into the driver's seat. I glance into the rear of the car; the back seats are empty except for a lime green golf umbrella and the Welcome Home placard. The phone screen lights, filling with text and missed call notifications. She presses the home key and enters a four-digit passcode glancing up at me as she does so. I watch her scroll through messages, mine over the last thirty-six hours, missed calls from Will and Jack, several from Nicola today.

'Nothing much here,' she says. 'I'll give it to the police if they want it.'

She drops the mobile into her bag as she watches Jack

walking around the front of the Jeep. He stops beside me.

'You're looking well, Nicola.'

'Jack,' she says with a tight smile.

'We're planning on walking to the harbour, see if there's any word of Luke in town,' says Jack.

Nicola stares straight ahead at Seahurst, clouds scud across the face of the building.

'How long are you and your son staying?'

'Our plans aren't fixed, but we'll travel back before the 6th.'

A ghostly outline of Adam stands beside Alfie at the glass. Can she ask us to leave? We're Luke's guests, this is his place, not hers. She gets out of the Jeep, and I step away from the car. She walks to the rear and opens the boot. I stand beside her and look at a pair of walking boots and a navy wax jacket. She slams the door down, locks the vehicle.

'As his mother, I'm his next of kin. The police will contact me if they have any news, you should do the same.'

She walks around the Jeep to the Audi, the lights bleep on as she nears it. Lou is making a pretence of mopping out the Beetle, but I see her watching through the windscreen. Jack follows Nicola. He says something, his words carried away from me on the salty air as she pulls open the driver's door. She looks into his face then past him to me. She gets into the car and pulls the door shut.

Jack steps back as the Audi pulls away and turns to the track. I sprint past Jack, pull alongside the car and rap my knuckles on the passenger window. The Audi stops as Nicola looks at me. The glass lowers with a whir.

'I left you a voicemail with my number.' She continues to look at me. 'If there's any news, anything at all, you will let me know, won't you?'

CHAPTER THIRTEEN

I LINK MY arm with Lou's.

'You okay?' she says, pulling me close to her.

'I could be better, to be honest. A walk is good, the fresh air will clear my head, it takes a while to shake off a long flight.'

Molly is running up ahead, her red wool hat pushed back, her ebony hair flying behind her.

'Alfie needs a normal few hours, poor kid,' I say. 'Things haven't been great with Seth and me for a while.' I glance as Lou. She's watching my face intently.

'I kind of guessed something was up.'

I manage a flat smile and she squeezes my arm again. Molly stops at the bridge, turns back and waves, shouting for us to hurry.

'Remember when we were that excited?' Lou is looking out across grey mudflats as she speaks; wide at low tide, they flank the river as it weaves between reed bed and marsh.

'Do I remember? Come on, I'll race you!' I say, grabbing her wrist and breaking into a run. I need to lighten up, let the rest of them enjoy the morning.

'Hey!' she says, laughing.

I let her go and run the last few metres to where Molly stands with my old castle-shaped bucket and her fuchsia-pink net. The little girl's face shines with excitement, just like the Lou I first met.

'Come on!' she says climbing the steps onto the bridge. 'If

it starts raining Mummy will make us walk to the harbour.'

I look back at our little party; Jack points upriver, Alfie following his direction intently. The camera is in his hand, the case slung around his neck, the drama about his coat forgotten the instant it was found under a sofa. I wonder what they're talking about. Sometimes it's hard to engage with him these days, but he seems more relaxed now we're out of the house.

Adam has caught Lou's hand and is pulling her along. Beyond them, the land rises sharply to the Abbey. More of the site is visible on this side of the rise. Stones scatter randomly, a short run of broken wall here and there; and soaring above it all, the arch. Shadows play against the flint and stone, the light, low and dazzling. Someone stands with their back to the arch. They look out across the flat ground and straight at me. I squint against the glare, the sun blurring behind gauzy white cloud. A slight figure, long hair streaming in the wind. We haven't passed anyone since we left Seahurst. How would we miss them on this naked landscape? I blink and hold my hand up to shield my face. Try to focus. The light makes my eyes water.

'Hey!' Lou chases Adam. Their laughter bubbles on the dank air rushing across the marsh. I watch them, push the sudden rush of loneliness to one side and look back to the rise. The arch stands alone, a fragment of the past with its back to the sea. No one stands there. Nothing more than shifting shadows and bright light. I recall the person on the clifftop earlier: Jack saw no one though. Adam grabs Lou about her waist making her shriek, and I laugh with them.

Molly's rapid footsteps make the metal bridge ring, birds flap and rise into the air. I take hold of the handrail and climb the steps. The last time I came here, Dad was with me. We walked back from a day trip out on his boat. A scorching early-September day. The bridge was packed with end-of-season holidaymakers, the ones with pre-schoolers. The tide had been rushing in, people packing up, streaming back the way we'd come to catch the ice-cream van before it headed off to the housing estates for the evening. We walk without speaking for a while and by the time we reach the bridge the silence had grown hostile, too thick to break. We had argued all that last summer about everything and nothing. I'd slept over at Lou's more than at Seahurst, as much to be near Will as to escape Dad's low moods. I'd do things so differently now if only I could.

'Let's sit here!' Molly is kneeling, taking out her fishing line and greasy tendrils of bacon rind from the bucket. The bridge vibrates with footsteps as I kneel beside her and tuck flapping strands of hair behind her ear.

'Your mum's hair never stays in a scrunchie either,' I say, taking the line from her.

'Where's our magic stone?'

'In my rucksack.' I swing the bag from my shoulder and unzip the front pocket. I pull out one of the larger stones that had been amongst the pile on my bedroom floor. I thread string through the hole in the stone.

'You were always dead superstitious, Evie.' Adam squats beside us, watching me tie off the string.

'You can never have too much luck,' I say, as Jack thunks Dad's old fishing bucket down beside me. 'And you never know when you might need a bit of it either. You wait and see, Molly. We'll catch far more than the boys with their fancy line and weights!'

'You're on!' says Jack, kneeling down and pulling line from Dad's old bucket. 'Hold onto to that for me, Alfie.'

Alfie takes the reel from Jack, his face a picture. He's no idea what's going on.

'We don't often get the whole bridge to ourselves. Those crabs are going to be starving!' Lou says, leaning on the handrail and looking out across the mudflats to the heathland and a pale, never-ending sky.

I secure the rind to the line with a couple of knots. 'Ready?' Molly beams at me as I smile back. She drops the stone over the edge of the bridge. It hits the water with a plop.

'It works really well!'

'Don't talk too soon, Miss Molly. Let's see what your catch looks like first!' Jack kneels between Alfie and Molly as we all peer at the sandy grey water gushing towards the North Sea. Molly pulls her line up, the rind white and lank.

'Leave it until you feel it jerking, Mols.' Jack's voice is low and calm. I can't help but smile at Lou, it could so easily be us twenty-five years ago, focussing on the surface of the water. Waiting.

'Hey!' Alfie sits back on his heels.

'Keep a tight hold on the line, Alfie. Pull it up slow and steady,' says Jack.

Alfie looks uncertain, his eyes find mine. 'Smoothly does it,' I say. 'You might have a monster on there.'

There's much shuffling and jostling of bucket and line until we all admire a large brown crab in the bottom of Dad's old bucket.

'He needs a bit of water to keep himself cool.' Jack takes Molly's bucket and heads back along the bridge.

'I'll take a photo!' says Alfie, fumbling to take my old Leica from its case.

'Take one on your phone as well, just in case, Alfie,' I say, as he fiddles to focus the camera.

'We can't be too much longer if we're going to have any time in town,' says Lou, catching my eye.

Alfie and Molly instantly start to protest about the unfairness of life. We have barely been here ten minutes.

'Why don't we stay and see how many we can catch before these dull grown-ups get back?' Jack is striding back with a bucket so full, water sloshes over its rim. He wears a grin on his face like I haven't seen since we arrived.

'Can we?' Alfie and Molly stand together, an unlikely alliance if ever I saw one. I'm relieved they're getting along now.

'I thought you wanted to do a few things in town?' I say to Jack.

'Lou knows what I wanted to pick up. To be honest, I'd rather have some peace and quiet with these two demons than have to make polite conversation with all and sundry. It'll be busy today, first proper opening since Christmas.'

I glance at Lou, Jack stands just behind her and I know they have planned this. I'm not alone in my need to find out what the hell is going on with Luke.

'You won't get a better offer today,' Jack says, as Alfie lowers his line back into the river.

CHAPTER FOURTEEN

W E CROSS THE bridge and walk alongside the levies following the river towards the harbour.

'Is it me, or are these higher than they used to be?' I say.

'They've banked them up over the years, usually after a flood,' says Lou.

Adam strides ahead, and I follow Lou. The wildness of this place surprises me, something I didn't see as a child now starkly spreading out for miles all around us. Flat heath and marsh, singing reed beds and pale, wide skies, curlews calling, gulls screaming overhead.

'It's beautiful but as desolate as hell here this time of year,' I say, as my eye is drawn back the way we came – scrubland, cliffs and, barely visible now, the Abbey.

'It's the same during the summer, just more colour, blue sky, yellow gorse.' Lou's wellingtons squelch mud in all directions with each step. My ancient purple wellies are too short for me now, my big toe bumping the front of the boot, but I was relieved to find them beneath piles of old bedding in the bottom of my wardrobe. My trainers and old leather boots would have got ruined in this.

The occasional small boat has sunk low against the bank, waiting for the tide to turn and the water to rush back in. More vessels gather the further we walk. The harbour is at once familiar. Here the boats bustle for space at the quay-side, long rickety stages, grey wood poking out of thick mud.

Most vessels are shut up for the winter, some under cover on the shore. Jack's right about it being busy: dog walkers, pram-pushers, couples out for a seasonal stroll to shift the fug of overindulgence wander along the gravel walkway. There was a time when Jack would have been at the hub of all this, chatting with locals and tourists alike. I suspect his excuse not to come here today suited him very well. The path widens, Lou loops her arm through Adam's, and I find I'm the third wheel again.

'Miss Mathews!' A slim man walks towards us, taking long, effortless strides, a golden Labrador trotting at his heels. He raises his hand and waves, and automatically I wave back, some faint recognition stirring at the back of my mind. His hiking boots, waterproof trousers and jacket give no clues about who he is; standard kit on a day like today. We stop beside the harbour wall, my brain reeling trying to place him.

'You might not remember me: Simon Arthurton?'

I smile as fragments of memory tumble into place. Me, sitting with a book in my lap, its pages not turning, watching the receptionist and clients coming and going while I waited for Dad to finish his 'bit of business' with his solicitor.

'Yes, of course.'

He holds out his gloved hand. I shake it, his grip firm and brief.

'Nicola Symonds came by my office only half an hour ago – told me not to wait in for you both. I only have Luke's contact number, so I'm glad to bump into you. I don't work out of the local office usually, I'm based in Ipswich these days, but I still have my cottage just off The Green. Makes sense to meet you here. I'm sorry to hear about your brother. Rather a worry.' The dog nudges my knee. I bend to pat its silky head as Simon continues. I'm not sure what on earth he's on about. 'I wanted to check with you if there was anything you wanted to discuss?'

'Me?' I ask.

'When your brother made the appointment, it was for you both.' I must look confused; I certainly feel it. 'I assumed you knew of the arrangements? His mother picked up the appointment she says from his mobile phone this morning.'

Nice of her to pass that one on, then. 'Luke didn't mention an appointment,' I say.

Lou and Adam join us, all the usual hellos and handshakes as I remember Luke's rushed call as we hurried through the airport to the check-in desk. Something about Dad, things not being as we thought – was this what the meeting was about?

'How's Jack?' Simon has an open, friendly face, he's probably in his late fifties. No hint of the soft Suffolk burr that runs through Lou and Adam's voices, though. I remember feeling shy and tongue-tied when he and Dad came back into the reception. Simon invariably asked about the book I was reading, how school was going, all the usual lame things adults ask children they don't know too well.

'He's good,' says Lou. 'We've left him crabbing with Molly and Alfie. He didn't fancy battling through the holiday crowds down here.'

'It's even busier than usual, what with the cliff-fall that bought the green brigade out, and you've heard about the drugs washing up last night, just beyond Sizewell? A bit of drama never fails to pull in the crowds.'

Lou and Simon rattle on about it all, and I find my mind wandering, wondering what we both needed to see Simon about? None of it makes any sense.

'I've been meaning to give Jack a call and see if I could tempt him to a dram or two at the White Hart. I'm past sitting on the beach freezing to death these days.'

I join in with the laugher, and I wonder just how much time Jack has spent gathering his thoughts alone on the beach at night. Simon turns his attention back to me.

'I hope you hear from Luke today. His mother was understandably concerned.'

'Do you know Nicola?' I've no idea why I need to know or what difference it makes. I had thought Nicola kept herself separate from all things Suffolk.

'A little.' His smile is professional; all friendly openness has gone, his expression closed. 'When I left her, she was going to check the guesthouse Luke sometimes uses, although I'm at a loss to know why he'd stay there when there's Seahurst with its glorious views. I'm sure everything will turn out all right, there's usually some silly explanation behind these things.' Simon smiles, and I feel myself smiling back; a reflex thing.

'When Luke's back, give me a call and we can book another time to meet up.'

'What was the appointment about?' I say.

'I'm not entirely clear myself, I'm afraid. Just a date in my diary for when you were here.'

He assumes Luke is coming back, but after more than 24 hours, I'm less sure. These people know my brother, have spent time with him over the last decade, and I haven't. They are surely better able to second guess what he might do? No one says it out loud, but this is so like what happened with Dad. I wish I could shift the growing heaviness that seems to have made a home for itself in my chest, but I can't.

Simon holds up his gloved hand again as he strides off towards the marshes, the dog trotting behind him.

'I'm around until the New Year, so I can see you both anytime.'

'Shall we find a café and grab a coffee?' I say, suddenly feeling dog tired. There's not much we can do and Nicola is clearly two steps ahead of us anyway.

'Watch out, here comes Luke's mother,' Lou says looking just past the Harbour Masters hut. 'Don't reckon she got any answers, by the looks of her.' Nicola is almost breaking into a jog as she weaves between people along the harbour path. She passes the front of the Harbour Master's hut, the lights on the Audi blink at her approach. I hadn't seen the car tucked in between the black clapboard buildings. I bet every car park and side street in town is heaving today. I nip across towards her as she opens the driver's door.

'Mrs Symonds?' She turns at the sound of my voice and looks surprised to see me. 'Did you find out anything?'

She glances past me at Lou standing beside Adam. 'No news is good news, it seems, but it leaves me not knowing where Luke is.' She looks me full in the face. 'I was about to head back to Seahurst to go through Luke's room. See if there is anything that might suggest where he's gone.' She watches me for a moment. 'Did the policewoman look in there when she came by?'

'Briefly. Jack showed her while I was getting dressed – I'd just had a shower.'

'Did she find anything?'

'If she did, she didn't mention it.'

'This business down on the beach seems to have distracted everyone. The press have been up here. The nationals as well as the local papers, I'm told. No one seems to focus on what I'm saying about Luke. We must go back to Seahurst and make a proper search of the place.' Nicola sinks into the driver's seat. 'Get in. I'll drive the two of us over there now.'

CHAPTER FIFTEEN

NICOLA KEEPS HER eye on the track, weaving the car left and right, avoiding as many potholes as possible. We leave the harbour and head for the narrow road heading inland.

'We bumped into Simon Arthurton just now. He mentioned an appointment,' I say. Nicola continues to concentrate on the road. 'Were you planning on letting me know about that?' No comment, so I watch the landscape slide by. Familiar things: the heath dotted with gorse, a bobtail of a small brown rabbit, the water tower and lighthouse. The grand houses that watch over the common come and go as we pick up speed and head for the main road.

'Don't you think this seems similar to what happened with Dad?' I blurt out.

She glances at me, back to the road. 'No, I don't.'

Perhaps it's better to sit in silence. It's only a few miles to Seahurst. I pull off my gloves, too warm now in the wave of hot air spewing at me from the huge vents in the dash. The car is immaculate, the new smell of leather and polish mingling with the spicy scent I'd noticed Nicola wearing earlier. I shoot her a side glance. 'Why did Luke and Dad fall out so badly?' I'm pushing her too hard and fast, but it's only a short trip back to Seahurst along the coast road. If I don't quiz her now, I may never get the chance again. 'I only saw Luke that last summer at Dad's funeral. He never came to

Seahurst once while I was there.' Although I've asked Luke this several times, he always ducked and dived, avoiding giving me a proper reply. It's left me feeling like I was to blame in some way.

'I don't remember what they fell out about,' she replies.

'Luke had a talent for upsetting Dad.'

Nicola turns the car onto the main road, and we drive in silence. She must know about the times they argued, Luke disappearing for hours at a time or getting the train back home to Essex. The winter sun is low and white, light winking off the marshes as the car speeds by.

'Simon Arthurton didn't know why Luke made the appointment for you both. Marcus kept his business up here separate from our life in Essex. Luke continued in the same way.' She glances my way. 'Out of respect for me, as I'm sure you'll understand.'

Dad said little about his 'other' life, and Luke spent less time at Seahurst as he got older. Spending time with a much younger sister couldn't compete with hanging out with his mates. And Dad's old affair with Mum seemed to simmer constantly in the background between the three of us. Nicola concentrates on the road; it dips and bends, traffic coming at us so fast I have to stop myself flinching.

'Why did Luke stay in town rather than Seahurst?' She doesn't answer, and I'm fed up with being polite. I can sit in silence if that's what she wants. Brown broken banks of fern flash past the car window. When Dad drove us along here, or later when we got Betty, these were lush, green mounds of fronds.

'Haven't you searched Luke's room at all?' Nicola asks, a frown crinkling her brow.

'I'd have told you if I had.'

'I'm not suggesting you're lying. I just want to check we're not going over old ground.'

'What do you expect to find?' I ask. 'A note saying he's gone fishing?'

The muscles in her jaw tense. 'He has a second mobile, a business one that I've searched for at home. I'm hoping it might be up here.'

I'm amazed. Surely, this was something to mention earlier? 'Did you tell the police that?'

'Of course, I'm not an idiot, Evangeline.'

'Evie. People call me Evie.' I pull off my beanie, reach for the dash and turn down the heating. I half expect her to say something, but she just drives. 'Only asking as you didn't mention a second mobile to me.'

'If it's gone flat, I may have missed it.' She glances at me. 'It could be in a suit pocket or a drawer.'

'Why would he use that and not his own phone?' I say.

'I don't know. We need to check out everything we can.' None of this makes sense right now.

'Is there anything else we should check out?'

She glances at me. 'Do you know who Maurice Broughton is?' I shake my head as she slows the car to take a left turn.

'Why?' I ask.

There are a couple of calls to him on Luke's mobile. Probably nothing. I call him and check who he is when I have a decent signal.' I wait as it feels like there's more to come. 'You look the spitting image of your mother with your hair that colour – I suppose you know that. You're very like Marcus when it's natural, I thought so at his funeral.' Her voice is level, no hint of anything. As I watch her drive, I can see Luke in the jut of her jaw, the set and colour of her bright blue eyes.

'I get it's difficult for you.' I fold the beanie in my lap and unfold it, smooth it flat and fold it again. 'None of it's my fault. No one can help being born, right?' Nicola keeps driving. 'If we could just be civil for now, until we find out where Luke is. You're his mother, and I get that, but he is my brother too.'

'A half-brother you haven't had anything to do with for more than a decade.'

I look at her in surprise, her words spat out with such force. Does she know Luke got in touch a few years back? Admittedly, there had been nothing before then. No emails. No text messages. No phone calls. I had been as much to blame for the silence after Dad's death as Luke.

'You know about the Skype calls? Mostly once or twice a month, we have a long chat,' I say. Perhaps Luke calls when Nicola's not around or when he's up here? I call when Seth's at Maxwells. Maybe Luke's the same? If Nicola's surprised, she doesn't show it.

'You know Luke's selling Seahurst?' she says, her voice level again.

'He mentioned it.'

'He should have sold straight after Marcus died. I doubt he'll get anything much for it. Who would buy it now with it being so close to the cliffs? A pity, another mile inland and it would be worth a fortune.'

'I suggested he rent it as a holiday let. The sea views are amazing. It'd be good for that for a while, and he could use it sometimes.' I watch Nicola, but she keeps her attention on the road as we head into a deep bend.

'The business is expanding, and we're frantically busy. Luke doesn't have time to keep coming up here. He should be more focused if he's going to run things in a few years.'

Still trying to cut ties with Suffolk, then. Nicola slows the car as we reach The Street and pass the row of cottages. Lights twinkle from the pub windows as we pass by and turn down the narrow coastal track.

'Do you ever use Seahurst?'

'Why would I?' Nicola drops the car into second gear and turns onto the track to the house. The trees gather overhead, the car headlights come on, their beam streaming through pockets of mist hanging where the trail dips. 'Your mother chose the plot,' she says as we near the end of the trees, the hazy light up ahead growing stronger. 'And besides, whatever is there to do?'

I can't describe how time became elastic here; summers pulled out endlessly without ever a dull moment. If I try to explain what we did with all that time . . . I'll never make her understand.

'I'm sure Luke will be back, and everything will be straightened out before you head off to Canada, but if not, would you be out by the 4th? I'll arrange for you to leave the keys with the solicitor in town.'

'Luke said to stay as long as we wanted.' I haven't had time to even think about the situation with Seth. The last thing I want is to rush back too soon. 'I'll ask the solicitor to let you know when we hand the keys in.'

Nicola turns the car sharp left and heads along the cliff track, making faster progress than Betty ever could. She's going too quickly as she approaches the deep dip before the track climbs again to the house.

'Slow down a bit.' I grab hold of the dash. There's a dull thunk as the car exhaust scrapes along the rough ground, Nicola's bag flinging off the backseat and onto the floor.

'Christ's sakes!' Nicola hits the brakes so hard the bonnet dips, the headlights' beam bouncing between bracken and muddy wet track. 'If I ever needed a reason not to come here!'

We sit in silence, Seahurst's lights sparkling between the twisted black hedges up ahead.

'Just a short distance now,' I say.

She puts the car into gear, and we move slowly along again, the house coming into view. She parks beside Luke's Jeep. We don't speak as we get out of the car and head up the slate path with the wind at our backs. I pick up the key from beneath the large flat stone beside the front door, unlock it, and the door slides open. I glance back at Nicola. Her hands are deep inside her coat pockets, scarf pulled up over her chin. I step indoors.

'Do you know if Luke has had problems with the house? The pipes have been making a loud groaning sound, and the shower barely functions.'

'He hasn't said anything.'

'Hopefully Adam has managed to fix it.'

Nicola stands just beyond the sofa, looking out across the cliffs. The day is dying. A pale blast of low sunlight spreads across the sky. Shafts cut between the wicker fence, playing bright spots across the polished stone floor.

'Can I get you a hot drink?' I say.

'No, thank you.' She openly stares about the place, taking in the huge carved stone above the wood burner, the Abbey and the woods out back. 'How do you stay here?' She looks at me. 'The place makes me shiver. Everything out there looking in.'

Mum's goldfish bowl; maybe they can agree on something.

'I must admit it has been a bit unnerving being here on my own.' I glance at the rattle on the mantlepiece, feel sure Luke won't have mentioned that to her. 'I'm used to Dad being here. Luke and lots of friends about the place. It has a completely different feel in summer. Light nights make such a difference.'

She's watching the woods behind me. Their dark shifting shapes fill the glass, blotting out the light. It won't help to mention the rat problem.

'Let's get this done and I'll head home,' she says, unbuttoning the top of her coat.

'I'll put the kettle on and show you Luke's room. I could murder a cup of tea.'

As I turn to the kitchen, something catches my eye, more than just the shivering light. It takes a moment for me to realise what I'm looking at. Not just light, but water washing across the floor, edging silently towards where we stand.

'Shit!' I push past Nicola and run to the kitchen. The sink is overflowing, water cascading over the edge, down cupboards and across the floor. The cold tap gushes a steady stream of water along the work surface, running between dirty mugs and plates waiting to go into the dishwasher. I glance down at my feet, water seeping into my socks. I grab the tap and try to turn it. I can't make it move at all.

'Turn it off, for goodness' sake!' Nicola at my back, looking into the sink. She yanks her coat sleeve above her wrist and reaches into the water. It's as deep as her elbow. She claws at the plug. A snug fit, she won't raise it that way.

'There's a lever for the plug-release,' I say, fumbling to find it behind the taps. I haven't needed to use it. I've no idea how it got closed. The lever gives a fraction. I daren't force it - such a weight of water pressing down.

'Try the tap,' I say.

I drag open the cupboard doors beneath the sink, water soaking the cleaning cloths and tea towels. I swipe bottles aside. They tumble out, rolling away across the wet tiles. I grab the handle of Dad's old brown bucket Jack and Lou used earlier to mop out Betty and scoop a load of water from the sink. The level drops a fraction below the rim. It'll give us a moment to tackle the tap.

'Try and turn it off!' I shout, dumping the bucket onto the floor. Water sloshes over our feet.

'I'm trying!' The chrome shines as Nicola turns the tap. The flow stays the same. Won't stop. Nicola keeps turning, turning, turning. Eventually it slows, lessens, stops. She lets go of the tap and stands straight, looking into the sink. 'Why didn't you turn it off straight away?' There's no missing the accusing tone in her voice. Does she think I did this on purpose?

'It was stuck solid.'

'It turned easily enough for me.'

'Perhaps I loosened it? Lou thought they might need a new washer as we had problems the other day.'

Nicola scans the floor, the sleeves of her coat dripping. There's so much water.

'This needs sorting out straight away. It'll ruin the floor.' She glances back to the sitting area, the long bleached wooden floorboards already darkening in patches. 'I'd expect you to take more care as a guest here. Wooden floors don't come cheap.'

I won't apologise, not to her. To Luke, if we can't get this cleaned up and sorted.

'Try lifting the plug again. I'll see if the lever will shift,' I say. She looks into my face for a long moment. All I hear is the wind keening about the house. 'Then I'll help you check out Luke's room for that phone.'

CHAPTER SIXTEEN

NICOLA WRINGS A cloth into the sink and hangs it to dry over the tall curving neck of the tap.

'This is probably vintage by now,' I say, spooning peppermint tea into Dad's glass teapot. 'Looks like Luke still uses it, though.'

'He drinks that stuff all the time. I wouldn't be surprised if he hasn't blocked the drains with the dregs he tips down the sink.'

I look across the kitchen to where she stands, her back to the counter, arms folded across her chest.

'I can't tempt you to a cup then?'

She shakes her head. 'There's an odd smell, isn't there?' She looks into the sink, then back at me. 'Like stagnant water.'

'Luke seems to have had a bit of trouble with rats – did he mention that?'

Nicola pulls a face. 'He certainly didn't. This doesn't smell like rats, though.'

I tell her about the musty smell, the strange scratching noises and the traps we found this morning. 'Hopefully, it's all sorted now, but I'll call a pest control firm if it isn't.'

She pushes herself away from the counter. 'Maybe it is rats then. Let's check Luke's room. I said I'd let the police know if we find anything.'

'It's the room at the bottom of the stairs,' I say.

She heads for the staircase as the kettle boils. I should

mention Luke's laptop. The police might want to look at it, but something makes me hold back. I can look at it this evening – if I can guess the password. Let the police know myself if there's anything on there tomorrow. I pour water onto the tea leaves. They do make a mess, so maybe Nicola's right. If Luke slings this lot down the sink several times a day, the smell might not be just down to the rats. I assumed he'd got the new packet of tea for me. I leave it to brew and follow Nicola downstairs.

She has the bedside cabinet top drawer open, the contents spread across the bed as I stop at Luke's bedroom door. All the usual junk: passport, old flight tickets, a Norwich Castle guidebook, one red woollen glove and a creased black tie. Nicola scoops everything up and stuffs it back into the drawer. The second drawer is deeper. She lifts a paper file out, sits on the bed, and flicks through it. I've no stomach for this. I head back upstairs.

Dusk has turned the outside to shades of grey, shadows deepening, growing longer. I turn on the uplighters and the kitchen spots and pour a mug of tea. The floor looks better, the boards drying out, their pale colour returning. I pull open the small drawer beside the oven and root about until I find at the very back the tiny black remote I'd seen Dad use three, perhaps four times.

I hold it up and press the button. I press it a second and third time. No clanking, no whirring, the batteries long dead. The blinds probably don't work after all these years, but it would be cosier if they were closed. I open the back of the remote, the space for two triple AAAs is empty. I glance about the kitchen and the room. Would Luke have spares? I rummage about again in the drawer and find an ancient-looking packet of batteries.

'Evangeline!' I drop the remote on the counter and head for the stairs. Nicola stands at the bottom, looking down the corridor towards my room.

'Is everything all right?' I start down the stairs. Nicola looks up at me, her face full of surprise.

'I thought I saw you along there!' Nicola looks down the corridor. 'I could have sworn I saw someone.' The corridor is brightly lit and empty. I watch Nicola's profile, a frown pulling across her face. 'I heard a noise, a clicking sort of thing.' She's holding something in her right hand, and she raises it slightly as I stop beside her. 'His work mobile.' She continues to look away from me down the empty corridor. 'I'm sure I saw someone.' Her voice is low, and she raises a finger to her lips. 'I thought it was you.' The white painted brickwork arches to the ceiling, the flags running past the bathroom, my room, and the garage steps on the far wall. Nicola heads down the corridor, I follow. She stops at the bathroom door and glances back at me. It's ajar. 'That smell is stronger down here. Have you run the shower?'

'Yesterday and today. It'll probably take a while to clear.'

Nicola looks back at me. She switches on the bathroom light and pushes the door wide open. I stare over her shoulder into the bathroom mirror. I look like a crazy woman with wind-blown blond hair and wide, staring brown eyes.

'I'm sorry,' she says. 'I'm sure I saw someone standing just outside the door here. Obviously, I was mistaken.'

I smile at her in the glass, but she is pretty shaken, her face pale. 'Are you okay?'

'Of course.' She steps into the room and looks about. 'The clicking sound was so clear. A repetitive thing. It made me go into the corridor to see what it was.'

'What did it sound like?' I say.

The scratching is sudden and loud. We freeze as we stare at each other.

'That?' I whisper.

'No, not that.' She points to the wall below the wide square sink. The brick vent is barely visible, painted the same soft white as the rest of the room. Only the grid of small dark holes stands out. 'Coming from there?' she asks. The scratching comes again but from behind us. I jerk around to see the drain in the well of the floor below the shower head. The scuffing comes again, loud, like someone dragging something heavy across the floor.

'That musky smell gets in the back of your throat,' Nicola says. 'I've smelt it before in a property we were renovating for a client. We had to leave the site to Rentokil. There were rats in the walls, the roof space . . .' She stops speaking as she looks at me. I must look horrified. I certainly feel it. 'But there doesn't seem to be any sign here of them getting inside the house,' she says, looking about the floor and then back to me.

'I'm supposed to feel reassured by that?'

'Strange if they're causing the problems with the plumbing.' She walks out into the corridor. 'I'd keep the bathroom door closed and ask if your guy can take a look for you again.'

'Wouldn't Luke have mentioned this? I mean, rats in the place is hardly normal.'

'He's a grown man. He'd just deal with it.'

I follow her to the bottom of the stairs. 'I wouldn't think these are cavity walls, they're far too old for that, but perhaps some have been dry lined? Any gaps . . .'

My chest is tight, and I realise I'm holding my breath, my ears straining for the slightest sound.

'Can I leave you to get that looked into while we wait for

Luke to show up?' She's looking back along the corridor as she speaks. 'Send any account to me at the office. I'll see it gets paid.' She glances at the dark screen of the mobile in her hand. 'There was a little charge left on it. He hadn't made or received any calls. I imagine he left it down here when he arrived Christmas Eve and used his personal phone. I'll charge it and have a better look, but I don't think there's anything that'll help.'

'Luke was here for Christmas?' I'd assumed he spent the festive break in Essex.

'He thought you were coming over. You kept changing your plans.'

I don't respond, just study her closed expression. No way could we leave Maxwells at Christmas. I did change my mind backwards and forwards about coming over, but never the date.

'No calls to whoever the guy was?' I can't help it, but my voice sounds like I don't believe her.

'Maurice Broughton? No, nothing.' She turns to her left.

'What's in there?'

'Dad's room.'

She opens the door and stops just inside. She looks at the bed, the desk, the old computer and files. Despite the weird noises, I want her to leave, to stop nosing about.

'Couldn't you use this room while the rats are dealt with?'

'Luke kept it exactly the same,' I say.

Nicola looks at me, closes the door and walks past me to the stairs. 'Neither of you handled Marcus's death very well, did you?'

The stairs clang as she starts to climb them. I watch her, too astonished to move. I've no clue how Luke was in the months following Dad's suicide. I threw myself into setting up the restaurant, hiring staff, creating menus, attending meetings with the bank, lawyers, accountants. I barely recall that time at all. Even Alfie's birth is a bit of a blur.

'How did you think either of us would handle something like that?' I shout after her.

She turns mid-flight and looks down at me, her face startled. I've yelled at her, but what did she expect with a comment like that?

'I was barely eighteen. It's kind of young to lose a parent, and in that way, don't you think?'

She studies me, and I wait for her to say something. 'You're so like him. I've never realised it before.'

'Like Dad?'

'Luke.' I don't know what to say. Just stare back at her. 'Both of you were so self-obsessed you each assumed Marcus's suicide had to be all be down to you.'

'How could Luke ever think that?'

'Like you said, he had a talent for falling out with Marcus. They had a huge row earlier that summer.'

The first time I saw Luke was at Dad's funeral. Luke hadn't stayed at Seahurst that year, and although I plagued Dad with questions about when he would be coming over, there was never a straight answer. He stuck close to Nicola at the funeral, barely speaking more than half a dozen words all afternoon. I'd been desperate to talk to him, ask his advice, what should I do? I felt utterly bereft as I watched his face slide by as I sat in the back of a cab heading for the airport.

'What did they argue about?'

'Does it matter now?'

'Yes, it does!'

Nicola's jaw tightens. She turns away from me and starts back up the stairs. 'It was about you, actually. I had wanted to go on a family cruise. We hadn't taken a holiday in years, we were so busy with the business. Marcus was always up here every summer.' I chase up the stairs after her. 'I wanted it to be just us, my family. Marcus wouldn't hear of putting you off until after the holiday.'

'And Luke said he should have done?'

She picks up her bag from the sofa and drops Luke's mobile inside.

'They argued about Luke's role at the firm. Luke wanted a year out to travel, he wasn't sure following in his father's footsteps was for him. You followed on from that.'

'How?' I say, determined she let me understand this.

'Marcus sent Luke home to Essex after they argued up here and refused to let him come back. Luke was furious you were here when he wasn't.'

Dad hadn't argued about my staying over at Lou's for most of that summer. I'd assumed he just wanted rid of a grumpy teenager, but was there more to it? Was Dad depressed, but what did Luke mean when he said there was stuff I should know?

She puts on her coat and winds her scarf about her neck. 'I have to go. I want to make it to the main road before it's completely dark,' she says. The cars outside are hulking black shapes now, the day's colour drained away. I follow her across the room.

'We could try the Maurice guy's number,' I say, suddenly wanting to delay her departure. The unease at the thought of being here on my own makes me shiver. Nicola looks at me for a moment. 'I can usually get enough signal.' She rummages in her bag and pulls out Luke's personal mobile.

'Luke texted to say he'd left a message. Could this guy return his call as he was staying in Suffolk over Christmas.'

She presses dial and puts the phone to her ear. I hear the faint ring, the click as the call goes to voicemail.

'Have you Googled him?' I say.

Nicola shakes her head. 'No signal earlier.'

I pull out my phone and put Maurice Broughton into the search engine. A few names come up on LinkedIn and SM. 'Nothing that looks likely. A guy in the US, but that's about it.'

'Maybe a client, although Luke wouldn't usually use his private mobile. When I'm home, I'll check the company database and let the police have the name.' She looks at me, and I hold her gaze.

'What?' she says.

'Maurice is an unusual name, and I'm sure . . .' I step across to the coffee table and pull out a couple of Dad's notebooks. I flick through the pages of the one Will borrowed when he went fishing with Jack. Dad's scrawl and sketches are like hieroglyphics scattered at various angles across the pages. I turn to the inside cover.

'Here!' I say, glancing up at Nicola as I stand. 'Only the Christian name and a Norwich number. Seems odd Luke's trying to catch up with someone of that name, doesn't it?'

I hold the notebook open. Nicola stands beside me and squints. 'I need my glasses.'

I point to the number as she dials it into Luke's phone and puts it on speaker. We listen to it connect and click straight through to the Norwich Castle Museum and a list of opening times.

'Will and Jack Maynard said Luke was following up Dad's research,' I say as she disconnects the call.

'A waste of time, really it is. It isn't healthy, and I hope you don't encourage him. Luke's obsessed with Marcus's death, he's determined it was something other than suicide.'

I'm surprised at the ferocity in her tone. They've clearly had words about this, and I'd guess more than once. I think better of mentioning Luke's conversation as Alfie and I raced through Toronto airport.

'The floor looks okay,' she says as we pass the kitchen. 'Your friends and your son will be back soon?' She stops just before the front door and looks back at me.

'No more than an hour, I expect. It's already getting dark.'

For a moment, we stand in silence, looking at each other. She opens the door, and cold air rushes in as she steps outside, clutching her scarf about her throat. It was cold earlier, but the temperature has dropped along with the daylight. She pauses a few steps along the path and turns back.

'They both loved you, Evangeline.'

She doesn't wait for a reply, and I'm not sure I have one. I close the door and watch her through the glass as she climbs into her car and drives away.

CHAPTER SEVENTEEN

ALFIE TRAMPS OFF down the path as Jack fastens the collar of his waterproof.

'Sure you won't come?' asks Jack.

'I haven't shaken off the jet lag. I'll potter and then maybe get my head down.' After Nicola's visit this afternoon and all the weird stuff here, I feel unsettled. I'd rather be at Seahurst anyway in case Luke shows up.

'We'll be further along the bay if you change your mind, and for God's sake, keep away from the cliffs.'

I pull a face at Jack as he heads off after Alfie. I fold my arms across my chest against the damp air. I won't be making that mistake a second time.

'Have fun, both of you!'

My old yellow windcheater is a little too big for Alfie, but my ancient purple wellingtons are a perfect fit. In the dark, he didn't object too much to the colour. The security lights come on one-by-one as they walk away down the path; Jack laden with rods, a rucksack and brolly, Alfie, a bucket and camping seat. Jack holds up his hand, Alfie waving as they head past the cars, the darkness folding around them. I close the door and double-check it's locked.

I head back into the kitchen. It's an unfamiliar space with the blinds down, but much better with the dark beyond the gauzy material. I switch off the Xbox and TV and put the Leica back in its case. The film canister lies on the table.

Alfie's likely to be so disappointed when it's developed if there's nothing to see.

The large brown crab Lou and Adam bought back from the stall at the harbour cools beside the hob. There had been no contest for Alfie between helping me dress it or going night-fishing with Jack. Once I have it sorted and in the fridge, I'll have a look at Luke's laptop while Alfie's out of the house.

I pull out my mobile. 21:43. Seth will be at the restaurant, busy with pre-service prep. I put in my earphones and pick up the playlist from where it left off. I lay the first crab on its back and twist off a leg. With everything that's been going on, I've not had a moment to think about Seth. I have to speak to him, it's cowardly to tell him over the phone, but he knows it already. He knew it Christmas Day. He knew it long before that, so why not let us go?

I look up and stare blindly at the room. For a moment, I think something caught my eye, a movement, but no, there's nothing here. I look back at the partly dissected crab. I'd planned on speaking to Luke about it all. Now I'm using his absence to delay, but nothing will change what I want to do. Luke was only ever going to be a sounding board, approving the decision I'd already made. Seth saw it all coming. With Alfie there and a gorgeous ring, the proposal was designed to push me off course yet again. Not this time. Not after Christmas day.

The crab is splayed out on the chopping board. I tear off the dead man's fingers. Better to make it sound like it's coming from Seth, not from me. If it's his decision, it'll be easier. Maybe he's already spreading that version of events. There's been nothing from the guys at Maxwells, but I'm beyond caring what people think. Let Seth calm down before we head back to Toronto. That was the point of coming over. He can't touch me here, can't shout at Alfie.

I open the cutlery drawer, find a spoon, and scoop soft brown flesh into a side bowl. The tap turns smoothly, water running ice cold. Is there a hint of something musty and stale? I let it run, clear and fresh, the system working properly at last. I fill a saucepan and put it on to heat. A quick check on the internet earlier had confirmed boiled water is safe to use.

I rinse my fingers, pull out my mobile and pause the playlist. Maybe I should call Mum and see if she knows what Seth is up to? I can't face another ear-bashing right now, and she'd call if there's any significant news. I scroll through recent calls until I get to Seth's number. If he's in the office or dining room at Maxwells, he'll put on a performance for anyone in earshot. Just be clear, keep it simple, don't let him take over the conversation. I press dial and wait.

My heart is banging in my chest like crazy. I pull in a deep breath and try to keep calm as the call connects and rings – words spiral through my mind, my hand tight around the phone. I listen to the droning tone, the line cutting to voicemail. Seth's familiar message to leave a number; he'll return the call as soon as he can. Stupid not to have something ready to reel off. The silence draws out.

'Seth, it's Evie.' I pause for a moment, not wanting to scramble my words. I must sound clear and confident. 'We got here okay. I think Mum let you know that already. We need to speak.' I stare at the crab's dissected body. Turn off the dripping tap. 'You know I've wanted out for a while. We're not good for each other. Christmas Day proved that to us both. When we fly back, we'll stay with Mum until we can sort things out – with the apartment, Maxwells and stuff.' I take a breath to stop my words from spilling out so fast.

'Neither of us are happy, we haven't been for ages. This is the best thing for Alfie too. I'll call you before we fly back as we'll need to pick up Alfie's school uniform and a few bits from the apartment.'

I cut the call, my hand shaking. I log into my emails and find the one sent a few days before Christmas to the letting agent. I open and reread their reply. Is this why Seth suddenly proposed? Did he know of my plans to move out? Alfie's convinced he monitors my account. I send a short email asking if the small two-bed apartment is still available. Would they let me know how to put down a deposit?

I switch the playlist back on. I should open a new email account, change all my passwords for banking and stuff, in case Alfie's right. I chop the crab's body in half, spoon out the white meat, and try not to think about how Maxwells might be going. I've only ever been away a few days at a time since we opened, the longest just over a week when Alfie was born. Usually, the staff are in touch all the time, but there's been no texts or calls. There was nothing on Maxwells' social media earlier: silence on Instagram and Twitter. Seth will have closed all of that down the second we left.

I smash one claw, then the other, remove the meat, drop the shell, and scraps into the stock pan. I look up from the chopping board and scan the room, a horrible sense of unease creeping over me in waves. With the blinds pulled, I thought it would feel cosier, Mum's goldfish bowl sorted out. No one can see in from outside. I pull out my earphones. The room is silent - only the sound of the wind against the glass.

The kitchen is pooled beneath the white light of the spots; beyond it, the room bathes in a softer light. No dark corners, the metal banister gleaming as it twists away to the floor below. With the blinds pulled, there's no moon or cloud to cast light and shadow. My tired brain playing tricks, imagination running riot. Just thinking about Seth is making me edgy. Nicola's comments earlier don't help. She seems so self-assured, not the fanciful type, yet was convinced she saw someone in the corridor. I turn back to the counter and reach for the spoon and find my fingers curling around the jagged edge of a broken handle. I cry out and drop it to the counter. *Click-clack.*

The creamy bone thing rolls to the edge of the chopping board, the miniature ball inside the dome *click, click, clicking* with each turn. I stare at it. How did it get here? I'm certain I'd have noticed it when I was working. I'm not a messy chef. Nothing on my bench is here unless I need it. I glance back across the room at the wood burner. The logs have sunk into a hot yellow glow. The mantelpiece has only the TV remote on it. I look back at the worktop. Surely Alfie didn't put this here? He was too upset to play a practical joke. The skin on my arms prickles, and my hand is shaking. It's just an ugly old thing, but I don't want to touch it.

I snatch the tea towel from the oven rail and wrap it around my hand, but I can't make myself reach out. *Fuck it!* I can hear Seth's laugh in my head, his mantra about how useless I am. He might have a point. I can see now it isn't a stone in the dome. Somehow the same bone has been used as the rattle inside the intricately carved globe. Was this once a pretty thing? I shudder and put out my hand, fumble for a moment, finding it hard to take hold of through the tea towel.

I wrap it up not wanting to look at it. My underarms are sticky, heart racing ridiculously fast. Calm down. Breathe! The muffled *clink clink* as I hurry with it across the room makes me shudder. What the hell's wrong with me? I shove it, still wrapped in the towel, onto the mantelpiece. Would Luke mind if I threw it away? Why did he keep it? For all I know, it might be valuable. I step back from the shelf, the heat from the wood burner roasting my legs through my jeans. I stare at the bundle of tea towel. Why had Alfie reacted as he did? Molly was fine, but Lou wasn't keen. I can't stand here all night, and with it wrapped up, what harm can it do?

I walk to the kitchen but can't help glancing over my shoulder. I lean against the worktop, fold my arms across my chest and look at the mantelpiece. Hardly surprising the towel is still there. It hasn't moved. *Click-clack. Click-clack.* I gasp, my focus still on the bundle of material. The sound is sharp, not muffled. *Clickety-clack. Clickety-clack.* It's a beat before I realise the sound isn't coming from in front of me. *Click Clack. Clickety-clack.* I jolt away from the worktop and stare across the space towards the stairs. Is the noise coming from down there?

I stand still and listen. The house, so quiet, I hear each shallow juddering intake of my own breath. *Clickety-clack.* It is coming from downstairs. And something else, a lower sound, so faint I wonder if I imagine it. I keep listening. Not even wind. There's always wind here. It's the backdrop to this place. Never total silence. A soft, crooning comes again, almost like the wind keening about the house, but it isn't. Surely it has to be the wind? I grab an empty milk pan from the stove and walk swiftly towards the stairs. The rubber soles of my shoes don't make a sound. I stop just before the top of the staircase, feeling slightly absurd brandishing the pan.

The first few steps are visible from where I'm standing. The weird scraping sounds have to have been rats, but this was different. I hold my breath and listen, pressing my body against the side of the banister, clinging tightly with my free hand. The vertigo is always worse if I'm stressed or tired. I dare not move to the head of the stairs. Better to lean over here and look down. Adam's assurances that no one ever comes down the track here are poor comfort right now. The internal door from the garage is locked, but the outer doors are only closed. I would hear anyone down there unless, like me, they stand silently listening.

I focus on the whitewashed brickwork opposite, following the rows downwards, keeping my eyes away from the spiralling stairs. Light flares up the walls from the uplighters, I left them on earlier in my room, the corridor and the bathroom. Luke and Dad's doors are shut; it's better not seeing inside their rooms each time I pass by. A glimpse of flagstone floor, the arched ceiling to the corridor. I spring back from the banister, gasping. A dark shape at the entrance to the passage; someone standing there looking up at me. The pan shakes in my hand. My ears strain against the silence; even a tiny child's footfall would be loud if they climbed the stairs. I can't hear anything at all, no wind, no rain battering against the glass.

What do I do now? I wait for what feels like hours. I have no choice but to look again. If there's someone downstairs, I have a head start on them if I have to run for it. I step silently back to the banister, searching the widening space of the stairwell. I bend my knees and sit back on my heels. I can see a further stretch of the passageway through the metal rails. A darker section fills the space from the head of the corridor for as far as I can see. One of the uplights has blown. The bulbs will be old now if Luke's never had to replace them. All I saw was the darker space, nothing more. No one was standing down there. *Idiot*.

I step back from the stairs and silently make my way across the room. The bundled tea towel is still on the mantelpiece. I stand before the kitchen counter, looking back at the stairs.

I should go down there and check around properly. It's the only way I'm going to feel comfortable here tonight. My parka hangs along with my rucksack on the back of a kitchen bar-stool. I'll feel a complete fool if I wimp out. Alfie is wearing my waterproof, and if Luke shows up . . .

It comes again, a low crooning, rising and falling in pitch. A soft, melodic sound. Not the wind. I'm sure of it. *Clickety-clack, clickety clickety clickety-clack*. A thin wail – I think of Alfie as a baby, exhausted, fighting sleep. The cry turns to a whimper. The crooning drifts on. Melancholy and mesmeris-ing, it soaks into the walls of the building and I hear nothing.

My heart pulses in my throat, and it's all I can make out in the silence of the house. The air is thick and cold as I glance about the room, brandishing the pan in front of me. Everything looks so normal. The fire glows, the crabs half prepped on the counter, but the stillness unnerves me. And I sense it, a change in the light. The air seems to solidify, too thick even to breathe. A darkening as if a shadow drifted across the room, but there is no moonlight. No cloud. I can't move, can't make myself turn around. A scream, a long shrill-ness, slashes the silence, rasping in my throat. I spin around, the pan flies out of my hand and hurtles across the floor, smashing against a section of flint and stone wall.

I glance urgently all about me. The room is empty, no one here. What is wrong with me? Am I going crazy? Wind whistles about the house, a great gust thudding against the glass. Nothing is going to make me feel okay here tonight, not on my own. I grab my parka, kick off my shoes and jam my feet into Dad's pair of old wellies. With a last glance at the half-prepped crabs, I run for the door.

CHAPTER EIGHTEEN

THE FABRIC ROOF of the little tent snaps and shakes in the wind. Despite being tucked up inside here, sunk deep into a camping chair and wrapped in a scratchy wool blanket, I'm still cold. How anyone does this for fun, I don't know. Moonlight spills across the sea, Jack's line cast beyond where the waves start to gather and rise.

'You can cook, that's for sure, Evie. Your dad and I used to look forward to you coming down with bacon rolls and fruitcake as the dawn broke.'

Jack hands an empty soup mug back to me as I repack the flask into the rucksack. I gently pull Alfie's mug from his fingers. He's snuggled into his scarf up to the bridge of his nose, his wool hat pulled low, muffling his ears.

'Kids these days, no stamina,' Jack chuckles to himself and settles back to watch the waves rolling up the shingle. I remember waking, dozing and waking, hearing the soft murmur of Dad and Jack's conversation before the rhythm of the sea tugged me back into sleep.

'I'd better take him back if he doesn't wake soon,' I say.

'Give it another ten minutes. I'll head back with you if the boy hasn't woken up.' I zip up the rucksack and buckle the straps, thanking my good luck we won't have to go back to Seahurst alone. 'So, what got you down here tonight?' Jack watches the sea as he speaks. It's almost as if he could read my mind. I've been distracted while we've been sitting here, trying to rationalise what happened earlier. It seems crazy now I'm away from the house.

'Nicola thought she heard someone downstairs. Probably the rats.' I wait for Jack to say something, but he just watches the sea. 'I don't know, Jack. I'm so jumpy what with everything that's happened. The plumbing is still not working; the taps need fixing for sure.' There's no movement from Jack, but I know he hears me. 'I didn't tell Nicola about Luke's laptop. Maybe she doesn't know he has one. I probably can't get into it anyway. It'll have a password. I don't know why, but I want to check it out before I hand it to the police.' Jack turns to face me and waits, his eyes deep in shadow. No way can I begin to explain what I thought went on tonight without sounding like a mad woman. 'I'm worried something bad has happened to him, Jack.' My voice wavers, and I take a breath. 'An accident, you think?'

Jack turns away to stare out to sea. 'Can't think what else would keep him away all this time.'

'Was there anything he said that would give us a clue?'

'Nothing I haven't told you already. I saw him though, walking near the Abbey when I was packing up my gear.' I'm astonished, Jack's never mentioned this. 'Will didn't want me to say anything. Didn't want you to worry.' Jack turns in his seat to face me. 'He reckons my memory's not so good. There was a time when it wasn't, but I've been far more myself lately.' Jack's face is in shadow, but I know he is looking into my face. 'I know what and when I saw it, Evie.'

'Why would he be up there then, and in that weather?'

Jack sits very still. The waves crash and boom beyond him. 'I can't think of any reason. I remember thinking he was cutting it fine if he was going to make it to the airport for your flight.'

My throat is thick, and suddenly I need to be out of this cramped space. I push the blanket from my knees and tuck it around Alfie's legs and feet.

'I'll walk for a minute before we head back. I won't go far. Just warm up a bit.'

'I'll start packing up,' says Jack. 'Take the torch.'

I leave them cocooned in the low lamplight beneath the umbrella. It takes my eyes a second to adjust to the soft white light of the moon. Now the sky is clear, the temperature has plummeted. My parka isn't much protection against this raw weather. It's a relief Jack knows how worried I am about Luke, but his reaction scares me.

Water froths about the ankles of my wellies, chills through my woollen socks to my toes. Way out across the water, lights blink, people are out there working on tankers, fishing vessels and rigs, the field of huge wind turbines, lost against the dark horizon. We've been here two days already; our third will be breaking in a few hours.

The cliffs start to rise here, encroaching further down the shingle, great hulking towers of ancient land growing taller the further I walk, their base dissolving into the waves. Seahurst is just visible, set back from the cliff edge, its lights glowing against a dark landscape. The ruins and the arch are lost in the darkness, and although I point the torch where they must stand, its beam is too weak to find them. Jack would be able to see someone standing amongst the ruins in daylight.

I swing the light to travel along the foot of the cliffs, close to the site of last night's collapse. The water is high, the tide turning. I crunch across the stones, keeping the torch trained ahead of me. The beam picks out one of the triangular metal signs that dot along the coast. The skull and crossbones frightened me as a tiny child; images in my head of skeletons creeping out of the crumbling cliffs, tapping bony fingers on my shoulder when my back was turned. I can't stop a shudder running through them now.

Moonlight brightens the scarred cliff face, layers of yellow and brown earth. A long section of plastic tape streams in the wind. As I get closer, I see it's tied at one end to a post driven into the base of the cliff. Yesterday's fall must have been cordoned off, the rest of the posts and tape snatched away by tonight's high tide.

I hear something so faint I'm unsure if it's the wind or my imagination. I look back along the curve of the bay. Jack's camp is a dull glow. I can just see him standing, too dark to make out if he looks this way. Alfie runs along the line of flotsam, waving.

'Mom!'

I make my way back to where the waves spill onto the beach. Alfie stops running, his feet slow and uneven in the deep shingle. He has so many layers beneath my windcheater he looks like the Michelin Man.

'Wait for me!' He's panting heavily as he pulls up beside me.

'I thought you were sound asleep.'

'I'm awake now.'

'So I see,' I say as we link arms and fall into step.

'How long are we staying here?'

'Until you head back to school.'

'Not forever then?' He lets my arm drop and splashes into deeper water, the surf sucking about his calves.

'Why do you ask that?'

'Jack wanted to know.' Alfie takes big deliberate steps, meeting the surge of each wave with a light jump as we walk. 'Jack says something's going on.' Alfie points out to sea. More lights pierce the dark horizon, the lighthouse blinking across the water. 'The supply helicopter has gone out, he says.'

'Don't go too deep, Alfie. You'll freeze if your jogging bottoms get soaked.'

He moves up the beach a little, and we walk side-by-side, listening to the wind and hiss of the foam across the stones.

'Would you want to leave your friends behind in Canada and move here?' I thread my arm through his again. Alfie and the restaurant are the two things that have stuck out against coming here. Maxwells is as much my baby as Alfie, but there's no way Seth would walk away from the restaurant, even if I could afford to buy out his share.

'Not to live at Uncle Luke's. We'd get somewhere else, right, just for us?' Alfie kicks at a stone, pulling against my arm. 'Why do you like it so much? It's nothing like you said it would be.'

'How do you mean?' I want to know what Alfie thinks of Seahurst, not put words or ideas into his head. Surely what I thought happened there this evening was no more than my mind playing tricks on me.

'I just don't like hanging out there.' Alfie shrugs and lets go of my arm. He walks a little ahead of me and I know my son. Nothing more is being said about this right now. I pull off my glove and check my phone. No messages. No missed calls. Perhaps Seth hasn't seen his phone. Maxwells is fully booked tonight.

'Hey!' Alfie shouts as he dashes towards the waves. The beach is flatter here; the water surges in then dallies, reluctant to get caught in the back-draught before it slides away. 'There's something here, Mom!'

I swing the torch towards Alfie. Water is close to the top

of his boots. The next wave is rising and curling just feet from him.

'Alfie! Don't go out any further!' I sprint after him, water splashing up around my knees, sucking on the stones behind me as I run into the waves. The cold is furious, making me gasp as it penetrates through Dad's wellingtons. I grab Alfie by his upper arm. 'Just be careful. If you slip, it'll be difficult to get up again.'

Alfie points as the water flattens out. Foam swirls and bubbles across the surface and, for an instant, stops moving. 'See it?' he says, diving forwards so sharply I lose my grip on his arm.

The rip is rapid, tugging at my legs, pulling the shingle from beneath my boots. Cold water slaps my face. Saltwater in my throat, choking, a muffled roar in my ears. My shoulder smacks against something hard. I fling out my hands, try to grab onto anything that will stop me from rolling over and over. My clothes are a dead weight. Can't move. Panic surges through me as I'm dragged against the stones. I flip onto my stomach, shingle tearing through my fingers. My head breaks the surface, around me streaming white water rushes back to the sea.

'Alfie!' I'm choking, saltwater in my nose and mouth. It's no more than a metre deep, my knees grazing through stones, but I can't move my feet. My ankles are tangled in something. The weight of it dragging me into deeper water along with the current.

The water finishes its retreat. The next wave curling and black, reaching the peak of its rise, towering above me, the white crest breaking. I need to move. I try to drag my feet free. The black and yellow tape is wrapped about my ankle and something else. My welly's wedged in the crook of it. A great mass attached to the wood and plastic entangling my feet. Pale hair swirling in dark water. Weirdly white skin shrunken across the bones of a hand.

My scream is endless; it rasps in my throat. The whole of me is rigid, unable to move. The receding water drags it backwards. I brace my hands at my sides; try to resist the pull of it. My jeans are like concrete. The thing is too heavy; the waves sucking it back into the sea. Pain shoots through my shoulder and arm, my feet scrabbling beneath me.

'I've got you, girl.' My hair clings to my face as I clutch Jack's arm. The moon is a massive white circle behind him, his face in darkness. Wind buffets into my mouth as I scream, all of me shaking. My body, weighted like a stone.

'Evie! Calm down!' Jack's arm is at my back, holding me, pushing me up the beach towards the cliffs. I can hardly move my legs with the weight of my clothes. Alfie is at the shoreline, running at me.

'Alfie!'

He's saying something. His lips moving fast, both hands held out towards me. I let him take my hand. Let them both guide me back up the bank of shingle. My knees buckle beneath me as we clear the water. I'm shivering so hard my teeth are chattering. Alfie's are too.

'Mom! Are you all right?' Alfie squats beside me, his face pushed close to mine. His skin is pale beneath his woollen hat. Jack's at Alfie's back, hands on his knees, face creased in concern.

'I'm sorry, Mom. I'm sorry!'

I pull my son to me and hold him tight. He's shaking so hard I can't stop it. I stare across the sea, waves rolling in - nothing more to see.

'We need to move away from here, Evie.' Jack's deep voice

has an urgency to it. 'We're right up against the cliffs.'

I follow Jack's gaze. The current has swept us further along the beach. The overhang is deep here, we're below the ruins. I stare at him, at Alfie. At the water surging up the beach at our backs.

'You'll freeze in no time in those wet clothes.'

My socks hang limply from the ends of my feet. No boots. Jack's right. My bones feel like ice is running right through them. I don't move. The image in my head; surely I'm mistaken? Just debris washed about by the tide. They're speaking; Jack and Alfie. Talking to me and to each other. They pull me up, one either side of me. Their arms beneath mine, my legs somehow moving, walking between them.

'We've . . . got to go back.' My voice doesn't sound like my own. My throat is raw, salt on my lips, my words disjointed.

'Let's get you home, Evie, as quickly as we can.' I pull back against Jack's grip on my arm, shake myself free. I'm shivering so hard, trying to make the words come out of me.

'We need to go back.'

'Mom, you're freezing cold.' Alfie's voice is heavy with fear. I shake my head. He saw it too. I know he did.

'You don't understand,' I say, looking at Jack. 'There's something in the water.'

'What are you on about, girl?'

I gulp in a breath to stead my words. 'I think it was Luke.'

CHAPTER NINETEEN

JACK IS STRUGGLING to decide what to say. 'It'll be a bit of flotsam. A dead fish. Stuff like that washes up here all the time, Evie.'

'I know what I saw.'

There's doubt in Jack's face. He wants us off the beach, and I get that. I'm keener than he knows to get out of these wet clothes and this bitter, driving wind.

'We can't just leave it – can we?' I say.

'I'll go and look; you take your mother back to Seahurst, Alfie. I won't be long.'

Jack heads past where we stand. I watch him walk away, tempted to do as he says and head home. But I have to know. Alfie's staring after Jack's retreating back. I don't want my son stumbling in the dark alone trying to get back to Seahurst; either we both go or stay.

'It didn't have a face, Mom.'

Alfie's shaking violently. I pull him towards me and hold him tight to my chest.

'What do you mean?' There's horror in my tone. Alfie's head jerks up, his eyes scanning mine. 'I thought . . .' My voice is hoarse. 'It's so dark, in the moonlight – it's hard to see anything.' We stare at each other. His jaw is trembling. 'I thought it was face down, Alfie.'

Jack stops where the cliff juts out, where the beach narrows and the water laps the foot of the cliffs. He's looking out across the surface of the sea. He takes a few steps forwards, waves lapping at the ankles of his waders. He glances back at us; holds up his hand and jerks his finger for us to head back up the beach. He knows we won't go. He wades deeper into the water.

'It was all horrible – the eyes weren't in it.'

I hardly know what to say. Alfie isn't a fanciful child. 'Jack's probably right, it'll have been a dead fish washing up.' It's dark, and I only got a glimpse . . .

The sand is scuffed on the shore where they pulled me up the beach. Moonlight bathes everything in bright white light now. If it had been clearer a few moments ago, I might have been sure. I'm shivering badly, my hair hanging in wet ropes about my face. We should do as Jack says and head back to Seahurst.

'Hey!' Alfie darts forward, pulling away from me, running down the stones, splashing through the water to the left of where Jack stands. He dips his hands in the sea and snatches something up; holds it high.

'One of your wellies, Mom!'

'Stay on the beach, both of you!' Jack roars at Alfie.

My son staggers back a step and runs to where I'm standing. He stops in front of me, tips up the boot and pours water onto the stones. My hand shakes as he passes it to me.

'We should go back, Mom.' I lean on his arm, my wet sock making it a struggle to force my foot back into the wellington. 'I don't want you to die.'

'Die?' I say with a short laugh. 'No one's died getting wet.'

'They do. Hypothermia gets old people all the time.' I stamp my foot on the ground, the boot finally on. 'You've lost your beanie too.'

I raise my hand, feel only claggy wet hair. 'Bloody hell!' I say.

'Where's the torch, Evie?' Jack's gone out further now, water circling his waders well above knee level. I hobble down the shingle and shout back at him.

'I had it with me, Jack. I must have dropped it – sorry.'

I grope in my pockets; find water and sand. No mobile. There's an urgency in Jack's tone. I'd rather Alfie was out of the way right now.

'Have you got your phone, Alfie?' I ask.

'Where's yours?' Alfie's looking worried and starts searching his pockets.

'I think I lost it along with the beanie.'

'No way?' Alfie looks horrified as he frantically searches through his coat.

'I was taking photos of Jack fishing. Dad'll be mad as fuck if I've lost it!' Alfie turns away and sprints off towards Jack's little camp before I can get the words out to tell him off.

I wish I hadn't put the one welly back on, but it'll be too hard to get off. I hobble back into the waves. Jack glances over his shoulder. He's deeper than I can go, his waders chest high.

'Have you seen anything?' Jack is beyond where the waves break, water swelling around his hips.

'Don't come any deeper, Evie. The ground shelves here – water'll be up to your waist before you know it.'

My heart is thumping against my ribs. The image of pale hair in black water, white skin above the collar of a coat. A hand floating beneath the water is too clear in my mind. I will it to be a dead fish, something dredged from the seabed; a glimpse of something in low light I didn't see properly.

'Alfie's gone to get his mobile – it has a torch on it, Jack.'

'Here's something!' Jack lunges forward, one arm up to his elbow in water. He looks up at the swell and waits for the flow to turn up the beach. His back is towards me, pulling something with both hands half a dozen steps towards the shore. He stops as the water turns again. The rip gathering in strength, the flow sucking around him. He staggers a couple of steps forwards. I hear him shout, his words taken out across the water. He lets go of what he's holding. The water circles and sucks around him. Raises him a fraction, and I know his feet are off the seabed.

'Jack, come back in!' Behind me, a light plays across the water, Alfie with his mobile. 'Stay there, Alfie!' My son stops, his face startled by the ferocity of my tone.

'Evie!'

I turn back to the sea. Jack has both hands in the water again. He's staggering, being dragged deeper; the water waist-high.

'Jack – let it go!' I scream; words tearing from me. 'Jack!' He lets go and straightens, water sucking him deeper. 'Jack!'

I take a step forward and stop. The current is too strong, the seabed dishing away beneath me, my feet sinking, skidding through stone and shingle. At my back, I hear Alfie, his voice high pitched and fractured on the wind. The torchlight is a thin beam bouncing past me. Jack is wading back, the water turning again, swelling about him, washing him towards where I'm standing.

'Get back up the beach!' Jack bellows, his face creased in anger.

I trudge back towards Alfie, panting as I stagger the last few steps and stop beside my son. My legs are trembling with the weight of my jeans. The one welly full of water.

'What didn't you understand, Evie?' Jack has my upper arm, half pulling me further up the shingle bank. 'You know as well as I do how strong the current is when the tide is turning.' Jack's grip on my arm is powerful. I hear the panic in his tone.

'I'm sorry! I didn't want you getting into trouble.' Tears sting the back of my eyes.

'Did you see it?' Alfie is at Jack's side as he starts back towards the camp. Jack doesn't answer, the only sounds are the wind and the crunch of our feet on shingle. 'We aren't just leaving it, are we?'

'Too heavy to pull in against an outgoing tide, Alfie.' Jack's hold on my arm slackens as we make our way along the beach.

'Did you see it, though? What was it?' Alfie is running at Jack's side, looking up at him as he strides along. Jack lets go of my arm and marches ahead. Alfie looks back at me as I try to keep pace with them both.

'Got a signal on that mobile, Alfie?' says Jack.

'Not until we get further up the beach. Why?'

'We need to call the coastguard. They'll get the search and rescue out to bring it in.'

CHAPTER TWENTY

JACK TRAMPS AHEAD of us towards Seahurst laden with fishing gear. He's said nothing since he finished his call to the coastguard a few minutes ago. He stops beside Betty and dumps the rods beside her.

'Jack thinks it's Uncle Luke, doesn't he?' Alfie's face is pale in the moonlight, his eyes searching my face. Please don't let it be Luke. Don't let it be anyone, just something in the waves and the scattered light that fooled us all into thinking . . .

'I'm sure it won't be, Alfie. It can't be,' I say, pulling him close.

We reach Jack and head down the slate path towards the house. I grab the keys from beneath the stone and unlock the glass door. Alfie heads inside. I can tell from the way he moves he's suddenly tired again.

Jack stops a few feet from me. 'I'm going back down to the beach, Evie. It'll help if I show them exactly where we saw things.'

Jack's face is bleached white in the light streaming at my back from the house; shadows hang beneath his cheekbones and encircle his eyes.

'I'll get Alfie into dry clothes and off to bed.' Jack nods and turns away. I reach out and catch his forearm. 'Was it...?' Jack holds my gaze. He's so close I see grains of sand in the deep creases on either side of his mouth, the crows-feet at the corners of his eyes. 'I mean . . . how much did you see?'

I glance back into the house. Alfie is peeling off his jogging bottoms as he sits on the floor in front of the sofa.

'I can't be sure with it being so dark,' says Jack.

'Not someone, just a dead fish . . . or something, right?'

'Let's wait and see, Evie. No good speculating now, is there?'

I let go of his arm, and he turns back to the path. I watch him, wait for him to turn and raise his hand, but he melds into the darkness.

Alfie is struggling to pull off the windcheater. His scarf and jogging bottoms are on the floor near his feet.

'Let me do it.' I grab his coat and peel it down his back, tugging, so his arms come free. For once, Alfie doesn't argue, lets me pull his hoody, a jumper and then his tee-shirt over his head.

'Is Jack coming back?'

'We'll see, but you need to be in bed. You jump in the shower.' I'll put all of our stuff straight into Luke's washing machine and make some hot chocolate.

'We should go and help Jack,' he says.

'He can manage. We'd just be in the way.'

Alfie looks at the counter, the half-dressed crab still on the chopping board, the pan full of shell ready to make into stock on the hob.

'Quickly now, I need to shower after you,' I say. Alfie doesn't make a move, just stands staring at the counter.

'Is that weird thing wrapped up in there?' He's staring at the bundled tea towel on the counter. He half turns his head towards the wood burner behind him. I stare at the mantelpiece. Hadn't I left it there? Not on the worktop? He looks up at me. 'Did something happen?'

I'm tempted to say what does he mean, fob things off and get us to bed. Everything will be more rational in the morning, but Alfie got freaked out with everyone here in broad daylight.

'I can't really explain it . . .'

'Get rid of it, Mom.'

Alfie's right, there's no need for it to be here. I cross to the kitchen and snatch up one of the orange carrier bags I'd stuffed into a drawer, hurry past Alfie and stop before the worktop. I stare at the tea towel, a wave of apprehension flooding over me. I don't want to touch it, even bundled up as it is. I use the bag like a glove, make myself reach out and grasp the cloth. I can't feel anything. Is it still in there? I lower it into the bag and hear it, a dull *click-clack*. I drop the bag, step back from it as if it scalded me.

'Mom!'

I glance across at Alfie. His face, pinched and pale. He looks ill again. 'It's fine,' I say, trying to make myself smile. 'The noise made me jump.'

'That's what I heard downstairs when we first got here, not the scratching sounds.'

I hadn't understood that. 'Why didn't you say?'

Alfie is starting to shake. I don't want him to have another weird turn. I pick up the bag, 'Come on,' I say, forcing a can-do tone into my voice. 'Bring the wet clothes. I'll put this outside in the garage.'

I hurry to the stairs and head down the first couple of steps. Alfie stands rooted to the spot, as white as a sheet. 'Hey, you okay?'

He nods. I smile and wait while he scoops the wet clothes into his arms. We head downstairs.

'Leave the wet stuff beside the garage steps, Alfie. Take

what you need from Lou's bag. There's plenty of towels in there.'

I glance at Alfie, but he seems a bit more like himself again. I nip up the garage steps keener than I could ever say to be rid of this thing. I try the handle. *Damn!* The door has been locked all evening. I leave the carrier bag by the door and head down the steps and into my room. Alfie looks up anxiously, a clean towel in his hands. Lou's bag spills its contents onto the floor at his feet.

'The door's locked. You jump in the shower and I'll get rid of it, okay?'

Alfie nods and I step towards him. He lets me pull him into a hug. He's almost as big as me now. 'It'll be fine, really. Leave the bathroom door ajar if you like. I won't come in.'

I grin at him as we step apart. Alfie nods again and heads into the corridor. I sit on the futon and struggle out of my jeans as the whine of the shower starts up. I towel sand off my damp skin and pull on dry joggers, a tee-shirt and the thickest hoody I have. It feels much better with Alfie here, but I can't fathom why we'd both hate that thing so much.

The fusty smell is faint, the same as in the bathroom, and I wish it would go. I've smelt rats around the bins behind Maxwells so many times, it's just the same, but Nicola was right about the smell sometimes being different. Something wet. Rotting.

Three walls in my room are ancient, solid flint and brick, but the fourth between here and the garage is smooth plaster. A pale yellowish stain crawls along the crease where the wall and floor meet. I drag the futon away from the wall. The stain carries along the length of the room. What the hell is that? I shudder at the thought of dark, furry bodies nesting in the gap behind here. I rap my fist against the plaster: a hollow space. I crouch in front of the wall and run my forefinger down the surface. It's cold, the wall damp. I don't remember it being like that before, and Dad would have sorted it anyway. Maybe the garage extension caused a problem?

The garage keys and Luke's laptop are on the low bedside table. The tiny light on the charger has gone from orange to green. I lift the laptop lid, the screen lights, and the cursor blinks for a password. Once Alfie is in bed, I'll take a look while I wait for Jack to come back. It feels wrong that Luke would have left the laptop on the coffee table like that. Luke's many things, sometimes unpredictable, but he's also like Dad. Loves his gadgets. He wouldn't leave the laptop that way.

I gather my wet clothes from the floor, grab the garage key and hurry into the corridor. We can sleep in Luke's room; no need to use my room tonight. I resist the temptation to check Alfie's okay. He's thirteen. He'll yell if there's a problem. I gather the bundle of washing onto my hip and head up the garage steps. The orange bag is here – why wouldn't it be? Be rational, for goodness' sake.

The garage is the only part of the house I hadn't left lights on. I can't imagine why anyone wouldn't put a switch on this side of the wall – does Luke always expect to access it from outside? I take a breath and fit the key in the lock, turn it and push the door away from me. If rats are in here, they'll run from the light; more scared of me than I of them. I don't let my eyes linger in the black space as I grope on the rough wall until my fingers find the pull-cord.

Overhead, strip lights blink several times, fracturing the darkness with shadows and white light. I'm aware of my heart thumping a little too hard as I glance around the room. The ratty smell is more potent in here. The washing machine and tumble dryer are to my right. I pile the wet laundry into the machine and brush damp sand from my hands. I cross the room. The metal ring in the stone cover lies snug now in the indentation cut into its surface. Behind my old bike, the trap has sprung. The metal bar crushed the rat's neck, its body spayed flat and stiff on the dusty concrete floor. In the morning, when it's light, I'll empty and reset them.

The strip lights hum, the air cold and still. The double doors are closed, with no sign that anyone has tried to access them from the woods outside. I cross the room and push the recycling and waste bins hard up against the double doors. If anyone tries to enter, there'll be a whole lot of noise. I open the lid to the waste bin. Calm down, for God's sake. No one is here, but I can't explain what I felt upstairs. I grab the carrier bag, hold it away from me and run across the garage. I hurl it into the bin, flip up the lid and let it slam closed.

I feel stupidly relieved as I run back to the door, turn the key and try the handle. Locked. The whine of the shower has stopped, just the faint whirring of the extractor fan. I duck into my room, grab Luke's laptop and head back down the corridor. The soft moan of the water pipes starts up as I pass the bathroom door. Not so loud as before. Perhaps that's settling down now Adam's reset the system.

I stop at Luke's room, open the door and switch on the light. It's just as it was when Nicola was here a few hours ago. Then I was hopeful Luke would walk back into the house, his big stupid grin plastered across his face and an excuse explaining everything. After tonight though, it feels like I'm running from a nightmare.

'What are you doing?'

I spin around, the garage key flying out of my hand, clattering across the floor. 'Shit! What's the matter with you, Alfie? Why sneak up on me like that?'

166

'I'm not sneaking, just being normal.' Alfie's wrapped in a towel. His bare feet wouldn't have made much sound on the stone floor. He's right; it is me.

'Did you get rid of it?' Alfie looks at the laptop as he bends down and picks up the garage key.

'Yes. It's in the wheelie bin, and the garage is locked.'

'Can I wait up while you shower?'

I'm about to argue, to tell him to go straight to bed. But he won't settle, not on his own. Neither will I, for that matter.

CHAPTER TWENTY-ONE

ALFIE STANDS AT the glass, remote controller in one hand, a half-eaten banana in the other, staring outside. The moon is high, throwing white light across the choppy surface of the sea.

'There's loads more lights out to sea, Mom. What do you think's going on?'

'Drink the rest of your hot chocolate before it gets cold. I'm getting in the shower.'

'Where's Jack?'

'You know where he is. Keep the door locked, and don't let anyone in while I'm downstairs – is that clear?'

'Okay, Mom. I was only asking!'

The Xbox finishes loading, and Alfie's game blares out as I head downstairs. I'm constantly on a short fuse with him. This trip was supposed to be a fun time, an escape from all the strife back home. The last thing I want right now is Alfie letting in some random weirdo at 12:30 am while I'm in the shower.

Alfie's trashed the bathroom: a pair of abandoned boxers, overturned shampoo bottle, and two discarded towels on the tiled floor. How does one boy constantly make so much mess? I try not to go over what happened on the beach tonight as I snatch up Alfie's clothes. Now I'm finally alone: no Jack, no Alfie to reassure, my jaw trembles, tears sting the back of my eyes and choke my throat. In the dark, just a glimpse . . . Jack's right, no good speculating.

I dump Alfie's things by the door. The rank smell mingles with the scent of sandalwood. Alfie helped himself to his uncle's expensive body wash. I switch on the shower and leave it to run. Maybe the smell comes from the grille beneath the sink? I squat down and make myself look at the square holes. Nicola said most of the walls are solid, but this must vent somewhere. The darkness behind the grille is a velvety blackness. If I had my mobile here the torch might let me see a bit more. The blackness shifts behind the holes, like a wave rippling behind the grille. I reel backwards. Is something there? I grab Alfie's wet towel and ram it against the vent. I slide the laundry basket beneath the sink. Nothing's getting out of those tiny holes.

I rock back on my heels to stand. There's something on the wall below the sink just to the right of the basket. It's only visible at this angle; otherwise, the basin obscures it. The light plays on the surface of the whitewash. I peer closer, just a scratch in the stone, painted over when the room was decorated. I put out my hand and run the tip of my finger along the curving indentation. There are several of them, curving lines. I peer more closely, a broken outline of a daisy type flower. No surprise I've not seen it before. It's barely visible. The great chunk of stone Dad recycled from the Abbey ruins that hangs above the hearth upstairs has a similar pattern. Slim daisy petals within a circle. A decorative thing. I guess it has been here for centuries.

I stand and stare into the oversized mirror. For goodness' sakes, get a grip Evie Meyer. I scrub at the dried mascara streaks on my cheeks. My hair is a tangled mess, the tramline of auburn roots widening against the blond. There's no tenderness in the bruise now, just a fading band of yellowing skin. I don't think Jack saw it earlier; the light wasn't good enough. I should explain about Seth. Luke believed me, so why wouldn't Jack?

Luke's dressing gown hangs on the back of the door. I could let myself imagine him standing here talking to me, making plans for a day trip tomorrow. But he's not here. I need to get on, get Alfie and me to bed. I pull my hoody off over my head as a muffled round of explosions and gunfire from upstairs cuts through the steamy room. How loud does Alfie need that damned game? The brackish smell reminds me of rotting leaves and is quite noticeable, despite the shower running for a while. Is it getting worse? It's hard to tell. I glance at the basket beneath the sink. The smell can't be coming from there now. It couldn't have been like this when Alfie showered. I'd have heard about it for sure. I put my hand under the shower, warm water runs over my skin. The smell is different from the rat smell, like Nicola said. I guess there's no harm in it, and my hair is a sticky, tangled lump after my dunk in the sea.

I step into the hot water, let it wash over me, let it run through my hair and down my back. My skin tingles with the heat, my muscles relax. Just the smell. I lather shampoo into my hair, citrus scent mingles with the steam. I grab the sponge from a hook on the wall and lather soap until I can't smell anything except its scent. Will Jack have any news when he gets back? I close my eyes and raise my face to the water. Do I want to know if he does have any? Good news will be it wasn't Luke or anything to do with him, but that gets us precisely nowhere further than we are right now.

I recoil from the shower, the water suddenly icy. I arc my body away from the needle-sharp spray. Sour earthiness on my tongue as I blink water from my eyes. It pounds the tiles, pouring like a monsoon from the massive shower head. Grimy grey foam pools around the drain. How can that be? My skin wasn't dirty, only sea salt and sand.

I grab a towel and wrap it around myself. Turn the tap on. Brown water chokes into the basin, a rotting smell rising into my face. Spray hits my chest and I shudder, step back. Pipes start to groan and knock. Rivulets of water stream down the mirror. I turn off the tap and the shower. The foam is gone, but the stagnant stench is so pungent I cover my nose and mouth with my hand. The knocking is fading, the weird groaning subsiding. What the hell happened? I just want out of this room.

I'm facing the mirror, see the startled look on my face. The dark wooden door behind me fills one side of the mirror. Alfie was right to keep it ajar. I wish I'd left it open. This room is claustrophobic. I clutch the towel tight to me and rush across the wet tiles, push the door handle, force it up and down. The door, which usually moves so easily, doesn't budge.

'Hey!'

I'm not sure Alfie will hear me; his game on full blast as always. I tug and pull on the handle. The door rattles in its frame. I pump the handle, but it's not the problem. I glance behind me, not sure why I'm feeling so anxious. The mirror is heavy with condensation, and the basket still stuffed against the grille. I look back at the door, yank the handle as hard as I can manage – it's stuck solid at the top of the frame. Why I think of Alfie and his hatred of that old bolt, I don't know. Not helpful. It hasn't moved in God only knows how long, but something is making the door stick. I'm shivering, the air on my damp skin growing cold and heavy. I don't know what to do.

'Alfie!' I hammer my fist against the wood. Pull the handle. I can't make the door move.

'Alfie!' I kick out at the wood, but my bare feet hardly make a sound. The light changes, growing dim. I glance back at the room as I work the handle up and down. The light overhead and above the mirror are bright. I don't understand. How is the room becoming dark?

Panic surges through me. I hammer against the door, screaming my son's name. It's black as pitch in here, only a bright thread of light coming through the ancient keyhole. I drop to my knees and shout through the hole.

'Alfie, can you hear me? Let me out!' I hammer against the wood.

I look through the keyhole. Someone's out there.

'Alfie?'

Dark and light, as if someone stands on the other side of the door shifting from one foot to the other. I hold my breath. Silence. Are they listening too? It has to be Alfie. The house was locked. No one was here. I hammer against the wood. 'Alfie, open up before I get really mad.' Silence so dense it hisses in my ears. The weird stillness I sensed earlier was the same. The darkness at my back is thick. Cold. Coming closer. I try the door handle again, wrench it up and down.

'Alfie!' I hear the terror in my voice. It's freezing in here. I can't make myself look around. Are the lights still on? The air is sharp with the smell like a candle snuffed out. I slam the flats of my hands against the door as I scream.

Light blinds me as I fall forward.

'What on earth's the matter?' I stare into Jack's startled face. Alfie stands behind him, his face pale and dark eyes huge. I'm shivering so much I can't stop.

'I'll get more towels,' says Alfie, running off along the passage towards my room.

'Evie?' Jack is looking past me into the bathroom. I turn around and gape into the brightly lit space. Everything looks as it should. Lights on, the shower and taps turned off. A whiff of citrus. No hideous smell. No darkness creeping towards me. Alfie is back, Jack drapes a towel around my shoulders as I glare into my son's face.

'Did you do that? Lock me in there?' I don't contain my anger. Let Alfie have the full force of it. 'None of that was funny.'

'I was playing my game . . .' Alfie looks at Jack as he shakes his head. 'We heard the pipes and you yelling.'

'The door wasn't locked, Evie.' I frown at Jack as he continues. 'It opened as normal.'

'We heard you yelling, Mom. Kind of . . . screaming . . .'

I look at them both as Alfie steps closer to the bathroom and pushes the door a little wider. Water trickles from my hair, drips onto my neck. He glances up at the massive bolt that hasn't moved in years. What happened just now? Is it possible I didn't open an unlocked door in a state of total panic?

'All a bit of a commotion, I'd say.' Jack looks shattered, his skin so pale it's grey, his blue eyes watery and bloodshot. 'Why don't you get dry and into some warm clothes, Evie? I'll make us all a hot drink while you do that. Standing on the beach in that wind's frozen my marrow.' Jack takes Alfie by the elbow and they head off to the stairs.

I wrap my hands around the mug of hot chocolate. Alfie's finally asleep on the nearest sofa, and I'm beginning to feel warm as toast in my jogging bottoms in front of the wood burner. I look up at the jagged slab of stone Dad set in the wall above the mantlepiece. He recycled so much from the Abbey it's part of this house, something that was always here.

There is a pattern on the slab that was cut into it centuries ago. Narrow petals within a circle.

'You feeling better?' Jack's voice makes me start. We've been silent for the last few minutes. I thought he was dozing like Alfie.

'I'm fine,' I say, not wanting to go over what happened earlier.

'You've seen all the business out at sea?' Jack says.

'Alfie's been watching.'

'Seems the search and rescue got called out earlier to a small boat full of migrants trying to cross over from France – was taking on water.'

'Did they find . . .' I look back at Jack as I keep my voice low, but Alfie won't hear me. 'What we saw?'

'I only pointed out where we'd seen something. Tide had taken it out by the time I got back to the beach.' He looks into my face and smiles, a flat, defeated thing. 'They'll find it if there's anything out there. What with all the other business going on, there'll be news one way or other.'

'Could it have been one of the migrants?' I hate myself for saying it. Some other poor soul, not Luke.

'Let's wait and see.' Jack puts his feet up onto the coffee table, his thick socks floppy at the toes. He looks fit to drop and closes his eyes. The laptop is beside his feet where I left it earlier. I open the lid and the screen lights. I have no clue what password Luke would use. I try his name, date of birth, Dad's details and Nicola's as far as I know them. Each time the laptop buzzes as I press enter, the cursor continues to blink.

I sit back and stare at the screen. I can't think of what else to try. Will's right when he says it could be anything. I glance up at Jack. 'I thought you'd dropped off there,' I say with a smile. 'There's some of Dad's whisky left in the cabinet.'

His eyes hold mine for a moment, linger for a second on the side of my face. I look back at the laptop.

'Any luck?' Jack says.

'I don't know where to start with a password,' I answer. Jack pulls himself from the sofa and walks to the kitchen.

'What do you reckon is in there that'll help, Evie?'

I watch him find the whisky and two glasses and then come back to sit beside me on the sofa waiting for a response.

'Maybe nothing, but it has to be worth checking. She only mentioned a mobile, nothing about a laptop.' I watch Jack sipping his whisky. 'Maybe it's nothing, but I didn't want to give away his secret.'

'If there is one.' Jack raises his eyebrows.

'She knew the code to his phone. How weird is that? He's thirty-nine years old, for God's sake!'

Jack swallows some of his drink. 'Don't be too hard on the woman. She put up with a whole load of shit from Marcus.' I jolt with surprise, his words stinging like a slap around my face. 'I loved your dad, you know that, but he was no saint.'

Mum's hectoring voice chimes in the back of my mind, but I'm not getting into an argument this late at night.

'I first met your parents when this was no more than a scraggy piece of land, as you know.' Jack casts a glance at the room. 'I thought they were just married, your mum, pregnant. Later I find out he had a wife and six-year-old kid back home in Essex.'

'I wonder why Nicola hung around? She doesn't seem the type.'

Jack pours another measure of whisky into his glass.

'Join me?' he says, holding the bottle up a little. I shake my head. 'At the time, Nicola didn't work much in the business. If they'd divorced, she'd have lost that as well as a husband.'

'How do you know that?'

'She was rather frank at your dad's wake.'

I hold Jack's gaze for a long moment. 'Did Will find anything in the notebook? There are three older ones here.' I pull one from the shelf beneath the glass tabletop and flick through the pages. Luke doesn't seem to have marked anything in these. Just the one Will borrowed.

'He moaned about your dad's handwriting, but didn't mention anything else. Not sure he would, though, if there was anything to worry about. Keeps things close to his chest, does Will.' Jack swirls the whisky around his glass.

'Do you know a Maurice Broughton? Nicola says Luke's tried to call a guy of that name.'

'Can't say I do. Funny how Luke turned out the same as your dad.'

'The same?' I say, dropping the notebook beside the laptop.

'Being so interested in the Abbey.' He looks at the laptop. 'Have you tried Seahurst?'

I sit forward and type. I try it forwards and backwards. The laptop just buzzes each time I hit enter.

'Needle in a haystack?' says Jack.

'It could be anything. Numbers, words, something completely random.' I snap the lid closed and get to my feet. I feel dog-tired and should get some sleep. I cross the room to stand at the glass. The slope of the land between here and the cliffs is a black space, but the moon spreads a glittering wide path across the sea. The lighthouse blinks off to the left. The lights out at sea are too distant to make out in any detail.

'Luke has to be out there, Jack. I just pray that he's safe.'

CHAPTER TWENTY-TWO

I LINGER IN the doorway of Luke's room to stare along the brightly lit corridor. The planet is dying because of idiots like me, but no way am I killing the lights down here tonight. It helps that Jack is kipping upstairs, but Nicola was sure she saw something. Did that just spook me, make me irrational? In the bathroom earlier tonight . . . it all seemed so real.

I step into Luke's bedroom and pull the door half-closed behind me. The bedside lamp casts a soft glow about the room. Alfie lies on his side with his arm thrown over the pillow, his cheeks flushed pink with warmth. The camera and his mobile are beneath the lamp. Alfie wouldn't worry me with anything Seth's been up to, not unless something really bothers him.

Alfie's eyelids flicker. 'Mom?'

'Go to sleep. It's late.'

Alfie turns on his back to look at me. 'Why were you screaming in the shower room?'

'Oh, I don't know. I got panicky when I couldn't open the door.' I perch on the edge of the bed and tuck his arm beneath the duvet. I'm not surprised he wonders what happened.

'It wasn't the people in the walls?'

'What?' I say. 'There's no one here except us and Jack upstairs. You've been dreaming. Now go to sleep young man!'

Alfie stares at me, his eyelids heavy, fighting sleep. I pull the duvet higher over his shoulders and tuck it about his neck.

I wait for him to fall back to sleep. His breathing settles into a regular rhythm and I pick up his mobile, thinking how weird it is that Nicola has Luke's info. Alfie's a child. He knows that if he has a mobile he shares the passcode with me until he's older. Luke surely must want a private life of his own? I type in the four-digit code and see a whole string of text messages from Seth, the earliest yesterday afternoon. I scroll through them, the usual information-gathering. Who have we seen, what have we been up to? When do we fly back? Alfie's only message was sent this evening letting Seth know I've lost my mobile. There's no mention of the voicemail I left. I leave the phone beside the camera.

I should get into bed, but I'm wide awake, and I can't stop wondering about Luke's laptop. I'm alert to every slight sound. Alfie snuffles in his sleep, then his breathing drops back into a gentle rhythm. If I toss and turn, I'll wake him and that's the last thing he needs. I sit on the edge of the bed watching the slice of bright light from the passage. The head waiter at Maxwells is a computer nerd, but it's weird to ask him how to crack someone's password. All I can do is hand it to the police if Luke doesn't show up in the morning.

I stand and walk silently to the door, stop and listen. Only the wind about the corner of the house. I slip into the corridor and open the door to Dad's room. I always came in here when I couldn't sleep. I make my way to the desk and switch on the angle-poised lamp. Dad used to sit here in a pool of yellow light working most nights. I run my hand across the top of his easy chair and slide open the mirrored wardrobe doors. Dad's clothes hang neatly: trousers, jackets, battered tee-shirts. All present and correct beneath them are his scruffy beach shoes beside smart, polished brogues. I know, without looking, the bedside cabinet drawers will be full of ties, sunglasses; all Dad's small things.

I close the wardrobe, stand with my arms wrapped around my waist, and take in the room. I pick up the book from Dad's footstool and realise it's the one he'd sometimes read to me as a child. I flip open the cover. Several torn pieces of paper mark sections of interest. I glance through them. Suffolk myths: a great witch's stone in a graveyard and a satanic dog with fierce red eyes. The peeling of church bells beneath the sea warning of storms on the way. Dad loved the local legends as much as the history of the Abbey.

The desk still has neat piles of papers and files, the computer screen like something from the dark ages now. The keyboard is clean and oddly free of dust. The room isn't dirty, but the mirrors have a film and there's no shine on the bedside table. Did Alfie try and get this thing started? I wouldn't put it past him. I push the power button. Nothing, why would there be? It's way more than a decade since this was last used.

I pull open a drawer: pens, a ruler, stapler and a small brown bottle of pills. The label has Dad's name and address on it. Zolpidem – I didn't know he took any medication. The date is the end of June, just before I flew over that last time. The computer's blue power light comes on; the fan whirs. The screen starts to glitch and flash. For a moment, I'm transfixed, unable to believe this ancient old piece of kit is still working. I put the bottle on the desk, pull out Dad's chair and sit down.

It takes an age for the screen to load the homepage. The artist's impression of the Abbey in its heyday, before the storms ravaged the land and the town. Before the dissolution of the monasteries. Dad told me the names of the parts of the building, but I can't recall them now. The cursor blinks for a password below the user name – Marcus L. Symonds.

I pull the keyboard towards me, and my fingers hover above the keys. Dad let me use this the last couple of summers I stayed over. Homework, I told him. The old password – what the hell was it? I look at the image of the Abbey, the Arch and type – Sea Siren. No way would that be any good as a password now, but it was fine back then. The coloured ball spins on the screen as the computer chugs beside me. Our desktop in the apartment would have loaded a dozen times over by now. Chances are the password was changed, or I've forgotten it after so long. Dad would switch it on and go to make coffee or top up his whisky while it loaded. I can understand why.

The desktop starts to appear, and I feel elated, so surprised it's loading. I stare at the familiar picture, my breath catching in my throat. Her strong features and bold dark eyes gaze past the files that scatter the desktop. I'd forgotten about her on here; her face is so familiar. Dad's obsession with the history of this place going back centuries never interested me back then. I'd forgotten about Sibilla.

'Evie?'

I jump to my feet, the chair tipping backwards, cracking on the flagstones. Jack stands just inside the door, a blanket wrapped about his shoulders.

'For God's sakes, you nearly gave me heart failure!' I say.

'Warned you I don't sleep too good, and I wasn't particularly quiet. What had you so enthralled?'

Jack looks past me at the computer screen as he hands me a glass of warm milk laced with whisky. I pick up the chair and sit back at the desk.

'Can you believe this old thing is still working?' I say

'I remember that last trip to the Castle Gallery like yesterday,' says Jack. He rests one hand on the desk and leans in to look more closely at the screen. 'Your Dad was transfixed by this painting, do you remember?' I glance up at Jack, but he's focusing on the monitor. 'The original's probably still on display there. It may be worth a trip while you're here?' he says.

The artist's impression of a girl only a few years older than Alfie was with a group of Victorian impressionist portraits in a busy gallery section. Sibilla sits in one of the nooks at the base of the Arch. The Abbey, in all its glory, is behind her. There was no sign back then of any threat from the sea or a King breaking away from Rome. She holds a child just out of babyhood on her knee and, standing beside her, a boy a little younger than Alfie is now. His smiling face is turned towards her, his arm circling her shoulders.

'She does demand your attention,' I say, taking in the thick coil of dark auburn hair that lies across one shoulder to rest on the front of her green tunic. Mine was a similar bold colour until Seth persuaded me to go blond.

'Rather romanticised,' says Jack, standing straight.

I click on Dad's old email account. 'I wonder if they knew why he didn't answer their emails?' Jack's voice sounds strange, and I don't look up at him as I sip the milk. There are dozens of messages, mostly spam. I scroll through to ones sent just a few days before Dad died.

'Maurice Broughton!' I say, clicking on an email. 'Nicola says there were missed calls on Luke's mobile to a guy with that name.' The circle spins and spins. How did people have the patience for these things? 'Luke's been on here at some point,' I say, glancing back at Jack. 'He's forwarded these emails to his own address.' There's excitement in my voice, and I take a breath. Calm down.

Jack leans forwards, the blanket around him brushing my back as we read. 'I've never met him, but Maurice Broughton helped out with your dad's research about the Abbey. That name didn't ring a bell when you mentioned it.

Luke has forwarded every email from Maurice Broughton to his account. Nothing else seems to have interested him. I click on a couple and scroll through them. The footer says Maurice was the curator at the museum. I have no clue what Dad got up to while I went clothes shopping in the city or the cinema with Will, Lou and Adam. I scroll past short exchanges until I find the original message.

'This is just two days before Dad died,' I say as I read:

'. . . *folklore starts somewhere, Marcus. We know a co-lossal surge hit the town in 1286, followed by a massive storm in early 1287. In December that year, another fero-cious storm battered the whole coastline. These lead to the port silting up and a gradual decline for the town over the centuries. These are the facts, and coastal erosion is evidenced.*

Sibilla is a different matter entirely. If she existed, and we have nothing concrete here, she seems to have been from this period. How the early storms could have been laid at her door is something we are not likely to ever find out. The belief in magic goes back through the ages, long before the witch trials of the 1600s. The populous used healers, midwives and herbalists as a matter of routine, but if things went awry, accusations of dark magic and consorting with the devil were common. Folklore suggests Sibilla was from a long line of healers. Or witches as they were called when the authorities, usually the Church, turned against them. Witches are supposed to be able to control the weather, and the storms during this period

182

were frequent and devastating. Draw your own conclu-
sions as you choose, Marcus.'

'I recall your dad becoming more interested in the old folktales
rather than the architectural history of the Abbey. Medieval structures aren't a passion of mine.' I glance at Jack as
he chuckles. 'Bit of light relief, to be honest.' I turn back
to the screen and scan through the shorter messages that
tail off from the primary email. 'Bangs on a bit, doesn't he?'
says Jack.

'This last one . . . Dad must have sent it only a few hours
before he died,' I say. I sip the warm milk to clear my throat as
I reread the last emails between Dad and Maurice Broughton.

'Is there no way to establish a connection between Sibilla and
Seahurst?'

'Unlikely. IF she existed, Marcus, and that's a big one,
she wasn't wealthy. Records for the illiterate poor don't
exist. I've found nothing to connect her to the Abbey or
Seahurst.'

'Where did all that come from, Jack? I don't recall Dad speaking to me about it. I point to the bottle of tablets beneath the
screen. 'Was Dad ill?'

Jack shakes his head. 'Didn't sleep good and was anxious
those last few weeks. I think he'd have said if anything else
was wrong, health-wise. I put it down to the business; worries
about you and Luke. Nothing out of the ordinary for him.
Just life, you know?' I sit back in the chair and look at Jack.
The lines around his mouth are deeper, a frown pulling his
thick brows together. 'So many times I've wished I listened

more closely to him, Evie, asked him about what was on his mind, but I didn't.'

Jack's voice is thin and reedy. I put my hand over his as it rests on the desk. Luke, Jack and I all quietly shared the blame for what happened. How I wish I'd listened to Luke at the airport. Not cut the call but asked him what was on his mind about Dad.

I close the emails and open a file named Seahurst.

'Dad showed me some of this stuff about the house, but I didn't pay much attention.'

'He complained more than once about it.' Jack sounds more like his usual self as I scroll over the architect's plans.

'Simon Arthurton helped out in the early days,' says Jack. 'There were loads of legal issues with it being so close to the Abbey.'

The date and client details are at the bottom right corner of each plan. I look up at Jack. 'Mum and Dad instructed on this?'

'Of course, it was their 'baby', if you like, before you were born.'

'But Mum hates Seahurst.'

Jack shakes his head. 'They had a weekend up here in the early days, like I said. Your Mum fell in love with the area, the coast in particular. So they found this plot and decided to build here.'

'She calls it the goldfish bowl.'

'Her idea, as far as I know. The site was just what they wanted for the sea view. She was crazy about recycling, using any old Abbey stonework that had fallen here over the centuries. I thought she was barmy wanting one of those living walls where the garage is now. Never got built as they separated just after the building work started.'

Jack shrugs and raises his eyebrows. I turn back to the screen and read letters from my parents to planners, builders, notes of meetings and telephone calls. Mum was Dad's secretary. She kept this file in the same way she would for any client. I sit back in the chair, still staring at the screen.

'You'll have to ask her about it, Evie. Tread carefully, though. I don't know what caused them to split up. Your dad was pretty closed about it, but I gathered it was his decision.'

'That's not likely to happen. Mum never has had a good word to say about Dad. I'm sick of hearing her go on about it all.

'Your mum assumed Marcus would leave Nicola. Perhaps he would have if it weren't for Luke and the business. Tricky position to get into.'

Luke has been in this file. The last dates opened and modified were only a few days ago.

'Luke sent this file to himself as well,' I say. 'It would be easier to navigate on his laptop than this ancient old piece of kit.' Jack squeezes my shoulder. He has to have heard the wobble in my voice. 'It's all such a mess, Jack.' I glance up. Jack's eyes are very bright. He presses his lips together, and again he looks at my cheekbone.

'You telling about that?'

I stare back at the screen, the cursor blinking in slow motion. 'What did Luke tell you?'

'Luke? Nothing.'

I focus on the cursor and its rhythm and try not to think about all we saw tonight. 'Alfie then?' When Jack says nothing, I look up at him.

'Alfie didn't say anything. It's pretty clear something's not right from all you haven't said about things back in Canada.'

I turn back to the screen and the cursor. Close the Seahurst file. Sibilla holds my gaze. When I've tried to explain things to Mum, I've felt more cornered than ever when she didn't believe me. Jack's coming at this from a totally different place. Keeping it secret isn't doing me any favours. Luke believed me. I'm sure he did.

'Things haven't worked for years, not on a personal level. The restaurant is a roaring success, but we've been falling apart for so long I can't remember when it was ever good between us.'

'Seth did that to you?'

The silence drags out. Even the wind is quieter. Maybe it's finally dropped a little. There's so much to explain it's hard to know where to start.

'Just the slightest thing sets him off, and when he's been drinking . . . I'm forever walking on eggshells.' My voice has grown husky and low, my words sticking in my throat. 'He's pushed me a couple of times, but Christmas Day . . .' I swallow and take a breath. 'It got out of hand. I worry about Alfie. It's not good to be stuck in a war zone. To see and hear all that . . .'

'What about you?' Only Luke has asked that before. I glance up at Jack.

'All our finances are tied up together, the restaurant is in joint names, we share the same friends, you can imagine how it is, but when he asked me to get married . . . I just froze right there and then on Christmas morning. I can usually do the right thing to keep him calm, but I just couldn't. He went crazy, Jack. Utterly berserk. He's never hit me before, not quite like this. Alfie raced upstairs. It ruined the whole day, and as soon as I get us over here, there's no Luke, and it's all weird . . .' My throat is so tight it feels swollen. I close my eyes and suck in a breath. Jack must see I'm shaking. 'I've left him twice before, and both times I've given in and gone back. He doesn't love me, and I certainly don't love him. God knows why I let him treat me like that.' Jack puts his hand on my shoulder. The relief to have said all that out loud, although I can't stop trembling. 'Each time I think if I try a bit harder. If I stop irritating the hell out of him, it will work out. It sounds crazy right now, sitting here talking to you. I want Luke to say it's okay to throw away the last fourteen years.'

'You don't need anyone's permission to do that, Evie.'

'It's hard, Jack. I can't explain it. Outwardly we have a perfect life and a business doing well. We've been looking at buying a place in Prince Edward County with more space. Maybe open a second restaurant, but none of it makes me happy, and it's bad for Alfie. When I'm away from it all, I don't get why I stay.'

I look up at Jack. Behind him, Alfie stands in the doorway. He's very still until he realises I see him. He rushes forward and stops behind my chair, craning his neck to get a better view of the screen.

'Kind of cool, isn't it?' Alfie grins at me. He will think that, but how long has he been standing there? I stare back at the screen into Sibilla's dead gaze. How much of our conversation did Alfie overhear?

CHAPTER TWENTY-THREE

I SIT BESIDE Alfie on the sofa, fastening my running shoes. Pink-grey clouds streak the lightening sky, and now that the wind has dropped the sea is as flat as a board.

'Come for a run with me?' I say.

Alfie's brow crinkles with a deep frown as he hunches over the coffee table staring at Luke's laptop screen. 'It's locked out again.'

'Leave it, for now, Alfie!' The irritation in my voice is plain but entirely lost on my son.

'He might have a computer-generated one, you know, just random stuff,' says Alfie.

I reach across and close the laptop lid. 'Did you hear me? I said leave it for now.' I stand and pick up the coffee mugs. Jack snores, shifts in his sleep and settles again on the opposite sofa.

'Sure you won't come?' Alfie shakes his head as he picks up the Xbox controller. 'Keep the volume down then while Jack's sleeping. Can I borrow your phone?'

The Xbox screen is loading, Alfie's attention draining fast. He pulls his mobile from his pyjama pocket and waves it at me. I should insist that he comes with me. He hasn't said if he overheard our conversation last night. I should find out. But I need time alone. Time to think.

'Do you know your number if you need to call me?'

I watch my son as I wait to see if there's a reply. I don't want to snap at him. I'll only feel more miserable than I do already if we fall out. He's trying to help in his own way, after all, but there may be news of Luke while I'm running.

'Alfie?'

'Write it down, Mom.'

I sigh, which I know annoys him, and head to the kitchen. The receipt for Luke's shopping is still on the windowsill. Stupidly, a lump rises to my throat. I find a pen and press the home key on Alfie's mobile. Several more messages have come in from Seth, all unanswered. At least it isn't just me Alfie ignores. I take a look at a couple, just the same as last night. The last one was sent less than half an hour ago. Maybe it was a late one at Maxwells. Seth has to have picked up my message, but there's no mention of it, which is a massive relief. None of that has anything to do with Alfie. Lots of emojis and jokes about being bored around 'Mom'.

I write down the mobile number and leave it tucked under the kettle along with the pen. Jack will spot it here if it's needed. I find my scarf and put on several layers. My wind-cheater and parka are still wet from last night.

'I'll be forty, fifty minutes, Alfie.' Gunfire. Electronic voices. No answer. I look across to where my son sits with his legs tucked beneath him and it catches my eye, the pattern carved into the stone above the mantel. I should find out what that is.

'Alfie?'

'Okay!'

I pick up keys and head into the hall. I need to get out of this house and clear my head; get some perspective. Jack's right; we can't assume it's Luke. I stop in front of the mirror beside the door and tie back my hair. My roots are shocking. The yellowish bruise is barely visible now, but I'm so glad Jack knows. Should I put some make-up on it? Lou and the crowd might arrive before I'm back? Fuck it. They need to know. I head outside.

I stop at the Arch and lean my back against the rough flint wall. Breath rasps in my throat, my lungs on fire. Gorse spiked with bright yellow blooms shelter me from the wind as I pull out Alfie's mobile. Thirty-five minutes for the loop to the beach car park and back isn't bad. Salt wind chafes my hot face as gulls circle and cry overhead. Out across the grey water, a bright band spreads up from the horizon, the moon a pale disc dipping in and out of thin cloud above the power station's nuclear dome. The sight of it always put me on edge; even now, it looks alien, like something from a Sci-Fi movie. There's no sign at all of last night's drama. Has anything been found? I bite down hard on my lip as it trembles, determined not to lose it. If I give in, let myself howl, it feels like giving up all hope – it will be Luke if I let myself cry.

I shove the phone and my cold hands into my pockets, my fingers curling around the small hag stone. I rub my thumb against the smooth surface, feel the irregular hole, too narrow for my index finger to find a way in. It's illogical, but it feels better having it with me. I push away from the wall and walk around the giant pillar.

I jolt to a halt, gasping in surprise. I hadn't expected to see a soul out here at this time of day, let alone him. He sits, elbows on his knees in one of the nooks at the foot of the pillars, staring right at me.

'You scared me half to death, sitting there.' I put my hands on my thighs as I try to catch my breath.

Will stands and brushes down the back of his jeans. I stare up at him. He seems so tall, but his eyes are familiar hazel-green, fringed with dark lashes. 'Jack called us about last night.' He pushes his hands into his coat pockets, the same one he wore to Lou's the other night. 'I wanted to check you're okay. I thought you'd probably come back this way.'

'I'm fine. Running helps.' Will is no fool, why would I be okay? I follow his gaze past the waist-high post and wire fence to the vast expanse of sky. I walk up to the fence for no reason other than for something to do. How much has Jack told him? Just about Luke, or me going crazy in an unlocked room? Will comes to stand beside me.

'I thought you'd have all those gadgets Luke sports when he's running.'

I force myself to laugh, not sure why I suddenly feel so unsettled. The knot tightening in my chest is nothing to do with a hard run. I don't want Will thinking I'm deranged. Why should I care, though?

'We left in a hurry. They're still on the side table in the apartment back home.' I look at my feet. 'Lucky this old pair were still here. There was only one running shoe in our suit-case.' The wind tugs his dark hair back from his face as he frowns against the force of it. 'Good thing this ground is soft, it's all concrete back home.' I turn away from him and walk the few steps to the flagstone path where it dips beneath the wire. I don't know why I find him so hard to be around after such a long time.

Will catches my forearm. 'Don't get too close.' He drops his hand. 'Sorry,' he says, looking uncertain. 'The weather over the last few weeks has battered this section of cliffs.'

I step away from the wire, my gaze following the line of flagstones through the tufts of rough grass to the cliff edge. 'Seems crazy we used to run along there, doesn't it?' His voice is deep, the warmth in his tone just the same, and I see us all chasing towards the tower, the sun on our backs and wind in our faces. It feels like a lifetime ago.

'Did Luke go over – like Dad?'

There's a beat before Will answers, but I can't pull my gaze from the horizon to look at him.

'Why would he, Evie? He had no reason to.'

'That's what I said about Dad. No one listened!' My voice is shrill, a ring of accusation all too clear. 'Jack said he saw Luke up here.' I turn to face him, see the shock on his face. I'm practically shouting at him. I try to gather myself, take a breath, but tears wet my skin. 'I'm sorry, it's not your fault . . .' A sob chokes out of me as drips fall from my chin onto my hoody. I scrub at my nose with the back of my hand, but the wave keeps coming. I realise with horror, I desperately want him to hold me. I cover my face with my hands. This has been building since we got here, but why now? 'I'm sorry, I shouldn't be yelling at you . . .'

'Hey.' His arms fold around me, pulling me into him. I bury my face in the gap between his shoulder and neck. The wool of his coat is soft, warm, and I scrunch my eyes tight shut. Tears leak out, there is nothing I can do to push back the tide. Everything I've boxed in, Dad, Luke, Seth, spills out.

My breathing finally settles, and the tears stop. We stand motionless, the wind moaning about the Arch overhead. I should be the one to move. But it's warm and safe with his arms around me. Gulls scream. I've missed this, someone to turn to. His weight shifts very slightly. I straighten and pull away, wiping my wet face with my palm.

'Sorry. I've needed to do that for a while.' I risk a glance up at him and see the wonky Will Maynard grin. I must look a fright. I meet his dark eyes, and they hold mine. I crank out an embarrassed grin as I rummage through pockets for a tissue.

'I can tell,' he says.

'Was Luke all right when you saw him?' My voice is hoarse, but thank God it's level, no sign of another meltdown just yet. 'You would tell me, wouldn't you?'

'He was fine, Evie. Just a bit annoyed you'd started to wobble about coming over again.' I stare up at him. 'Annoyed isn't probably quite it, more concerned. He really wants to see you.'

I can't think of anything to say. His eyes hold mine again, and I know for sure Luke has said something. For months we've spoken about all the strife with Seth, but I can't go there right now. Will's gaze moves a fraction. If I hadn't been looking right at him, I'd have missed it. My cheekbone is bare, no make-up covering it today.

'I told Jack about that,' I say. Will says nothing, and I look past him as gulls cry, diving beneath the cliffs. What must he think of me? He pulls his mobile from his pocket, the screen lit with a text.

'We should head back. Jenna's thinking I've got lost,' he says with a crooked half-smile, 'and you're shivering.' I'm cooling down too quickly, standing in the shadow of the Arch. 'Lou will be wondering where we are as well,' he says as we turn and follow the flagstone path. It's instantly quieter as we leave the Arch and head out across the Abbey grounds, weaving between the bones of old rooms, the sea booming at our backs. Grey reed beds up ahead whisper and chatter, seed heads nodding in great rippling waves beneath a clinging white mist.

'It's just so hard, not knowing about Luke,' I say.

'We'll call the police when we get in, see if there's any news. Not much else we can do for now other than wait.'

I tell him about Dad's iMac. 'Did Luke mention any of that historical stuff when you saw him?'

'I've wracked my brains since reading your dad's notebook. Luke said something in passing that last time I saw him, but looking back I wonder if there was more to it.'

'In what way?'

Will shakes his head. 'I don't know. I might not be right about it. You know how you can look for something that's not there?' I watch his profile as we walk, a frown creasing his brow. 'There's nothing much on the net other than some old wives' tales about the medieval storms being part of a hex to punish the town.'

He stops so abruptly I end up slightly ahead of him, looking up into his face. 'Dad mentioned Marcus's fascination with the painting at the Castle Museum. All I could find was a sketchy tale of a girl accused of witchcraft cursing the town. We all heard that story dozens of times as kids. Why your dad and Luke were both so interested in her, I've no clue.'

'Luke mentioned her?'

'I think so. I should have paid more attention, but he'd marked your dad's text. He wasn't staying at Seahurst, and I'm not really clear why that was. He made a joke about the place feeling weird in winter. Dark nights and shadows and no one there. Not like the light, busy place of your dad's day. None of this is likely to be connected to Luke not being here, though. I can't see how it could be.'

'Do you know why Luke stood you up that last time?'

'No idea. I called him, but no reply. You know what he's like, but Dad saw him several times after that, and he seemed fine.'

You can never pin Luke down. When we were kids, he was so much older, more complicated and dismissive of a much younger sister and her friends. But the number of times we've ended a Skype call and I'd been none the wiser about him, his life, what he actually does with himself. Even I must admit he can be infuriating.

'You worry you haven't been in touch, but you've probably spoken to Luke more than I have. He mentioned you above anything else. Anyway, Lou's got today mapped out, as you'd expect.' I listen to his voice as we amble along the path – pub lunch, a walk, all the usual things. 'Alfie's need to go beach-combing for hag stones is proving a bit of a challenge, though. Lou's not used to her plans being messed with.' Will's grin is broad as he indicates for me to go ahead.

I climb the stile and try to avoid the worst of the mud as I jump down the other side. As he climbs, I look back at the Arch. Clouds race great shadows across the undulating ground, swallowing the walls, path and Arch. They're almost invisible against the glare of the horizon.

'Alfie needs to be out of the house,' I say. 'Away from the Xbox. Maybe we go crabbing again?'

Will jumps down beside me, and we head down the slope towards Seahurst. 'He's a great kid. Molly is a huge fan, and he's good for Dad.'

I shoot a glance at Will and realise I'm holding my breath, but he's looking at the ground, avoiding the worst of the mud. Tiny crinkles, so like Jack's, are at the corners of his eyes, and I wonder what has made him laugh in the years since I was last here. Molly has something of him with her dark hair and eyes.

'Jenna seems lovely. She suits you,' I say, keen to steer the conversation onto solid ground before we reach Seahurst. The last thing Alfie needs is me turning up in a tear-stained mess. 'She has very good boots.' I look at him as we pass Betty and Adam's van.

'If it weren't for that fancy footwear she might have come to meet you too, but you're right, Jenna's a good person.'

Does he mean you're not, Evie Meyer? I'm over-analysing everything, just keep it calm now we're back here.

'I assumed she would be! You'd hardly get engaged to someone who wasn't.' As the words leave me, I'm aware of Will looking at me. All I can do is focus straight ahead.

Molly waves through the glass as we head up the slate path. Will runs towards the door making the little girl giggle and jump back as it slides open. I follow them inside, surprised to hear so many voices. The slightly stilted laughter and raised tones make me think of guests arriving at Maxwells, meeting up, needing a drink to hold and a barstool to sit on.

Will kicks off his boots and joins them, standing with his back to me beside the nearest sofa, his arm around Jenna's waist. Alfie runs towards me, his face pale and tired. I stare at the group, my heart in my mouth. Alfie stops in front of me and hugs me like he's five years old. I pull him close as the faces all turn towards me.

'Hello, Evie. I grabbed a last-minute flight. Thought I'd come over and surprise you.' Seth strides across the room towards me, his smile hard.

CHAPTER TWENTY-FOUR

SETH CRUSHES ME into a fierce hug. Over his shoulder, I see Lou and Adam side-by-side, Jenna pulling Will down on the sofa beside her. No sign of Jack.

'I'm so sorry to hear about your brother. Can't leave you dealing with everything here on your own, can I?' Seth speaks loudly enough so everyone will hear. He lowers his voice. I barely catch his words. 'You didn't say anything about the bump to your face on the kitchen cupboard door.' He releases me and smirks as he looks into my eyes.

My heart is racing, heat rushing to my cheeks, although I'm shivering head to toe. Alfie stands so close his shoulder bumps my arm. I pull off my bobble hat, Seth's eyes focusing on the thick line of dark roots. He frowns, and I'm glad of them. Glad it will annoy the hell out of him.

'When did you get here?' It's all I can think of to say.

'About ten minutes ago.'

I wish I could stop trembling. He must notice it. I sit with a thunk on the Ottoman and start to unlace my muddy running shoes. Alfie hovers beside me. He would have freaked out when Seth turned up out of the blue.

'Where's Jack?' I say to Alfie.

'Gone for a walk.' My son's voice is subdued, his eyes hold mine, and I see the fear there – the same as he must see in me. Molly sits on the floor, building some sort of marble maze. Alfie was obsessive about a similar thing at that age.

'Go and help Molly,' I say. Alfie nods. He knows the drill: do as I say and keep out of the way. Alfie glances back at me as he heads towards where Molly sits in the space beyond the sofas.

Seth has my hand, pulling me to my feet and into the room. I'm aware of him talking nineteen-to-the dozen, his words buzzing, Lou laughing at something he's saying and wrapping her arms about my shoulders, hugging me tightly. I should have told her about Seth. As we pull apart, she looks into my face.

'Are you okay? Dad says there's no news yet.' I nod, manage a fleeting smile. She studies my face for a second, so I smile again.

'We were just saying about coming over here for a while, weren't we?' Seth is saying. Lou looks from me to Seth. I've no idea what he's on about.

'That would be so exciting, wouldn't it?' Lou's smiling at me, taking my arm and rubbing my hand. I daren't look at her. I can't risk another full-on meltdown. 'The three of us here for the summer – what do you say, Evie?'

I smile, an autopilot thing, not really hearing what they say. How had Seth sussed Lou out so fast? Had I said something, maybe Jack or Alfie even. He can't mean it, he's blocked us coming over here for years, but he's such a good liar. None of these people know him, yet he has them hanging onto his every word. Seth's barrage of warm humour and charm is already exhausting me. All I want is to run from the room.

'You're cold, Evie,' says Lou as she rubs my hand between hers.

'Let's get some more coffee on, get you warmed up.' Seth glances at Will. 'Coffee?'

'Great, thanks,' says Will. 'It's raw out there today, bitter up on the cliffs.' I try to catch Will's attention, but he only has eyes for Jenna. How much does Will know? Maybe Jack hasn't said anything. Perhaps they don't believe me. Seth's easy front-of-house charm has clientele coming back to Maxwells in droves, and it's working a treat here right now. Everyone crowds around the kitchen, pulling out barstools, chatting and making themselves comfy. Seth has the fridge door open, finding milk and ground coffee.

'Your ring's here, Evie, did you know?' Seth picks up the ring from the dish and walks towards Lou and me. 'Jenna says she hasn't seen it. Haven't you been wearing it?'

I look down and see the ring in Seth's hands. He holds it up for all to see, takes my left hand and wiggles it onto my finger. I imagine pulling my hand free, yanking the ring off, throwing it across the room. It bouncing across the floor-boards. But that's not happening. Dad was forever pointing out how overactive my imagination could be.

Seth has his hand in the small of my back, pressing me forward, showing off the ring, turning my hand this way and that, the stones catching the light. Alfie is watching as he sits on the floor beside Molly.

'It's beautiful, Evie. Isn't it strange how similar they are?' Jenna holds out her hand. Her small nails are glossy and red. Mine are all different lengths and desperately in need of a trim. I pull my hand free from Seth's.

'Evie never wears jewellery when she's running.' Seth sits between Lou and Jenna as the coffee drips through the percolator.

'I'll get changed,' I say to Lou. She's still looking concerned, and I don't trust myself right now, not after the scene on the cliffs. 'Then I'll check in with the police if we haven't heard any news.' I don't wait for anyone to respond but head straight for the stairs. I need time to think. Decide how the hell I'm going to handle Seth. I glance through the metal spindles as I round the spiral. My eyes meet Alfie's. He is okay for now playing with Molly.

I'm relieved the bathroom door is closed as I hurry along the corridor and turn into my room. Usually, I'd shower after a run, but no way can I face that room after last night. I sink onto the futon, drag the ring from my finger and drop it on the low table. *Shit!*

I put my head in my hands, my fingers tearing at my hair. Seth will be as mad as hell about the voicemail. Why didn't I think that silence might mean he was following us over here? I've been so preoccupied about Luke I've barely thought what Seth might be up to. Stupid – no way would he be ignoring it all. Does Mum know he's over here? Surely she'd have let me know?

A burst of laughter comes from upstairs. The murmur of conversation resumes. Hesitant footsteps on the stairs. I head out into the corridor, and Alfie hurtles towards me.

'Mom!'

'Shush!' I grab his hand and tug him towards Luke's room. 'What are we going to do?'

I stop just inside the door, Alfie beside me. 'We can stay at Lou's or the pub,' I say in a voice that sounds far more certain and calm than I'm feeling. Alfie's eyes are huge in his pale face, and he's nodding like crazy as I look at him. He must be frightened after his conversation with Seth at the airport.

'Pack your rucksack and stash it in Betty's boot when you can. Don't be obvious about it, okay?' Alfie's nodding continues. I pull him into a hug, and we stand very still for a long moment. He's shaking as much as I am. 'We'll be okay this time. You'll just have to trust me,' I say.

We pull apart, and I hold his gaze, raise my eyebrows, and he nods. I can't mess up, not again. I glance at Luke's bedside tables.

'Why are we in here?' he says.

'Something Will said just now.' I move towards the bed, pull open the top drawer of the low table. I don't remember seeing anything while Nicola searched through here.

'Will says Uncle Luke has running stuff, but I haven't seen anything. I'd have borrowed it if I had.' Alfie comes to stand beside me and watches me close the top drawer and pull out the lower one. 'Look around, will you?'

Alfie walks around the bed and opens the top drawer of the matching table. 'Dad's cooking breakfast, you know?'

I glance across at Alfie; there is nothing obvious in the drawer he has hanging open. 'Is he?' I say, forcing a neutral tone into my voice. Seth rarely cooks, although he's pretty good, to be fair. A handful of times, he's stepped in at Maxwells to help out when one of the chefs is off, but never at home. Alfie's not daft. He knows what Seth's up to. I've not seen any running shoes or gear other than the sports hoody over the back of the chair.

'Hey!' Alfie holds up a small square box. 'This is dead cool!'

'Is there anything in there?' I ask. Alfie pulls off the lid. He shakes his head and looks at me across the bed. 'It's like the one you looked at buying,' he says. Luke clearly didn't spare the budget, the Garmin smartwatch is a beautiful thing, but I had to think about spending that much just on me.

'What did you see, Mom, last night?'

I look back at the drawer and push it closed. My legs are wobbly, and I slump onto the bed.

'I can't be a hundred per cent, Alfie. It was so dark, just a glimpse but maybe an armband.'

'What's going on?'

I jump up from the bed like it's electrified me. Seth stands in the doorway holding a steaming mug of coffee. He moves into the room, pushing the door closed at his back and holds out the mug. I take it from him.

'Looking for Luke's running gear.' I can't look up into his face as I speak. The surface of the coffee shivers.

'We need to have a chat, Alfie.' Seth's voice is cold, calm. He almost speaks in slow motion. 'About your behaviour at the airport.' Coffee nearly slopes over the edge of my mug as I take a drink.

'Careful with that,' says Seth. He brushes his fingers beneath my chin, only the lightest touch, but I shudder as I look into his pale blue eyes. 'We need to talk too, Evie.' I don't reply. Wait to see what comes next. He can't do much with everyone upstairs. 'I suppose you know you look like shit?' He's eyeing my hair. His gaze drops to my cheekbone. 'Sort yourself out, will you? The rest of us have to look at that.' I stay silent. 'What were you doing running about with Will Maynard so early this morning?'

'He's engaged!' I blurt out. His smile is humourless, and I thank God we're not alone here right now.

'Jenna's no idea what you're like, has she? Pretty girl, though. Beautiful ring.' He looks at my bare hand then back to my face. 'Wear it, Evie or I'll think you didn't like it.'

The vibration is deafening, the whole building consumed by it. Surprise turns to shock on Seth's face.

'What the hell is that?' The groaning starts, an undercurrent to the vibration, growing louder. Alfie runs around the bed to stand beside me.

'It's probably the boiler, it's been happening a lot.' I leave the coffee on the table and head into the corridor. 'I'll find out what's going on.'

Adam is sprinting down the spiral stairs. The sound is different down here, like it's in the walls. I grab the banister, vibrations shiver through my hand and into my bones. I hope Adam knows what he's doing. It feels like the whole place might cave in.

'It sounds worse than it is,' Adam says.

I hurry after him down the passage. The bathroom door opens, and Jack steps out. He's dressed in dark jeans and a heavy knitted sweater.

'Good to be so popular,' says Jack with a frown. 'That set off when I turned on the hot tap to rinse my hands.'

The noise stops abruptly. Adam steps past Jack and into the bathroom. I'm aware of Seth close behind me. Adam turns on the cold tap, water gushing into the basin.

'All good until that racket started up,' Jack says.

Adam turns off the tap and stands with his hands on his hips, staring into the mirror. Seth is so close I move away, step into the bathroom. The silence is oppressive after so much noise. The shower looks just fine, the taps aren't dripping, even the towels are straight and tidy on the rail, the shampoo bottle and conditioner lined up on the shelf. Jack, I assume, sorting things out.

'Do you know what that was?' Seth leans against the door frame.

Adam looks past me to Seth. 'A valve sticking. Probably needs replacing, to be honest, but I'll see what I can do.'

'The rank smell is still here,' I say, looking about the room. 'It was a whole lot stronger earlier when I realised it was in my hair. Stank like rotting vegetation.'

'Always the drama queen, Evie.' Seth's genial smile reflects back at me in the mirror. I imagine turning around, slapping him hard across his grinning face – the shock of it in his expression. 'Girls and their hair,' he says, looking at the line of dark roots.

'The noise shouldn't have anything to do with a bad smell. That has to be something else,' says Adam.

'Would it leak out of those holes?' I point at the brick beneath the washbasin. Adam squats down to take a closer look at the air brick. The pattern cut into the wall isn't visible from here.

'There's no obvious reason for that to be there. Probably something to do with an abandoned system. Jack tried to help me lever the old stone lid up in the garage earlier to see what that's all about.'

'It's a dead weight though, needs a lot more muscle to shift it,' says Jack. Alfie has vanished. Escaped back upstairs, I would think, while Seth's distracted.

'Maybe Will can give me a hand after breakfast,' says Adam. 'More the merrier, Seth, if you're okay to help out?'

CHAPTER TWENTY-FIVE

I HOLD ALFIE'S mobile in front of me, the speaker on full volume. I like the police liaison officer's matter of fact style. It makes it easier to handle what and when we might hear something. The fence is behind me on the cliff edge, my back to the wind. Alfie is indoors, standing at the glass, watching me. I raise my hand and wave. Clouds race across the face of the building, and he vanishes. I wonder if he waved back or turned away, gone to find Molly or Lou. He won't go into the garage with the guys, I'm sure about that. Not with Seth there.

'We have his mother as next of kin, Ms Mathews. We'll call her as soon as we have any information,' the police officer says.

'She may not let me know.' I explain briefly why things are not so straightforward between Nicola and me.

'I'll check with her that she's calling you when there's some news. She might prefer, as you say, to suggest I call you back.'

'This phone will be on all day. The signal is patchy here, so please leave a message if I don't pick up.'

As we end the call, a regular hammering rhythm starts up in the garage. I turn around and watch the steel grey sea, the sky only a little brighter. Seth turning up is the last thing I need on top of everything else. I don't even want to go into the garage with him there. The other guys are with him, though. Jack knows, and I'm pretty sure he will have spoken to Will.

I turn back to the house, walk past Betty, Adam's van and

Luke's Jeep. Luke's the main priority right now. I try to push the memory of what was in the sea out of my head. I'd have felt far happier if we'd found his running gear earlier. Was it a smartwatch I saw last night? They are common enough. It doesn't mean anything, even if I could be sure what I saw.

Along the side of the house, the woods are strangely quiet. Both garage doors are open, and I can hear the men's voices beneath the clang of hammering.

'The garage must have been planned later then?' Adam is speaking to Jack as I walk in.

'Marcus had been thinking about it for a while. The build started the May before he died.' Jack is watching Adam hammering around the stone cover on the floor. He glances up as I stop inside the garage door.

'Still having trouble by the sounds of it,' I say.

'Adam doesn't want to bust the lid. Not easy to get a replacement. It's not a standard thing,' Will says.

Cold air seeps in from the woods at my back. It feels colder in here than outside. Adam is on his knees beside the round stone lid. Seth stands on one side of him, a metal jemmy in his hand. Will is on his knees watching Adam chip away at the concrete around the edge of the lid with a hammer and chisel. Only Seth watches me. I won't look back at him. He picks up on stuff so fast, almost like he can read my mind. He's not mentioned the text message, but he's read it. I'm sure of that.

'We're getting there,' says Adam pushing himself back on his heels. 'It's still cemented on this side. That's why it's not budging.' Adam starts tapping away again around the rim of the lid.

'What did the police say? Any news?' says Will as he pushes himself to his feet and comes to stand beside me. Seth watches us over Will's shoulder. He's never met Will, but he knows we went out for a while. Seth has a talent for making something of nothing. I need to be careful.

'They'll call when they have something,' I say.

Adam stops tapping around the edges of the stone. 'Try it again, Seth.'

So typical of Seth to have the jemmy. He hooks the end of it beneath the stone and puts his weight behind it – shards of stone snap and crack from the edge of the lid.

'Leave it!' says Adam. 'Let's not risk busting the whole thing.'

'Why would it be so hard to raise? Surely it might be needed for access?' I say as Will and I move closer to the men around the lid.

'If it's an old well, it's probably backfilled. There'd be no reason to lift it,' says Adam. He hands the hammer and chisel to Will. We all stand and watch him tap the head of the chisel with the hammer for a minute or two.

'Let's try it now,' Will says, standing and brushing pale dust from his black jeans. Seth wedges the jemmy between the edge of the lid and the floor and leans his weight onto it. Nothing seems to happen as far as I can see.

'Take it slowly.' Adam grasps the metal ring in the centre of the lid. Seth leans his weight on the end of the jemmy and rocks up and down. A grinding kind of popping sounds and the cover shifts sideways. 'That's it!' says Adam. He reaches towards Seth and takes the crowbar from him. He hooks the metal bar through the ring, glances at Will and Seth, who both grasp the jemmy. The three men heave the lid. It tilts as the men step backwards, dragging the stone across the floor.

'Let it down slowly,' says Adam, his breath short and sharp. They lower the stone to the floor, and we all step towards the circular dark hole in the ground. The top of the shaft is lined with narrow red bricks, row upon row falling away into darkness. I step back, find Will's arm behind me.

'All right, Evie,' he says, and I catch a glimmer of a smile as he leans forward to see into the hole. The air is cold. The damp smell of a dead space rising up from the floor makes me shiver. I step away from the men as they huddle together.

'Anyone got a torch?' Adam looks at me across the space of the well as he kneels at the lip of the hole.

'I'll have a look back here.' I head to the crowded shelves at the back of the garage, glad to be away from the gaping black hole. The bottle of fabric conditioner is on top of the washing machine where I left it last night. I'd forgotten the laundry needs hanging out. Just in front of the bottle is the horrible bone thing I threw out. I gape at it, not understanding how it got here. I turn back and look towards the garage entrance. The bins stand side-by-side. Someone will have moved them out of the way when the men came in here. Did someone take it out of the bin and the orange plastic bag? Why would anyone do that? I turn back and stare at it on the shelf.

'Try this.' Will's holding his phone out towards the top of the well. The men's conversation sounds miles away. How do I get rid of this thing?

'I'm surprised it hasn't been filled – makes it easier though to check out. Evie? Are you listening?' I turn around, Adam is looking up at me, but I can't concentrate on what he's saying. All I want is to get away from here, my skin shrinking as if a thousand tiny insects crawled across me.

'You all right, Evie – you've gone as white as a sheet?' The concern in Seth's voice is so syrupy I could vomit. He steps towards me, lays his arm across my shoulders, and a silent scream goes off in my head. Why can't I tell him to shove his false concern?

'Hates heights,' he says to no one in particular. Will looks up, still holding the torch above the hole as I step away from Seth.

'It's nothing to do with the well,' I say in a far too aggressive tone. The men all look at me. 'Does anyone know where this came from?' I ask.

'What is it?' says Seth, picking it up and turning it over in his hands. I want to yell at him, tell him to drop it. Don't touch it. I'll look like a crazy woman, though. 'Looks like an old kid's rattle. Bit scuffed though,' he says, dropping it back beside the bottle of conditioner. *Clack.*

I feel the noise in my chest, like it's trying to stop me from breathing. I have to move away.

I try to calm down.

'No sign of a torch here,' I say. 'I'll check the rat traps while you guys take a look down there.'

I concentrate on checking the traps along the back wall of the garage. Only one has sprung, but it's empty. I kneel on the dusty floor and reset it while the men behind me try to see down the shaft. It makes no sense that any of them would go rifling through the bin. So how did the rattle get on top of the machine? It wasn't there last night. I'd have seen it.

'We need a flashlight or a decent torch,' says Will. 'We can't see anything like this.'

'I have one in the van,' says Adam, heading out of the garage.

'You all right, Evie?' Jack comes to stand beside me, his eyes on my face. I look at him, see the concern in his expression and know his question is about so much more than this great hole in the floor. I can't ask about the rattle, not here. Not now.

'That smell,' I say, looking past Jack to where Seth and Will stand beside the stone lid. It's so weird seeing them together. I look back at the rat traps. 'The rat smell.' I catch Seth's eye, determined to sound sure of myself. 'We smell it around the bins in the back ally at home. It's really distinct, isn't it?' I hold his gaze and wait for him to reply.

He shrugs. 'What are you on about, Evie?'

'What I'm saying is it's nothing like the smell coming from there,' I say, pointing to the open hole in the floor.

'Why would it be?' Seth laughs.' Are you expecting rats to come teeming out of here? I think you're letting your imagination get the better of you, Evie.'

'No,' I say, keeping my voice level and calm. 'You're missing my point.' I look at Jack. 'This is the same smell we get here in the bathroom, isn't it?

Jack's nodding, stepping across to stare into the old well. I look towards the woods at the sound of Adam's heavy footfall. A mobile buzzes. I snatch Alfie's phone from my pocket, but the screen is dark.

'Better take this,' says Jack as he passes Adam on his way outside.

'Let's see what we've got then.' Adam kneels at the edge of the hole. Seth and Will stand opposite, hands on knees peering into the darkness. I move to stand just behind Adam. He switches the flashlight on, the beam a white tunnel moving around as he leans forward to look deeper into the hole.

'Doesn't look like it's been filled; pretty deep, though. Jesus!' He sits back on his heels. 'The air's not good down there.'

'It's the same in the bathroom. Do you think it's venting through the grille beneath the sink?'

'Maybe. Luke's going to have to get this checked out,' Adam

says, looking up at me. 'I'm surprised it got built over like this.'

'Dad had the foundations built, didn't he?' I say. 'Maybe Luke didn't get it opened?'

Adam stands and switches off the flashlight. 'I'm pretty sure he didn't. Leave it with me. There's an engineer I know who can probably help with it.' Adam smiles at me. 'Don't look so worried, Evie. We'll sort something out.'

Jack stops beside the garage doors, the mobile screen bright in his hand. 'Nicola's on the phone,' he says, looking at me. 'She has some news.' Jack backs away towards the path, and I know he wants me to follow him. I find my feet don't move. I stare at Jack, and my stomach turns over. Jack walks away, disappearing along the side of the house. The three men look at me.

'Shall I come with you?' says Seth.

'No,' I say and hurry after Jack.

I catch up with Jack at the fence as he stares out across the sea. He holds the mobile out towards me. 'Nicola says it's easier to tell me, but you need to hear this for yourself.'

I take it from him, and he walks away along the cliffs to where they drop down to the beach. I don't really hear what she says; just follow behind Jack. I stop where the marram grass meets the shingle and listen to her voice – the details of what she's been told.

Jack walks to where the waves wash across the shore. I hear myself, words spilling out: 'How can they be sure?' and 'What happened, do they know?'

I must end the call as Lou is here taking the mobile from me. She has her arm around my shoulders, and she's yelling to Jack. Waving for him to come back. It's too cold, she's saying, to be standing outside.

'The water must have been freezing,' I say to Lou. 'Luke was in there all that time.'

Lou is taking my hand, not really listening to me. Will and Seth are coming down the rise, hurrying towards us. Lou shouting to Will. I take his hand and let him lead me back towards the house. How long had Luke been out there, in the sea on his own and in only his running gear?

'I should've come over sooner,' I say to Will.

He has his arm around my shoulders. 'Let's get you inside, Evie.'

'I left it too late.' My voice is weird, shrill and too loud. 'If I'd come over sooner, Will. It's all my fault!'

CHAPTER TWENTY-SIX

I STARE OUT of the café's steamy, wet window. Betty is parked on the opposite side of the green, her bright red paintwork slick with rain.

'I'm making a habit of this today,' I say, balling the soggy tissue in my fist. 'I did the same all over Will first thing this morning.' I raise a brief smile.

The waitress hovers a couple of feet from our table, notepad and pen in hand. Red and green Christmas garlands hang from the low ceiling above her head. She's busy, the other half-dozen tables full of customers escaping the biting wind and rain.

'Can I get you ladies anything else?'

Lou orders more coffee, peppermint tea for me, second slices of lemon drizzle cake. My chest aches from crying. I haven't managed to eat half of the first slice. I don't have the energy to say I can't face any more.

'It was the right thing to get you out,' Lou says. I pull my gaze away from the window; there's concern in her eyes. I must look a sight. I realise she's been talking to me. 'Poor Alfie was so worried when you started howling. Kids aren't used to seeing us like that, are they?'

I shake my head. 'I hope he's okay. No way did he want to go out with Seth today.'

'Dad will keep an eye on things.' Lou puts her hand over mine. 'He'll be fine. Molly will be in her element bossing the guys about. She loves spending time with her granddad.'

I nod and scrub at my nose again with the tissue. Jack's idea to get the film out of the camera and take it to be developed proved too tempting for Alfie, and he finally agreed to go with Seth for a couple of hours.

'After Nicola's call, you needed some space, Evie.'

'It wasn't a surprise, not really, though, was it?' Lou stares at me as the coffee machine screams, steam hissing so loudly I wait for it to stop before I continue. 'I'm dreading the inquest, Lou. Going over everything just for them to say it's the same as Dad.'

'You don't know that'll be the outcome. Nicola didn't know how he died.'

'It'll be just the same, whatever they find. If Luke climbed over a fence and kept going, that's what they'll say – all over again.' My fingers tremble as I scrunch up the tissue. 'I can't bear to go through all that again, Lou. I can't!'

Lou glances across the café. I was almost shouting. The waitress has stopped ringing up someone's bill to look at us. Customers stare. I look back at the small plastic Christmas tree on our table and lower my voice. 'Sorry.'

'Don't be. It's a dreadful thing to have happened, but wait to see what the inquest finds before you jump to conclusions. There's no reason to think that way. With the weather we've had, the cliffs are lethal in places.' I look up into her hazel-green eyes and so want to believe she's right. 'An accident seems far more likely, Evie.'

The waitress stops beside the table. A quick glance at me, and she seems satisfied I'm not about to alarm her customers again. She empties her tray: a fresh pot of tea for me, a cup of coffee for Lou. They chatter away about the wet weather as Lou moves the milk jug and sugar bowl out of the way. What

I saw in the sea was Luke. I knew it that night and know it for sure now. A running top hitched halfway up a white back, arms splayed out either side of the head, hair swirling like seaweed. The Garmin glinting on a wrist. Luke had been running that morning. He'd spoken to Jack. Why didn't he shower and change? Why go out again and in such dreadful weather? It makes no sense.

'Hey?' Lou looks so sad, her eyes, bright.

'Sorry. Did you say something?'

'Will you be all right with Seth? On your own at Seahurst?' I blink at her, confused by the sudden change of direction. She's been nattering away, and I've not heard a word. 'Dad says things haven't been good. You're welcome to stay with us, you know that? I don't like to think of you at Seahurst on your own.'

I stare out of the window. A small boy points at the Beetle, looking back along the narrow pavement at his parents as they walk towards him, smiling.

'I sent Seth a text just before he arrived to say I'm leaving him.' I look back at Lou. 'He's never lashed out before, not quite like he did on Christmas Day. He's much worse when things are slipping out of his control. It's made it difficult to leave.'

'Stay with us, just for a couple of days. It'll be so hard at Seahurst anyway after what's happened.' I'm shaking my head, watching her hand twirling a spoon in her coffee cup. I know she's right. It's Luke's place, his stuff everywhere. 'I've put it off before, too many times, Lou. I can't do it again.'

'Just get the inquest opened and out of the way first?'

'If I wait, Seth will be back in.' I put my head in my hands and screw my eyes shut. I get all she's saying; it makes so much sense. 'I have to do it now, Lou. For Alfie.'

'You need to take care of yourself, Evie. You're no good to Alfie if you give yourself a nervous breakdown. Let us help out, look after Alfie for you. The kids will love it.' My throat is closing up again. All I can do is nod and look out of the window. The little boy and his family have gone, the street is empty now. 'I could stay over at Seahurst. Adam wouldn't mind.'

'I appreciate the offer, Lou. Really, I do. I'll sort it out tonight with Seth and then see how things are. He's not going to try anything with you all knowing what's been going on. Hopefully, he'll sod off back to Canada when he realises it's for real this time.' I force a smile. 'You're so lucky. You do know that don't you?' I say. Lou looks surprised. 'Adam loves you; he's a good guy. You're okay, though, aren't you?'

'We'll be fine, don't worry about us, not right now.' Lou pokes at the brown and white sugar lumps in the bowl with her teaspoon.

'He's worried about you,' I say, keen to change the subject away from me. Easier to talk about other things right now. I blow my nose into the soggy tissue and shove it back into my pocket as the bell above the café door jingles. A young couple hurry in searching for a free table.

'I know, Evie, but this is not the time.' She looks at me, raises her eyebrows. 'You're the one we need to worry about right now. Stop ducking the issues. I know you, remember? So the thing with Seth. You turned him down, didn't you? Dad's not keen, says he's too good to be true.'

Does she get what Seth's like? He'll be doing the usual right now, promising Alfie a new phone, Xbox and games, being the perfect father and guest, fawning over Adam and Jack, subtly sowing seeds of doubt about me.

'Mum says if it's as bad as I say it is, I'd have left years ago.

That's the worst of it, never knowing if people will see it for what it is. I can't explain how impossible it is to leave.'

How scared I am, that I won't cope on my own. Seth's always been there, so much older and more experienced than me. That I'll lose the restaurant and Alfie. If I follow through this time, what will Seth actually do? I take a breath and look back outside.

'Luke got it all and begged me to come over. He was worried about Seahurst. Something about Dad's death he needed to speak about. I could tell he was also concerned about Alfie and me. He said he'd help us out, help us get away. Now he's not here, Lou.'

'We're all here for you, Evie. We always will be, you know that, don't you?' She puts her hand over mine, and I nod, too overwhelmed to reply.

'We haven't relaxed at Seahurst since we got here. The place feels scary, if I'm honest. I've been hanging onto a dream, Lou. All those summers here with you guys have gone.'

'You were the one who said people grow up, but we still miss you,' Lou says. 'That summer after Mum died, when you got here, Will wasn't so sad, and Dad had Marcus to talk to. Every year after that, when you left, and we went back to school, Will closed off, and Dad would sink back into depression.' She looks back at me and shrugs. 'When your dad died, you were gone straight after the funeral – I'd have been there for you like you were for me, but you shut me out.'

'Dad's death was very different from your mum. She fought so hard to stay with you and Will . . .'

The tears at the back of my throat will overwhelm me again if I don't stop talking. I pick up the fork and push the cake around my plate. The guilt drove me away more than anything. The arguments Dad and I had that summer, the distance between us hollowed me out. Now Alfie is growing up I see the teenage me being difficult and sullen.

'Anyway, you weren't speaking to me at the time, I remember.'

'You'd just dumped my brother. He was heartbroken!'

'He dumped me. He was planning on a wild time when he started uni.'

'Hardly, Evie! That's not Will's style.' Lou's suddenly angry. She's always been close to her brother, and she's so adamant about this. Why would Will say I dumped him? He's such a straight-up guy. It didn't make sense at the time, but it all got lost in the chaos of Dad dying.

'Jack had a bit of a go at me the other day,' I say. I glance out of the window then back at Lou. 'He was cross about me not keeping in touch. I should've answered your letters. I'm sorry about that, Lou. I tried to get back here the following summer, just for ten days or so, but Seth's a clever guy. If he doesn't want something to happen, he puts stuff in the way. Little things at first, things that didn't really register, but the more I tried over the years, the more he blocked it.'

'Why?'

'I don't know.' I think of the guys at Maxwells. I've not heard a word from anyone and realise I never really expected to. They know Seth will find out if they contact me. If push comes to shove, what he says goes, and they're worried about their jobs. I get that. I look into Lou's face and wonder how to make her understand.

'Go on,' she says.

'He has to have his own way.' I hold Lou's gaze. 'I didn't work it out, not properly, from the start. Eighteen and pregnant isn't great, but by the time Alfie was at nursery, when he was three, maybe four years old, I wanted to get away but just couldn't.' I look across the green, the rain is getting harder. 'He was so charming and attentive in the beginning and being ten years older – he's always looked after us. Even with hindsight, it's difficult to see how he gradually manipulated things.' I look at her and force myself to smile. 'I was so jealous of you that last summer!'

'Of me!'

'Is that so hard to believe?'

Lou's eyes are wide, her brow in ripples across her forehead. 'Everyone wanted to hang out with beautiful Evie Meyer.'

'Beautiful? Steady on, Lou!' I try and laugh, but my throat's too clogged still from crying, and a croak comes out instead. Seth would be howling with laughter at the suggestion I'm even vaguely attractive. I watch her over the rim of my cup as I drain the last dregs. 'Everything was falling apart that summer, right from the start, though, wasn't it?' She shakes her head; she clearly has no idea what I'm on about. 'We were all moving on, exams done, uni places or jobs waiting for us. Even if I came over the following year, no one was likely to be here, let alone with the whole summer to roam about like we used to.' I clatter my cup into the saucer. The young couple are leaving, bored of waiting for a table to be free. 'Seth was a mistake, a rebound thing when I got back to Canada. I'd known him from a part-time job. He'd hung around a bit too much . . . Knew how to flatter a silly younger me.'

I look at Lou, and she nods for me to go on. I start telling her about Christmas Day as I watch the young couple zip up their coats. I hear myself speaking, words falling between us, Lou's expression snapping from surprise to a deep frown. Anger. The bell tingles as the girl pulls open the door and steps out into the rain. She pauses as she opens a bright yellow umbrella, the man rushing forwards, ducking beneath it as the door closes at their backs.

'I worry Alfie will turn out like Seth. They say that, don't they – if children grow up around all that?' My smile is tight. 'Luke got how bad it was.' I rummage in my pocket for the tissue. 'Give me a sec.' The last thing I want is to lose it again, but just talking about him . . .

'Take your time, Evie.'

The bell tinkles, the door opening on a gasp of cold air. He smiles at me, moving between tables, coming towards us. Why do I smile back? Seth stops beside us as Lou looks up at him and I realise how stupid all my talk has been.

'We're getting cold on the beach, and the rain just keeps coming. I thought I'd come and see if you're feeling any better, Evie?'

CHAPTER TWENTY-SEVEN

ADAM RELEASES ME from a bear hug as the front door slides open.

'I'll be back tomorrow with the engineer. If you're still at the solicitor's, we'll access the well from the garage, if that's okay?'

'Seth will probably be about. I'll let you know when I'll be back from Ipswich.'

'Bloody hell, it's freezing! I'll wait for you in the van, Lou.' Adam jogs the length of the slate path, the security lights cutting through the darkness as he passes each one. Lou fastens her coat.

'I don't like leaving you here on your own, Evie.' She's looking past me, back into the house. Seth sprawls across the furthest sofa, an empty whisky tumbler limp between his fingers.

'We'll be fine, don't worry. Alfie's in bed, and I'm heading there right now.' She frowns at me. 'Seth's out for the count,' I say, looking towards where he's sleeping. 'He probably won't wake for hours, what with jet lag and booze.'

I hug Lou, my eyes suddenly hot. I'm still all over the place about Luke. I wish I'd taken her up on her offer to stay. 'Anyway,' I say as we step apart, 'Seth knows you guys are over tomorrow, and we have to sort things out at some point – I need to get that done as soon as possible, for my sanity's sake.'

Adam's headlights cut through the black glass, the beam streaming across the space of the sitting room as the van turns towards the track. I walk silently towards the coffee table crowded with spent beer cans, dirty plates and glasses. Seth's head rests on the back of the sofa. I jolt with surprise, he's awake, his pale blue eyes following my progress across the room. I pick up a tray as I pass the counter, head towards the low table and start to load it with glasses.

'What were you saying, Evie?' he drawls.

My fingers tighten about the neck of Dad's bottle of Glenfiddich. I put it on the tray, Seth's tone like a warning siren blaring inside my head.

'Sorting out plans for tomorrow. Early start. I'll drive Betty to the station, take the train to Ipswich from there.' I crowd glasses onto the tray, a bowl greasy and smeared, a few peanuts in the bottom.

'Like hell you were, whispering away on the doorstep. You were talking about me, weren't you?'

He swings his legs off the sofa, his knee jolting the table leg. Glasses clatter. He slams his tumbler on the table so hard I jump. How it doesn't shatter beneath his hand, I don't know. *Keep calm, don't irritate him any more than he is already.*

'We thought you were asleep – didn't want to disturb you talking in here.'

'Bullshit!' He thrusts his hand towards me, palm upwards, fingers beckoning. 'Give me your mobile.'

I stare at him. 'I've lost it, you know that!'

'You think I'm that dumb?'

'Jack and Alfie will both tell you!' My voice is shrill. Alfie's only been in bed a few minutes – he'll probably still be awake. *Don't let him rile me, don't react, or this can only go one way.* Why hasn't he mentioned the text message?

'You've been using Alfie's – get it.'

'Do you really think I'd put stuff on Alfie's phone, even if anything was going on?' I straighten, glasses clink on the tray. 'I'll get the mobile. You're welcome to go through it like you always do, but there's nothing to find. You read the text I sent you?' My heart is thundering against my ribs. I grip the tray so hard, try not to let it shake or the glasses will clatter. He doesn't answer. We both know he has. 'The phone's on the counter. I'll get it.'

The tray jolts, china clinks as Seth's hand thrusts forwards. He hears my sharp intake of breath, a self-satisfied smirk across his features. We're inches apart; a day's stubble across his cheeks and chin, his eyes bleary with alcohol. The horror of Christmas Day nudges its way into my head. *Don't panic.*

'Leave the bottle,' he says, snatching the whisky from the tray.

I head for the kitchen, trying not to seem hurried. *Stay calm.* The counter is piled with dirty plates, the dishwater, only three minutes until it's done – no space for me to dump the tray. We need to sort things out, but not while he's this drunk.

'What's this, Evie?'

I hadn't heard him behind me, his bare feet silent on the wooden floor – the mobile slides from the back pocket of my denim skirt. Seth holds the phone up to my face. I can't focus. I hadn't realised I had the mobile on me.

'Let's take a look, shall we?' His breath is damp against my cheek, fetid and stale with liquor. He punches in a four-digit code. The screen buzzes. He frowns, tries again. 'You've changed the code?' He squares up to me, blocking my way.

'Alfie did. Said he didn't like anyone messing with his phone,' I say, forcing myself to look up into his face. He won't do anything. Not here. Not with Lou and the crowd coming over tomorrow. I tell him the code, keep my eyes on his and my voice steady. He taps the glass again. The screen lights, last summer, a bright sunny day, Alfie's thirteenth birthday party, a crowd of his friends pulling faces at the lens. The image flips to a list of recent calls. Alfie rarely phones anyone, just the few I made this afternoon after speaking to Nicola.

'You've binned them, haven't you?' There's nothing on the mobile to find. Nothing deleted. No calls, messages he can't see. I try to step forwards with the tray. He continues to stand in the way. 'You make me do these things, Evie, when you lie.' He's looking at the side of my face. Nothing to see there. A little make-up earlier was a patch repair for Alfie's sake after the café meltdown.

'I'm not lying.'

'There you go again. Don't treat me like an idiot. I can see what's going on here.' His voice is syrupy smooth, and slightly too high as if he were speaking to a child. I don't try to move: stand still and wait.

'What's going on with Will?' His face jerks into mine, and it takes all my resolve not to step back. 'Don't mess with me, Evie. You two getting back here together all smiles like you *bumped* into each other on the clifftop. What will Alfie think when he hears his mother's a two-timing slut?'

'He's engaged!' I shout. 'Over the moon with Jenna. Even you must see that.' He looks surprised for a second, not used to me firing back. He frowns, blond brows hooding his pale blue eyes. My heart races, my cheeks burning. *Don't shout. It only makes it worse.* He knows my son is my weak spot. Hold my nerve, sort this out before he goes off on one and wakes Alfie. 'I was a hot, sweaty mess when I stopped to catch my breath, hardly a romantic encounter.'

'I don't appreciate him poking his nose into our business.'
'Who, Will?'

'Don't pretend you don't know, Evie. Spreading tittle-tattle about me. No one believes a word you say.' He jerks his fist backwards. I keep totally still. Not even breathing. 'You did that to yourself, and you know it.' So he's figured out they believe me. Will must have said something. He knows they see what he is. If anything happens to Alfie and me, they know – Jack, Lou and Will. I force myself to hold his gaze. He drops his fist to his side, grabs the edge of the counter to steady himself.

'I didn't say anything to Will. Jack must have spoken to him. Will and Jenna have been spending some time at Lou and Adam's over Christmas, they've headed back to Norwich now, so I don't suppose we'll see them again this visit. This thing with Luke has hit us all hard.'

Seth shrugs. 'Looks like Luke's the same as your father.' He cups my chin in his hand, his skin cool against mine. He leans forward. Stale alcohol breath bathes my face as he presses his lips to my forehead. He stands straight and smiles. I want to reach up, scrub the damp imprint from my skin. 'That fucked-up brother's scrambled your brain. That's why you texted me that crap, right?'

My eyes sting; he knows which buttons to press. If I disagree now, anything could happen. The closer we get to leaving him, the scarier Seth gets. Christmas Day all over again. Alfie's terrified face, so pale and drawn, his eyes on mine as he rushed upstairs. The sound of his bedroom door slamming.

'You've got me and Maxwells. I'll take care of you.' He looks at my hand as I hold the tray – no engagement ring. The click of the dishwasher makes me jump. The tray tips, Seth catching its front as crockery slides forwards. 'Calm down, Evie.' He smiles, pulls the dishwasher door open, the end of the programme, steam gushing out. I need to put this damned tray down. I move past him and slide it onto the hob. I pull in a deep breath as I unload the tray. I have to get on top of this situation. 'Make us some coffee, Evie.'

I turn around and watch Seth's unsteady gait as he makes his way back across the room. His leg bumps the coffee table again as he tries to move past it to the sofa. He's barely able to stand. It's now or never. I can't let the moment pass. Not again.

'It's too late for me,' I say, my voice, steady and calm. 'You know where everything is if you want to make yourself some.' Seth jerks around, his eyes bleary and red. He looks startled, I don't usually refuse to do as he says. 'I've sorted out some temporary accommodation for Alfie and me for when we get back to Toronto. You can buy me out of Maxwells and the apartment. Keep it all.'

He laughs as he slumps onto the sofa. 'So you can open up next door? Take all the trade? Do you think I'm an idiot?'

'The lawyers will sort all of that out, and you know it. If you don't want the restaurant say so.'

Seth watches me, elbows on his knees. He won't call my bluff and refuse to take the restaurant. He went too far Christmas Day. He knows there's no going back. Seth's thought this all through. He doesn't want me, otherwise he'd never give up this easily. He guessed I'd give him all we have just to get away.

'Think about it and let me know what you want to do. I'll fix a meeting with the attorney when I get home.' I push myself away from the counter feeling euphoric. At last, I've said it.

Seth sits back on the sofa. 'I've an early start, so I'm going to bed. You're welcome to use Dad's old room or bring a pillow and duvet up here,' I say, as I walk to the stairs. I switch off the uplighters, desperate for Seth to sleep and not bother Alfie or me tonight. Shadows flit across the floor, filling the spaces between the kitchen and where Seth lies. His eyes are closed, and I can tell from the slow rise and fall of his chest he's asleep. I tiptoe back across the room, pull his jacket from the arm of the sofa and lay it across his shoulders. As I turn back to the stairs I see it. The bone rattle on the coffee table lying between the empty whisky bottle and Seth's glass. I gasp, horrified the hideous thing is here.

'Did you bring this up here?' I blurt out. Seth grunts, shifts a little, eyelids flicker. He knew I hated this thing, probably thought it was funny to dump it here to upset me. I stare at the rattle. What should I do? No way am I picking it up. It seems impossible to get rid of the bloody thing. I retreat silently across the room to the stairs and look back at him. With any luck he'll be out cold for hours. I'll put the rattle in the wood burner next time it's lit.

At the bottom of the stairs, I turn into the passage. Shadows rush across the brick ceiling and sneak along the walls as I hurry towards the bathroom. The blown light needs fixing, too many dark corners with it out. Alfie's left the bathroom light on, there's no hint of a smell in here now. I leave the door open and hurriedly wash and clean my teeth, turn off the tap and make sure it's not dripping. No sound from upstairs. I look wrecked. Dark circles hang under my eyes, and Seth has a point about my hair - it looks desperate. I pull it back off my face. The ring of dark roots at my hairline has widened. It makes me think of Dad, of the younger, happier me. I try not to think about Luke. I'm cried out for now. Just need to sleep. But there's something niggling at the back of my mind. A feeling I'm missing something.

Luke's dressing gown hangs on the door at my back. I'm not sure why I focus on it. It doesn't help having his things about the place. I shiver, suddenly cold. I'm exhausted and need to be in bed, but my mind is all over the place. No idea if I'll be able to sleep. The wind is getting up, rising in pitch, shrieking along the passage. I gape at the mirror. It wavers as if water gushes down its surface. A section of it, dark, almost black, as if someone's shadow crept across the glass. I grasp the edge of the washbasin. It's disorientating. Thin rivulets grow thicker. Flowing faster. I reach out to touch it, unable to make any sense of what I'm seeing. I stop, my hand outstretched. It's not the glass moving. Not the mirror. My throat constricts, air trapped in my chest. The mirror is reflecting something behind me.

I grip the washbasin harder, unable to make myself turn around – my heart a hard knot it's pumping so hard. I stare into the sink, won't look at the mirror. I close my eyes for a second. Try to breathe. Steady myself. *Nothing is here, be logical.* The temptation to scream, call out to Seth or Alfie is overwhelming. I press the urge down inside me. *Stay silent.* The sensation of someone here grows more powerful – standing close to my back. The cold penetrating my hoody, my tee-shirt, freezes my skin. Nothing like I've known before. I'm not breathing. I sense, whatever it is, is waiting. How long do I stand here shaking from head to toe? I swallow, open my eyes and stare into the sink. The taps trickle with water, the familiar stench rising into my face.

Click-clack.

I spin around, pressing my back against the basin as I clasp my hands over my mouth. The sound that comes out of me is a whimper. The rattle is upstairs, not in here. The air is dank. The rank smell, so thick it's suffocating. I can't see anything except an empty room. But the sense of someone is so strong – as if they are standing in front of me. I don't know why her name runs through my mind. Why I silently say her name in my head. *Sibilla*.

The door to the corridor is ajar. Five, maybe six steps from where I stand. I let go of the sink and dash for the door. I wrench it wide open and stumble out into the corridor.

Click-clack. Clickety, clickety, clickety-clack.

I stare back at the room. No mirror. No brightly lit space. The wind whistles about the house, the sound strange and unfamiliar. Not the usual rise and fall but an ever-increasing pitch, growing louder. Shadows jump all around me. I can't drag myself away from the room. A dimly lit space. Light flickering against dark brick walls. A pool of melted wax on the floor. A candle burnt low, guttering. There is someone beyond the glare of the dying candle. The smoke-laden air blurs her features. Only her dark eyes are sharp and cold as they hold mine. A child, bundled in a shawl, is restless in her lap. A young boy sits beside her, the rattle in his hand. He shakes it at the child. *Clickety-clack.*

I blink, and the bathroom is here, halogen light bouncing off the mirror, my horrified face staring back at me. My heart is racing so fast my chest aches. I run towards Luke's room, wind wailing along the passage. The same weird crooning sound I'd heard when Alfie and Jack were on the beach. I feel it all around me, pressing my clothes against my skin. I put my hands over my ears, can't silence it. A terrified screaming going off in my head.

I burst into Luke's room, slam the door and stop dead in

my tracks. Alfie is out of bed, standing in front of me. His lips are white, his eyes, huge and staring.

'Alfie?' I whisper. He must hear me, we're only a few inches apart. I glance back over my shoulder. Nothing there, the door, closed. Alfie's arms hang by his side, none of him moving. Not even a rise and fall of his chest. I reach out my hand, not sure about touching my son. 'Alfie?' He doesn't respond, it's as if he sees straight through me. I let my fingertips brush the side of his hand. His skin is so cold. Alfie doesn't stir. Is he sleepwalking? He never has before. Is this what happened the other night? I take his hand in mine, and gently chafe the back of it with my own. Try to get some warmth into his skin. Alfie blinks, his eyes finding my own. That vacant, startled expression, just like before. Is he ill?

'Are you okay?' Alfie's face is so full of confusion as I put my arm about his shoulders and guide him back into bed.

'You're . . . coming to bed . . . right?' he mumbles.

I nod as I pull the duvet up to his chin. The iPad is beside him and I wonder how long he was on it. Did something scare him? What is going on in the house?

'Get some sleep,' I whisper. 'It's late.'

'You . . . You told Dad?' Alfie struggles to sit up, scrunching the duvet into a heap about his waist. *Is stress causing Alfie's strange behaviour, or something else?* I nod and smile, pull the covers back over him as he lays back down on his side. The relief that I've finished things with Seth is enormous. He'll remember what I've said in the morning. I'm pretty sure Seth got what he came for.

'Will he go back home then?' I try to concentrate on what Alfie is saying, but I'm straining to hear any sound in the passage.

'I don't know, let's hope so. There's no reason for him to

hang around now. Once I'm back from Ipswich tomorrow, we can sort out what we're doing.' Alfie is staring at me, his brow creased into a deep frown. The colour is coming back into his face, his eyes focusing on mine. I try to smile, don't focus on what happened in the bathroom just now. 'Maybe we should stay over at Molly's for a few days?' Getting away from Seth is one thing, but staying here is quite another.

'We should do that, Mom.'

'I'll speak to Lou.' I watch his face for a moment. 'We're going to be fine, Alfie.'

'Are you sleeping here tonight?'

'Yes,' I say, forcing myself to laugh. 'You asked that already. Snuggle down.'

'Can we pick up my photos tomorrow? Will you be back in time?'

'Hopefully, I won't be too long.'

Something rolls across the duvet. I shoot out my hand, miss it. The crack as it hits the floor sounds so loud in the silent room. I hold my breath as I look back at the door. Thank goodness it's closed. On the floor beside my foot is a hag stone.

'I took it from your room,' says Alfie.

I pick the stone up from the floor and look at my son through the jagged hole at its centre. 'Get some sleep.' I drop the stone into the palm of his hand.

I change into my PJs and crawl into bed. Alfie's already sound asleep. What is going on with him? I might have to get him to a doctor if it happens again. I've heard nothing upstairs. Seth won't bother us again tonight. I'm too wired to sleep, my mind trying to make sense of what I saw – thought I saw – in the bathroom. All the times I'd stayed here with Dad and Luke, nothing remotely weird ever happened. I can't toss and turn, or I'll risk waking Alfie – the last thing he needs. I pick up the iPad and put the Abbey's name and location into the search engine. Familiar sites come up; historical information about when it was built, its influence during its medieval heyday and its dissolution and inevitable decline. None of this is new to me and not what I want.

I search again. Abbey folklore and legends, tales of strange lights, hobby lanterns luring people towards the crumbling cliffs and a watery death. Ghostly voices of monks, their chants carried out to sea on the wind. The girl accused of hexing the wealthy medieval port to drown beneath the waves is mentioned on several of the folklore sites. I've heard most of these tales, either from Dad or locals, over the years. I smile as I recall Will scaring the rest of us shitless one night, creeping about the ruins with an old-fashioned lantern taken from his mum's garden. Perhaps there's nothing to find, but I feel I'm missing something. My eyes are dry and heavy. It's late. None of this is helping.

I search for Sibilla and the painting at the Castle Museum fills the screen. I can see why Dad loved the Pre-Raphaelite style painting. The girl's quite like the teenage me with my long auburn hair before Seth persuaded me to go shorter and blond. Was that the only reason Dad loved that painting? A romanticised image of a long-ago girl who probably only existed in folklore and myth. The emails on his computer suggest something more was going on. Will said Luke mentioned it too.

I try one last search. See if I can find anything about the flower carvings. Without knowing what they're called, it's difficult to know where to start. I follow a trail of breadcrumbs, one search leading to another. An image like the carving upstairs above the wood burner fills the screen. A hexafoil, sometimes called a daisy wheel. I read a few paragraphs about them, my mind in turmoil. Unable to take in what I'm reading, I switch off the iPad and snuggle up to Alfie's warm back. I put my arm around his shoulders and breath in the soft scent of him. The daisy wheel symbol in the bathroom bothers me. Why is a witch's mark in that room? Is that the link to Sibilla - was it her I saw in the bathroom tonight?

CHAPTER TWENTY-EIGHT

NICOLA SITS ON one of a half dozen low-backed chairs in reception. An untouched coffee is on the table in front of her, a well-thumbed magazine open on her lap. She doesn't look up as I approach the desk and tell the receptionist why I'm here.

I'm not sure where to sit. All the chairs are free other than Nicola's. She closes the magazine and drops it onto the table as I hover beside it.

'Won't you sit down? We're both rather early.'

'I didn't want to be late.'

'Not the sort of appointment one wants to keep, is it? I'll be glad to get today done and out of the way.' She watches me as I take the seat opposite her, lowering my rucksack onto the chair beside me. Her dark blue wool coat is unbuttoned over a black roll-neck and dark linen trousers. She's much smarter than me. Her flat patent pumps are similar to a pair I have back home. Mascara and pale pink lipstick do nothing to hide her sallow complexion, her cheeks somehow hollower, her face thinner than two days ago. Luke is her only child. I can't begin to imagine what state I'd be in if this were about Alfie.

'While we're waiting, perhaps I can speak to you about arrangements . . .' Her eyes are bright, and she drops her gaze to the cooling cup of tea in front of her.

'Arrangements?' I say.

'Will you stay on for the funeral? I hope we'll know a

bit more about the timing today . . .' She looks up at me, clearly searching for words. 'Until the coroner releases Luke . . . We can't do anything until then. I'd like you to be there, Evangeline, but I realise you have your little boy to consider.'

We both look towards the reception as Simon Arthurton walks swiftly towards us. Nicola and I stand, hands are shaken, condolences uttered. Coffee and tea are ordered, the reception-ist hurrying off along the corridor.

'My office is just along here.'

I follow Nicola a short distance to the room I sat in with Dad a few times before. It's been decorated since I was last here. The walls are painted magnolia now, the striped wallpa-per gone, dark drapes replaced with bone-white blinds. The furniture is just the same: three wooden chairs line up in front of a long desk, one end still piled with papers and files, the other now home to a computer and two monitors. Nicola sits on the centre seat where Dad always sat. I want to pull a chair up to the table as Simon used to so I could colour and draw while I listened to their conversation.

'Unfortunately, I have just heard that the opening of the inquest today has been postponed,' says Simon once we are settled in our seats.

'Postponed?' Nicola leans forward, holding onto the edge of the desk.

'I was surprised, what with the time of year, that it was to be so soon. It's rescheduled now for the 10th of January.'

Nicola looks at me. 'Will you be able to stay on that long?'

'I can probably sort something out. I'll need to speak to my son's school. Check he can start term a bit later.' I hadn't hung around for Dad's inquest. All the detail had come secondhand and a couple of weeks after the event. Deep down, guilt had eaten away at me like acid, leaving everything to Luke, letting Seth persuade me not to travel back to the U.K.

'The coroner only opens proceedings on the 10th – just a preliminary thing. You might need to attend the full hearing sometime later in the year, but we will know more in a day or two. What we can do today is read the will and get some of the formalities underway.' There's a document on the desk, Simon picks it up.

'Luke made his will very shortly after his father passed away and hasn't updated it since then.'

Nicola probably knows all this. She sits very still, her attention on the solicitor waiting for him to go on. Simon stops speaking and starts reading, his eyes working their way down the page. He stops after only a line or two. 'Did you realise you were his executor?' He's looking at me, waiting for a reply. I shake my head. 'It means you manage the estate, collect in all the assets, pay liabilities etc. I'll help you with it all, of course.' He looks back at the page and starts reading again. The words wash over me; all I seem to focus on is the rhythm of his voice. He pauses and looks up at us both. I glance at Nicola, but she neither moves nor speaks. 'I give to my sister Evangeline Matthews my half-share in the property Seahurst . . .' He carries on reading about bank accounts and investments . . . 'give absolutely' . . . 'to my sister, Evangeline Mathews.' I glance again at Nicola. She must have known this. Is it why she insisted I come today? 'To my mother Nicola Sarah Symonds all my interest in the business Symonds and Symonds.'

He's finishing now, getting to the end of the will, folding the thick paper again along the creases in the document, pushing it back into an envelope on his desk with Luke's name printed across the front of it. There's a knock on the door, and the receptionist comes in. We watch in silence as she places tea in front of Nicola and Simon, coffee for me. She leaves the room, the door closing behind her with a soft click.

'There's another matter I must discuss with you both.' Simon pauses and looks between Nicola and me. 'You are aware Luke made an appointment for me to meet with you, Ms Mathews?' I nod. 'He wanted to discuss the trust your late father made. All rather academic now, I'm afraid, but I gathered he had never told you about it?' I shake my head. For some reason my voice seems to have deserted me. 'Marcus left Seahurst to you both in equal shares, but due to your age, he left your half in trust until your thirtieth birthday. Luke was the trustee. Now, as you are of age and with Luke no longer being here, you own the property outright.'

I pick up my coffee as I can't think of anything to say as Simon looks from Nicola to me. My hand is shaking, tears sting the back of my eyes and I blink them away. Nothing had come my way after Dad died. I'd assumed it had all gone to Nicola and Luke. A little bit of hurt I'd carried for so long falls away. The drink is scalding. I clatter the cup back in its saucer.

'Luke left a letter of wishes alongside his will. I have copied it for you both to read at your leisure, but in essence, he says Seahurst is a property Mrs Symonds you would never want to use or enjoy. Luke also left you a letter the other day, Ms Mathews.' He hands a small white envelope to me, my name scrawled across the front of it. 'He didn't tell me anything about its contents but was emphatic that it be placed with his will for you.'

I look at the white envelope. My hands tremble, the paper shaking. 'Shall I open it now?'

'It might be better to do so, in case it shines any light on recent events.'

Death wasn't mentioned when people spoke about Dad. Always this skirting around the truth; his 'passing', your 'late' father. Occasionally someone would be direct and mention the D-word but only rarely. I run my finger beneath the sealed flap and pull out a white postcard. It's blank apart from a few words written across the front of it in black biro.

'Evie, You'll need to access my laptop. If you're reading this, it's yours now. All my research is on it – password:- 'Little Sister.' Love Lx'

I read it twice, the card shaking so hard between my fingers Nicola and Simon must see it. I'm holding my breath, a dull pain in my chest. This is probably the last thing Luke will ever send me.

'What does it say, Evangeline?' I look at Nicola. Should I tell her this? I've never mentioned the laptop. I haven't even told the police about it. I think I should have.

'Just Luke's code for his laptop,' I say. 'We tried to access it the other day – hoped it might give a clue to where he was.'

I push the card back into the envelope and hold it between my hands on my lap. Why did he drop this in so recently? Did Luke know something might happen to him?

'It's a practical issue these days, passwords and the like. Very difficult if the relatives don't have them,' says Simon.

'When we spoke on the phone before we flew over, he said there was stuff I should know – about Dad.' I watch Nicola's face, see her taking in my words, but there's nothing in her features to suggest she holds anything back. 'What did he mean? Do you know, Nicola?'

She shakes her head and looks at Simon.

'Perhaps his laptop might tell you more, Ms Mathews.' The solicitor smiles at me. 'If there's anything on there the police should know, you'll need to pass it to them.'

Simon begins to explain what happens next: he'll send paperwork to sign, no rush to make any decisions if I want to keep Seahurst or sell it, although due to its location, its marketability is questionable. He speaks briefly to Nicola about the business. They both stand. I do the same and follow them out of the office. Suddenly it's Nicola and me, standing outside the office on the high street, people ambling by window shopping, and cars crawling along the road.

'Can I give you a lift to the station?' says Nicola.

'Thanks, but my train isn't for ages. I booked it for after the inquest.'

We step back to let a man with a pram and two children pass by. A small scruffy dog tugs on the lead wrapped around the pram handle.

'There's an excellent coffee bar just along from here. Can I get you one?' A smile curves her lips. 'You look so surprised, Evangeline, and I can't blame you. I thought about what you said the other day. You had a good point.' She indicates for us to walk back the way I came earlier. 'The office is only a couple of streets away, but Nick's coffee is far better than anything we have.'

Further along the street is a square lined with small businesses and shops. I hadn't taken much in on the high street in my rush to get to the solicitor's. I follow Nicola into a tiny café at the entrance to the square. 'What can I get you?'

'An espresso, no sugar,' I say.

She nods towards a table and two chairs. 'I'll bring them over.'

I sit and watch people outside the window, the traffic bumper to bumper. It feels so alien, everyone rushing about, getting on with their lives, but Luke's no longer part of it. I pull out Alfie's mobile and text Lou.

'Catching an earlier train back. I'll text the time when I know. Can you tell Alfie?'

Nicola is chatting with the coffee vendor. I can't catch their words, just the man's laugh, Nicola's voice rising as she turns back to where I sit.

'He'll bring them over,' she says, pulling out the chair opposite me. 'I haven't told most people about Luke. Not yet.' She looks into my face. 'Makes it easier just for now,' she says, taking off her gloves and dropping them onto the table in front of her, 'to be normal for a while. Would you let me know what you find on Luke's laptop?'

'Do you have any idea what might be on there?'

She shakes her head. 'I didn't know he had one up here. There's nothing on the office computer. Luke spoke a lot about you recently. He mentioned he might have to travel to Canada.'

'Really?' I'm genuinely astonished.

'He told me things were difficult for you and when you cancelled coming over again just before Christmas – He said he might fly over in January.'

'He never said anything to me.'

'He was worried about you, Evangeline.'

'Evie.'

'Evie,' she says with a smile.

'We're separating, Seth and me. It's for the best,' I say, not wanting to explain anything more.

'Luke would have been relieved to know that,' she says. Luke must have spoken about me more than I realised. 'Luke hadn't spent much time in Suffolk until he decided to finish renovating the place where Marcus left off. About the time you two got back in touch. Did he say anything to you about Marcus?'

'Not really.'

'Nothing at all?' She looks surprised and disappointed all at the same time.

'Nothing beyond a bit of reminiscing. We were both rubbish talking about Dad.'

'He become convinced Marcus's death wasn't suicide. We fell out about it just before Christmas. He stormed out and drove up to Seahurst. We didn't speak again . . .' Her voice peters out, but her eyes hold mine – blue just like Luke's and very bright. 'You know Marcus left a lot of debts. The company really struggled for a while.'

'Luke said something about it a while back, but nothing recently.'

'When Marcus bought Seahurst, he took out loans against the business premises. I didn't know about it for years, long after you were living in Canada, but he always refused to sell the place and clear some of the debts.'

'Did you know about the trust?' I ask.

'I was an executor under Marcus's will.'

'Why didn't anyone tell me?'

'Don't blame Luke. It was my doing entirely. I was furious Marcus left Seahurst to you and the debts to me.'

'Is it okay now then?'

'Absolutely – all cleared off a few years back. That's what never made sense. Yes, there were debts, but we weren't going bankrupt, no bailiffs at the door.'

'Two espressos, ladies.'

Nicola smiles and chats to the man as he puts cups and napkins on the table. She's so much better at keeping calm and carrying on than I am. The man nods at me before hurrying away towards a couple waiting at the counter. Nicola picks up her coffee, sips it and places the cup back in its saucer.

'Luke says the debts had nothing to do with what Marcus did.' She looks at me closely as she continues. Both of us – Luke and me – thought we had somehow contributed to Dad's death, but Nicola made her point clear about that last time we met.

'Luke became convinced that Marcus's death – that stepping over a wire fence and walking several feet to the cliff edge – wasn't a deliberate thing.'

I can only gape at her as Alfie's mobile starts ringing on the table between us. I glance at the screen, decline the call. Luke had never even hinted at that.

'Nothing to do with money worries, nothing to do with you or Luke. Do you need to get that?' she says looking at the mobile.

'In a moment, yes. So what was Luke saying?'

'It sounded crazy to me. Luke was clutching at straws, obsessively looking for any reason for it not to have been suicide. I do understand how hard that must have been for both of you. A parent doing that.' My mobile pings, a text message coming in. 'Luke was suggesting there was something at Seahurst.' She studies my face closely as she stops speaking.

'Like what?' I say. Luke had been too vague when we spoke before catching our flight. Why hadn't I stopped a second and listened to my brother? Too freaked out by Christmas Day. Alfie running ahead through the crowded airport.

'I laughed when he tried to explain, it sounded so fanciful,' she says. My heart thuds against my chest. All the weird stuff at Seahurst. Even Nicola thought she saw something, but does that relate to what happened to Dad and to Luke? Alfie is there right now with Lou and Adam. 'I won't repeat this at the inquest, Evie, but Luke would want you to know.'

The mobile vibrates again, the screen lighting. Another text from Lou. Nicola sees it.

'Please call Evie. ASAP.'

I look back at her, wait for her to go on.

'Luke thought there was something at Seahurst that caused Marcus to do what he did. He wasn't clear about how or why. I don't think he really knew himself.'

Alfie's mobile starts ringing again.

'Sorry,' I say, picking up the phone and looking at the screen. 'It's Lou. I'd better take it.'

Nicola nods and sips her coffee as I push back my chair and take a couple of steps away from the table.

'What's up, Lou?'

'Are you on your way back?'

'Not yet. I'm having a coffee with Nicola. Why?'

'There's been an accident at Seahurst.'

'Is Alfie okay?'

'It's Seth. Get back as soon as you can.'

CHAPTER TWENTY-NINE

I PARK BETTY alongside Luke's Jeep, her engine juddering into silence as I grab my rucksack from the passenger seat. People are moving around inside Seahurst. I can't be sure who they are, shadows in the kitchen, near the sofas. I climb out of the car, lock the driver's door and run up the path. Lou stands just inside the front door with her arms crossed, her face free of make-up and creased into a frown. Thank God I won't have to deal with this on my own.

'Seth's going berserk.' Her voice is low as she glances over her shoulder into the house.

'On the phone you said he fell down the stairs. He wasn't speaking?'

'When we arrived, yes. Let's just say he's fine now.' She rolls her eyes and I follow her inside. The kitchen counter is a mess of dirty dishes and mugs; the TV screen paused mid-game.

'Where's Alfie?' I say.

'Keeping a low profile in your brother's room.'

Quick steps on the stairs. Seth appears, his arms full of crumpled clothing, a towel draped over his shoulder. He glares at me as he strides towards the nearest sofa. His holdall is open on the seat, half stuffed with boots and clothes.

'Are you okay?' Other than an angry welt along his left cheekbone, he looks just as he did last night. He shoves more clothing into the bag. 'What happened?' He keeps shoving, tugging at the zip, the fabric of a tee-shirt catching in the teeth. 'Can I do that for you?' For an instant, he stops moving, is totally still as if frozen. He looks up. His eyes bore into mine. 'The zipper is stuck – if you want me to have a go?'

'Where's Alfie's passport?' He stands straight, hands on hips. He's got to be nuts if he thought I'd go to Ipswich and leave Alfie's passport here.

'Lou says you had quite a tumble down the stairs.'

'I'm good. Passport?' He thrusts his hand towards me, palm face-up, fingers beckoning. Clearly his plans to stay a few days have changed.

'He's not going back with you, Seth. We're here until New Year.'

'Let's get this straight.' Seth glances past me to where Lou stands awkwardly beside the kitchen counter. 'You flew him over here against my express wishes. You're lucky I didn't arrive with a court order.'

'He doesn't want to go back with you.'

'He hates this shit hole, and I'm with him on that. He's getting his stuff together downstairs. Taxi's due in less than ten minutes.'

'Shall I go and see what he's up to?' says Lou.

'No, it's fine,' I say, holding Seth's gaze. 'You've no interest in Alfie. We can be clear on that.' I walk to the top of the stairs, my stomach tightening. Does Seth not remember our conversation last night? He was hammered. Maybe he'd snatch Alfie anyway, just to be a total shit. No way is Alfie wanting to go back with him. Surely he hasn't changed his mind? God knows what promises Seth's made.

'Alfie? Can you come up here? Are you travelling back to Canada today?' My voice echoes down the stairwell. Seth's wearing that confident smirk as if he knows something I don't. He tolerates Alfie at the best of times, too engrossed in himself to have genuine interest in anyone else. 'Alfie?' I want him up here to make it plain to Seth and with Lou as my witness that my son does not want to fly back home right now. Surely a court would consider what a thirteen-year-old wants to do? I should find out just what trouble Seth can bring down on my head as he surely will if he can.

'Alfie!' I'm clutching the handrail as I stare into the spiral. Luke's door is open. At this angle, I can't see into the room. 'Alfie?'

Hurried footsteps in the corridor, getting louder. Jack stops at the bottom of the stairs. 'What's up, Evie? I thought Alfie was up there with Louisa?'

I shake my head and look back at Lou as she comes to stand beside me at the top of the flight.

'He said he was coming down to look at the well with you while Adam fetches the engineer,' Lou says.

Jack shakes his head. 'He's not been down here. I've been sitting out back waiting for the mug of tea he promised me.'

I look at Lou. Concern is clear from the frown on her face. I try to keep calm, ignore the unease that turns my gut to jelly. I glance at the TV, paused mid-game, something Alfie never does, something about losing the level. Seth stands with his hands in his pockets beside the overflowing holdall.

'Where is he?' I say, not attempting to hide the accusation in my tone.

'How the fuck should I know.' Seth walks towards Lou and me. I can see from the suspicion on his face this is not what he was expecting. I run down the stairs and slow at the bottom of the flight. Jack steps backwards into the corridor. Luke's bed is unmade with Alfie's usual mess of clothes and underwear over the floor. No sign of any packing happening.

Even though the room is empty, I walk into it and around the far side of the bed – no Alfie.

'He can't have gone far.' Jack's standing in the doorway as Lou, then Seth, pull up behind him. Seth moves away, and I hear him opening Dad's door.

'We'd better check around,' says Lou, heading off towards the bathroom, calling for Alfie. I hear her quick footsteps echoing along the passage as Dad's door slams. Seth looks past Jack at me, a scowl on his face.

'Think you're clever, Evie?'

'What?'

'Make him disappear, hide his passport?'

'I've not been here! You've been in charge for just a few hours, and he's vanished.' I stride past Jack and follow Lou into the corridor. She's coming out of my room, running up the steps to the garage. I hurry past the empty bathroom, Jack and Seth hot on my heels. Has Alfie run off to avoid going back with Seth, or has something happened?

I run up the steps into the garage and find Lou standing beside the open well. The stone lid lays on the ground beside it. I keep a few steps back and stare at the gaping hole.

'There's no sign of him out back, Evie, not unless he's gone up to the Abbey – would he do that without telling anyone?' Lou follows my gaze to the well. Blood pulses in my throat.

'He's not gone down there, Evie,' says Jack, his hand on my shoulder. 'I opened the well with Adam earlier. I've been out here all this time.'

'Are you certain?' I demand.

Seth stands beside the well leaning forward on one foot to look down it. Jack points to an upturned bucket beside the open door. 'Been sitting there waiting for my tea.'

A car horn toots, and we all look towards the garage doors.

'That'll be my cab.' Seth dashes back towards the steps and into the corridor. I watch his back for a second, then turn to Jack.

'Do you know where he is?'

Jack shrugs. 'There was a whole lot of shouting upstairs when we were opening this up.'

'Seth went berserk, like I said.' Lou's looking at me. 'He told Alfie they were leaving and to get packed right away.'

'What did Alfie say?'

'Not a whole lot, it was difficult for him to get a word in edgeways, to be honest,' says Lou. 'Just that he wanted to go back with you, which set Seth off in a frenzy of shouting and swearing. I was still trying to sort out the bump on his face at the time. He must have really smacked himself when he fell.'

'You're totally sure about the well, Jack?' I glance back at the hole.

'I wouldn't be standing here if I wasn't.' Jack's so unconcerned. He knows something, I'm sure of it. 'He's a sensible lad, one that's not going home without his mother.'

I walk out of the garage doors and peer along the side of the house. I can't see the parking area, the trees crowd too close to the building. Where would Alfie go? He probably would take off rather than go home with Seth.

'He won't have gone far, Evie. He knew Seth was under time pressure once he confirmed the flights and booked the cab.' Jack stands beside me and stares out into the woods. It's impossible to see far, twisted trunks and tangled branches cling together in an impenetrable embrace. 'He can look out for himself for a couple of hours.' Jack raises his eyebrows as he looks at the soft, crumbling dark earth and a narrow break in the undergrowth. Something has trampled the brown fern fronds to the ground.

'Seth's on his way back.' Lou's voice is low. I only just catch her words.

Seth stops on the garage steps. 'A word, now, Evie. I don't have much time.' He doesn't wait for an answer, turns back down the steps and into the house.

'Shall I come with you?' Lou looks so worried.

'I'll be fine,' I say.

Seth is moving fast, starting up the stairs as I reach the corridor. I glance into my room, push the door wider, then follow him upstairs. He's zipping up the holdall as I clear the top of the flight.

'Have you thought about what I said?' I say. 'Keep Maxwells and the apartment. Alfie stays with me.' My heart races, but my voice is steady. I lean with my back to the banister and cross my arms. 'You can fight about it through the lawyers if you want, but you know it's an offer you can't beat. Like I said, you've no interest in Alfie.'

'Left you a bundle, has he?' Seth practically spits the words at me.

'Luke?' He knows how painful it is to talk about this. I swallow and try to keep my voice level. 'Just a property which is falling into the sea and not much else. The business is his mother's.'

Seth glances across the kitchen. The taxi is parked just beyond the Jeep, the driver leaning against the bonnet smoking a cigarette. Seth walks towards me and stands so close I see the grey that has begun to sprinkle through the hair at his temples. He's showered using Luke's body wash. I can't step back, and he knows it. I don't move a muscle.

'I won't make a better offer,' I say. 'All I'll need is a few clothes for us and Alfie's school stuff. The rest is yours.' His blue eyes focus on my face, my hair. The dark roots must be screaming at him. 'The lawyers can send anything I need to sign to Mum's address.'

Seth turns away, snatching his things from the kitchen counter. He pauses for a fraction of a second. Air is trapped in my chest; I can't seem to breathe. He reaches for something, turns to face me holding it up between his thumb and forefinger--diamonds glint. He shoves the ring into the front pocket of his jeans and heads for the door. I think he'll look back, say something. I'm surprised when he doesn't stop but goes straight outside.

I still have no idea why he's leaving so fast. Did he think he could snatch Alfie? Probably. But what happened here? Was he drunk? Is that why he fell downstairs? My scare last night nudges into my mind. I push myself away from the banister and run after him. As I pass the counter where Seth picked up the engagement ring, I see the rattle. Why is that thing everywhere? Is it Seth? I dammed well hope it is.

Seth's slamming the boot, the driver behind the wheel. I pull up beside the open passenger door. Seth strides towards me. I stand my ground and stare into his face.

'Have it your way, but there's no coming back from here.' His voice is so low I doubt the driver can hear us.

'Absolutely.'

He looks at me, his hand on the open cab door. The welt along his cheekbone is angry and red, a darker colour blooming beneath it.

'What the hell happened?' I say, my eyes lingering on the side of his face. I can't shake the fleeting image of the bathroom from my mind – that dark room. The woman there, her cold, empty eyes. Too much has gone on at this house.

Seth stares back at me, the anger in his face becoming

something else. Uncertainty, confusion? I can't read him. It's so fleeting. Seth's voice is soaked in sarcasm as he glances past me to Seahurst.

'Speak to Alfie, if you find him. He knows.' He smiles, a humourless thing. 'I also left a message with the old guy.'

'Jack?'

'Told him your mucky little secret. Told him to pass it on.'

CHAPTER THIRTY

THE MURMUR OF the taxi engine dissolves on the wind as I run along the slate path. The glass walls are filled with clouds as if the sky has emptied itself inside the building. What happened to Seth? He never misses a chance to make himself the centre of attention. It's such a relief he's gone, but where the hell is Alfie?

I rush indoors. Lou is opening the fridge, the kettle boiling. No sign of Alfie or Jack.

'All sorted?' Lou says.

'For sure. Any idea where Alfie is?'

She looks back at me over her shoulder. 'I think he shot off to avoid heading back to Canada. We didn't realise you'd be back so soon.' He's probably fine, doing precisely what I would have told him to do, but I need to know he's all right. He was so strange last night, what was wrong with him? If he's been taken ill again . . . 'I could've sworn you had a four pinta in here earlier, Evie. We have some if you're out, but Dad'll have to have his tea black for now.'

I reach past her and pull open the salad drawer where we keep spare milk, cheese, and I'm sure we had a packet of ham. Just a bunch of wrinkling carrots and two red chillies. Lou looks at me, waiting for an answer. I can't worry about this right now.

'Jack knows something about Alfie. Bring his tea, Lou.' I hurry downstairs and back to the garage. Jack leans against one of the open garage doors and walks towards me as I clear the steps. What has Seth said to Jack? Maybe nothing at all. I wouldn't put it past him either way; Seth has a talent for spiteful, but Jack seems his usual self.

'So, where is he?' I say. Jack holds up his hands as he stops just a couple of feet in front of me. I dodge around him and head out of the garage. I kick away the beaten-down bramble and fern and push my thumb and two forefingers into the holes of the giant hag stone. I stagger forwards, surprised by the weight of it as I lift it up. 'This is my bedroom doorstop. It didn't get here on its own.' I glare at Jack. Deeper into the trees, a faint trail of crushed foliage winds between tree trunks. A deer or something has come through here recently. I drop the hag stone with a thunk into the leaf litter at our feet.

'He dashed up here before we had that well open,' says Jack. 'Had his rucksack with him. Said he'd lay low till you got back. That boy's nervous of Seth.'

I stare at Jack. 'You didn't think I needed to know that?' Lou stands at the top of the steps, a mug of tea in each hand. 'Did you know?' I try not to shout. Lou looks astonished, shakes her head. Seth, Alfie. The solicitors. Don't take it out on Lou. Only anger is keeping tears at bay right now.

'She didn't know, and you didn't need to either. Not till that twat left. No chance of him finding out then, was there?' I look back at Jack. I've never heard him swear other than when he's fishing. He puts his hands to his mouth and bellows Alfie's name into the trees. I look between twisted trunks, but there's no sign of him.

'We have to find him, Jack. He could be anywhere,' I say, stepping through the gap in the undergrowth. Brambles snag my jeans; I stop after half a dozen steps. The dark scent of damp earth rises from the scuffed ground. The undergrowth is thick, folding over crushed fronds in places, but the line flows deeper into the trees. I kick back brambles and step over a moss-covered log. A rotten branch snaps beneath my boot. A movement catches my eye as Jack stops behind me. It's hard to see, my eyes aren't used to the shadowy gloom. The dank smell from the woodland floor reminds me of the rank odour at Seahurst.

'Alfie?' I take another step forward. I see it again: a yellow flash. My windcheater. 'Alfie!' I break into a run, the bracken knee-high and getting deeper. 'Alfie?'

My son steps out from behind a tree trunk and into my path. I gasp with surprise and pull him to me. The windcheater's fabric is cold and a little damp, but my son's cheek against my neck is soft and warm. He lets me hold him for a long moment before he starts to wriggle and squirm.

'You had me so worried,' I say as we step apart. I'm struggling to keep my voice steady, and Alfie knows it as he focuses on Jack just beyond where I'm standing.

'Dad's gone, right?'

'Seth left a few minutes ago,' Jack says.

'So we're staying here, Mom?'

I nod, still trying to get myself under control. Far too much has gone on today.

'So we can go fishing later then?' Alfie says to Jack.

'For goodness' sake, is that all you can think of?' Exasperation rings in my voice as I try to pull myself together. I don't want to make a drama out of this. Alfie was only doing what he's had to do too many times before.

'Let's get in. I'm gasping for my tea and something to eat.' Jack is already stomping back through the brambles towards the house. 'Your mother probably needs something too after the morning she's had.'

'You saw the hag stone I left you, right?' says Alfie. 'The doorstop one?'

'I saw it.'

'So you weren't that worried, not really? You knew, right? I knew you'd know it was me!' Alfie sounds thrilled as he heads after Jack. He clears the trees and runs into the garage where Jack stands talking with a tall, angular man in dark blue overalls.

'A note would be great next time!' I shout after him. I look back, let my eye travel along the curving path of trodden fern fronds. Alfie's rucksack lays on its side in a small section of flattened grass and weed. The four-pint carton of milk Lou wanted is beside an orange carrier bag. I pick up the milk and peep into the bag. Cheese, a packet of ham and a box of crackers I'd forgotten we had. I have to give credit to Alfie – he didn't intend to starve.

'Mom! Come and see this.' Alfie's voice sounds thin, fading into the trees. Jack stands outside the garage, his hands on his hips. He sees me and beckons with a great sweep of his arm to join them. I pick up Alfie's things and make my way to where Jack stands. He takes the bag and milk from me. 'You get everything sorted at the solicitor's this morning?' Jack says. He looks at me as he speaks. He has dark circle beneath his eyes. It isn't only me who's struggling with what happened to Luke. I nod and follow him inside.

Adam, Lou and an animated-looking Alfie stand around the well. Boiler-suit man is on his knees with his back to me, one arm down the open shaft.

'Everything okay this morning?' Adam looks up at me.

'Much as you'd expect, except the inquest isn't opening for a few days.' I glance at Lou and manage a wonky smile. 'Tell you about it later.' I stop beside the well.

'This is Iain. He's doing a quick survey,' Adam says.

'He's got a video camera,' says Alfie.

'It should find out if the well's caused any problems with the borehole,' says Iain. 'Then I'll be out of your way.' Someone, Adam most likely, has filled Iain in about Luke.

'And what's down there!' Alfie has his hands on his knees, bending forward from the hips, peering into the dark hole.

Iain grins up at him. 'I've been doing this job for a while, mate. Never found pirate gold yet, but there's a first time for everything.'

'I explained to Iain about the rat problem,' says Adam. 'All the weird scratching sounds.'

'You think they come from down there?' The horror in my voice is plain. Images of oily bodies squirming beneath the floor, scurrying behind the walls, invade my mind.

'If they are, we'll find out for you.' Adam looks across the well at me and winks.

'Not funny, Adam,' I say. I take a step back. The dark hole puts me on edge, the smell like a cold hand across my face. No one else seems bothered by it. Just me. Whatever happened in the bathroom last night, the rank smell was there.

'I skipped lunch,' I say. Any excuse to get out of here will do. 'Can I get anyone else something to eat?'

'I'd never turn you down, Evie,' says Adam. Alfie looks up from the well and nods.

'I'll go and see what's left in the fridge then,' I say.

It's such a relief to leave them to it. Their voices fade behind me as I walk along the corridor towards the stairs. I've had no time to think about Luke and the solicitor's appointment. I suddenly feel dog tired, and now I'm alone, a little weepy. Life seems relentless. Rushing on, without Luke. Just the same as it did when Dad died. If I could find five minutes to look at Luke's laptop, I might start to understand what was in his head. I put the coffee on and unload Alfie's carrier bag back into the fridge.

'Are you okay?' Lou's at the top of the stairs. I hadn't heard her.

'A bit tired, you know. It's been a stressful day.'

'Can I help out?' She walks across the room, stops beside me and puts her hand over mine. 'You look shattered. I'm sorry Alfie ran off like that, but he seems fine.'

I nod as my throat tightens. I can't cope with a meltdown right now. 'I just need to eat.' There's a huskiness in my tone. 'I didn't manage breakfast and skipped lunch rushing back here. Can you chop this? I'll get the pancetta going.'

Lou takes the knife from me and starts to slice the one large onion we have left. I find Luke's turmeric, red lentils and cumin and realise I have no idea if my brother liked cooking. There's so much I won't know about him now. Lou's nattering about Iain. Did I recognise him? He used to join us sometimes when we were kids. Married now, two children at Molly's school. I leave the pancetta browning and set mugs out on the counter. The horrible rattle is here. I nudge it to the back of the counter with the edge of a mug.

'Did you want another tea, Lou?'

'Yes, please, and for Dad.'

Lou adds the onions to the pan, the oil sizzles and spits. 'What are we making?'

'Red lentil and bacon soup. It's quick, filling, and there's bread we can toast. Would you take the drinks downstairs? Let them know food in about thirty minutes,' I say.

Lou picks up two mugs. 'Did you see Dad brought Alfie's photos back this morning?' She's looking at a colourful envelope propped up beside Luke's laptop. I'd seen it on the counter earlier but hadn't registered it. Too much going on with Seth. I pick it up.

'Some of the colours aren't great, which is a shame. There's some you must have taken before you went back to Canada last time.'

'Has Alfie seen them?'

'Not as far as I know. All the craziness with Seth was going off as we got here.' I flip open the envelope and take out a stack of prints. 'The ones that came out are on top. There's several that didn't develop at the back.' Lou stands with her shoulder brushing mine. 'Your eighteenth.' A few of the beach party, flames shooting sparks into the night air. The tower is still on the clifftop, the Arch tucked in behind it. 'That was such a good night,' says Lou.

I don't reply. The memory of Will and me leaving the party runs through my mind like it happened yesterday: climbing the cliff steps, the walk to the Arch, our last time together. And the gut-wrenching row that followed. Had we got our wires crossed that night, like Lou says? Misunderstood each other. Frightened of growing up, leaving the certainty of what we had here.

'You and Adam wrapped about each other – some things never change.' I bump my shoulder against hers.

'Keep going. There are a couple of great ones of Dad sitting outside here with Marcus. A shame the colours are off. Dad says you can get that sort of stuff fixed now digitally.' She moves away. 'I'll take these to the guys before they get cold.'

I find the ones of Dad and Jack sitting in the sunken garden, whisky glasses in hand. Lou's right about the colours; the whole image is stained yellowy-brown. Part of the space behind Dad hasn't developed at all.

The colours of the ones Alfie has taken are better: on the bridge crabbing, fishing on the beach, eating cake at the café. The final two are of Alfie on the afternoon we arrived here. The first hasn't really come out at all. No surprise if the film got damaged over the years. The second is better. Alfie grins at the camera, but some of the background is black.

I flick back to the photo of Dad. He looks happy and well, but he was dead within a day or two of this being taken. The image shivers as my hand shakes. I try to hold a sob down. If things were so bad, why didn't he say something? To me, Luke, Jack. Anyone. Did he speak to Nicola? I can't stop staring at the image. I put it on the counter and lay the one of Alfie beside it. There's something not right here.

The image of Alfie is sharper. He's standing close to the camera, and I've focused the shot well. The shadows on the white wall behind him contrast more starkly than the murky colours of the open house interior at Dad's back. Alfie's shadow is to his left, a smaller outline of my son on the whitewashed wall behind him. Dad has shadows beneath his deckchair but little else. Taken around midday, then.

So what is the dark blotch to Alfie's right? I assumed the film had deteriorated over time, at least at first glance, but now I look closer . . . In the gloomy interior of the house behind Dad, which I'd thought was dull due to damaged film, it looks like someone is standing a little back from where Dad is sitting. The shape is the same in both shots. Something about it makes me think of the slight figure standing amongst the Abbey ruins the other day. I peer more closely at the photo of Alfie. The shape has a strange quality and curves from head to toe, a shoulder, nipping in where a waist would be. Rivulets run down its front to the flagstone floor like folds in fabric.

My blood runs cold. The mirror in the bathroom last night was just like this.

I snatch up the shots, shove them into the envelope and drop it onto the counter beside the sink. The rattle catches my eye just beyond the envelope. As I stare at it, the tap drips.

CHAPTER THIRTY-ONE

A LFIE SHOVES SPOONFULS of soup into his mouth so quickly he might as well pick the bowl up and drink from it. The two bowls for Adam and Iain are cooling, a skin forming across the top. Lou and Jack are enjoying theirs, but my appetite has deserted me. What can be taking the guys so long downstairs?

'So exactly what happened with Dad, Alfie?' He throws a glance at me. Maybe we should have this conversation when we're alone.

'When we got here, Seth was leaning over the kitchen sink with a cloth against his face,' says Lou. 'I assumed he was still tanked up from last night, to be honest, when he said he'd fallen downstairs.'

Lou looks at her father, who nods and pulls bite-size pieces off his toast. I remember he always did that with bread, toast, crumpets. Never bit into them like most people do. The envelope of photos lies open on the counter between Alfie and Jack. I'd kept an ear open when they looked through them as I waited for the soup to finish cooking. Neither had said a great deal. Alfie's been silent for much of the time since.

'He wasn't drunk – at least I don't think so.' Alfie holds my gaze. Seth drinks a lot some nights, but to be fair, he wouldn't usually be any worse for wear the next day other than his temper, which I'd always put down to a banging headache.

'I was in Uncle Luke's room playing on Dad's iPad. Keeping

out of the way until you got back like you said, Mom.' Alfie drains the last of his soup. 'I thought Dad was still asleep until I heard him yelling.'

'Yelling what?' asks Lou.

Alfie shrugs. 'Don't know. There was loads of noise in the corridor. When I looked out, Dad was all crumpled. His head on the floor and the rest of him lying on the stairs. I couldn't get him to say anything, so I called Jack.' I can see from Alfie's face how shocked he must have been.

'Hey.' I slide off the barstool and put my arms around my son. He pushes his face into my neck, and I hold him tight as I stare at Jack and Lou. Both look concerned.

'Don't you worry, Alfie. He'd had too much to drink and had a nightmare, I expect.' Jack puts his soup bowl on his plate and hands them to Lou as she begins gathering the dirty dishes from the counter.

Alfie stays still, not the usual wriggling away as soon as I go near him these days. I wait for him to make the first move as Jack and Lou load the dishwasher.

'It'll be okay now,' I say, although the whole thing sounds disturbing.

Alfie pulls his head up from my shoulder. He's close to tears. I smile, hope I look more confident and reassuring than I'm feeling. Alfie glances over at Jack and Lou, who are busy clearing the counter and loading the dishwasher. 'I don't want to stay here anymore, Mom.'

'We'll get a couple of rooms at the pub. Hopefully the Christmas rush is done. I doubt there'll be an Xbox or anything much for you to do, though.'

Alfie's nodding as I speak. 'What if they don't have room?'

'Mum knows you can stay with us, Alfie. Will's staying over tonight on the sofa, but we can move things around if we need to,' says Lou. As much as I love her, we'd be better on our own for tonight. Let me have some space and time to talk to Alfie. Get him settled after everything that's gone on. I should call Mum and the guys at Maxwells, explain what's happened. I glance at Luke's laptop.

'We'll go fishing tomorrow night, lad.' Jack smiles broadly at Alfie, and I'm so grateful he's here. And he seems perfectly alright. I doubt Seth has spoken to him at all.

'Not tonight?' says Alfie.

'Storms brewing, according to the forecast. It'll blow itself out by midday tomorrow. You come with me, Alfie. We'll see what fishing gear is in the garage here.' Jack is striding towards the stairs as he's speaking, Alfie hot on his heels.

'If Will's here we'll try somewhere in town if the pub doesn't have anything, Lou.'

'He's only back for a couple of days.' Lou raises her eyebrows. 'He decided shopping in the sales could wait a while.'

'Is he all right?' I ask. Lou shrugs. I can't read her expression.

'Here's Adam and Iain,' she says, pointing to the rear wall of the house. The men stride along the path, around the corner to the front door. They come in, Adam banging his hands together against the cold.

'You took your time. I'm not used to my cooking being left to go cold,' I say, grinning. They sit at the counter. 'I can blast it in the microwave for a minute.'

Adam shakes his head between mouthfuls. 'It's good, Evie, just what I need.'

Lou pours more coffee. I pull out a stool and sit opposite Adam and Iain. The light is already becoming grainy outside, the day draining away.

'So, what's the verdict?' I say, not encouraged by their silence.

'Iain has to get someone down there to have a proper look,' says Adam. I recognise Iain now I see him without his head down the well.

'The video suggests the well is in bad shape,' Iain says. 'The two lines are right up close in one section, so Luke's building work might have been enough to cause a problem.'

'I'm hoping we can move into the pub for now,' I say. The two men exchange a glance.

'Good idea,' says Adam. 'Better to head up there while there's some light left. We can all leave together. Make sure you're okay before we settle down for the evening.'

I frown at Adam. I know when he's not being straight with me. I don't want to hang around here, but what's the sudden rush? He's the world's worst liar.

'What else?' I say, looking between the two men as Lou puts mugs of coffee in front of them.

'We can't be one hundred per cent sure, but there may be some bones down there.'

※

Our rooms at The Black Dog Inn are warm and snug. The sloping floors and wonky windows are the polar opposite of Seahurst. Alfie comes in from the twin bedroom, one of Jack's fishing manuals still open in his hands. I'm surprised to see him standing there, I thought he was already asleep. He'd spent most of the evening thrashing Jack and Will at various board games. Now he looks fit to drop, his face pale and tired.

'When are you coming to bed?' he says. 'The window keeps rattling.'

'It's just the storm, Alfie.'

He spots Luke's laptop beside the glass of gin and tonic on

the table in front of me. I'd hoped to take a look while he was asleep. His pyjama bottoms ride above his ankles, the sleeves well short of his wrists.

'You won't guess the password,' he says. 'Just a waste of time.'

I shrug and smile at my son. 'Then I won't be long then, will I? Now get to bed or you'll be too tired to go fishing with Jack tomorrow.' Alfie doesn't move. 'Are you still worried about things?' All evening the discussion had been about Seth, Seahurst and what Iain thought might be down the well. Most likely animal bones, but they had to be properly checked out. I thought Alfie seemed settled when we got back here, but it's enough to give anyone nightmares. Alfie shrugs as we look at each other. He takes a step closer to me, the book still open in his hands. 'I kept in Uncle Luke's room like you said, but I got so hungry . . .'

'Really?' I say, raising my eyebrows, hoping to lighten Alfie's mood.

'I was really quiet, but he heard me open the fridge . . .' Alfie's eyes glisten. 'He had that rattle, kept shaking it . . . Laughing about you not liking it, Mom.' He drops the book, puts his hands over his ears. 'I don't like the noise it makes!'

'Hey!' I say, holding my hands out towards him. He rushes at me, throws his arms about my neck.

'He wouldn't stop . . . I had to make him stop . . .' Alfie is trembling head to toe, and suddenly I feel terribly afraid. 'He chased me with it . . .' his words are muffled into the crook of my neck. I stroke the back of his hair and wait for him to go on. 'I pushed him, Mom . . . Just to make it stop. The noise . . . I had to make it stop . . .' I hold my son tight against me. 'He kind of fell backwards over his own feet . . .' Seth had a shed-load of booze last night, he would probably have been groggy this morning. 'I tried to grab him, but he had the rattle . . .'

'Shush!' I say. 'Seth is fine, as always. No real harm done, is there?'

'Will I go to jail?'

'No one's going to jail!'

'If Dad goes to the police?'

'He won't, Alfie.' I push him away from me to look him full in the face. 'Dad's not doing anything like that, not after all he's done to us.' Alfie nods. 'Come here,' I say, pulling him close again. He's still for a long time, and I listen to the soft rhythm of his breathing. How crazy to have thought something weird had happened to Seth at Seahurst. How had I rationally thought something unexplained caused his fall downstairs. He would be right about my all-too-vivid imagination.

Alfie wriggles free and stands up. 'There's stuff that's not right,' he blurts out. 'There's something behind the people you took photos of, Mom. There's nothing in the ones I've taken.'

I stare at him astonished, he's practically shouting at me. His sudden change of subject takes my sluggish brain a second to catch up. I snatch the packet from the table and spread the images beside the laptop. Photos Will took on the beach, the ones Jack and Lou have taken when we have been out and about. Images Alfie has taken – all clear backgrounds.

'The ones I've taken have been at the house,' I say. 'Indoor shots might not have had enough light.'

Alfie picks out some he'd taken in the kitchen. Jack and Adam grinning at the camera, Molly holding the giant brown crab they caught. Nothing strange in any of them. He picks out the ones I've taken of him and Dad and pushes them towards me. I leave them on the table. I can't bring myself to look at them.

'There's something behind me, in your room the day we got here,' he says. 'And behind Grandpa.'

'The film was ancient. You were lucky anything came out at all. You know that. Have you had a nightmare?' I should just come clean and let him know how concerned I am. But at this time of night . . . And I want to see what Luke has on his laptop before we get into anything too weird. I can see Alfie's trying to think of the right words.

'It's when you wake up all of a sudden . . .' All I can do is nod for him to go on and try not to show him how much this is freaking me out. Is this why he's been waking randomly the last couple of nights? Will said Luke didn't usually sleep at Seahurst. Alfie is struggling with what to say, his brow creased. 'When I wake up. Those times you've found me . . .' He looks at me. 'I've seen – something. But it's all gone. I can't remember any of it. I just know it was scary.'

'How do you know that? Maybe it was a nightmare? I used to wake up completely confused when I was little.' Alfie is shaking his head as I speak, a determined frown on his face.

'It's not a nightmare,' he says emphatically.

'Okay, let's talk about it properly in the morning. It's late, and we've an early start tomorrow if we are to have a decent amount of time to do anything before Jack takes you fishing. Go to bed now, Alfie.'

Alfie looks reluctant to head off. 'Don't you get it, Mom? They're watching all the time.'

'Who are?' I stand and put my arm around his shoulders. The hideous feeling of someone beside me in the bathroom was so strong, and Nicola was convinced she saw someone.

'I don't know! But they're watching me, aren't they? Standing right behind me. Like they were watching Grandpops in the photos.' All of this is insane, but I get where he's going with it. No wonder he can't sleep.

'No one's watching you here, are they?'

'Promise we don't have to go back there?'

'Promise. That really isn't going to be a hard one to keep.' We go through to the low-ceilinged bedroom, and Alfie climbs into one of the single beds. I tug the duvet over his shoulders and tuck it under his chin.

'You need new pyjamas. These are getting too small for you.'

'*Minecraft* is kind of lame too.'

'There was a time you didn't think that.'

We both look towards the window, the metal catch rattling, the neatly striped curtains moving as the wind finds its way between the gaps in the frame.

'Jack's right about a storm tonight,' I say. 'Goodness knows what it's like up at Seahurst.'

'Leave the light on, Mom.'

I switch the lamp off beside his bed. 'I'll leave mine on over there and the bathroom light as well. Get some sleep.'

'I'm sorry about Uncle Luke, Mom. Do you think the people in the walls were watching him too?'

CHAPTER THIRTY-TWO

ALFIE IS SLEEPING as I walk silently into the sitting room. I leave the door ajar, a crack of light spilling back into the bedroom. It's taken ages for him to settle. The lamp is on if he wakes. I grab a second miniature bottle of gin from the minibar and sit back at the desk. Alfie's gone on about the walls ever since we arrived at Seahurst. Nicola was convinced she saw someone, and I can't explain what I thought I saw in the bathroom. I'm sure Luke sensed something and stayed in town, not at Seahurst. It's been a hell of a day, and I need to sleep as desperately as Alfie. I pour the drink and brush my forefinger across the trackpad of Luke's laptop.

The screen glows, and I enter the password. The desktop fills the screen with only a few everyday files for car insurance and bank account statements. One is entitled 'Note to Evie'. I'm nervous about what Luke has to say. Why didn't he just call or speak over Skype? I open the file.

Hello baby sister.

I pick up my glass and sip the gin, my lips trembling against the tumbler. Still trying to annoy the hell out of me, Luke Symonds.

This is a weird thing to write, and I'm not sure what to say, so I'll jump straight in and hope it makes more sense to you than it does to me. If you're reading this, something has happened to me. I can't believe I've just typed that last line, and I hope you'll never get to read it. If you do, get out of Seahurst if you're there, and stay out. Don't think it'll be okay or that you can sort things out. You can't. Get yourself and Alfie away from that place. I use a decent guest house in town, or Lou will always find room for you. Only then, read on.

I stare at the screen, hardly able to process what Luke's saying. If he knew he was in danger, why didn't he leave Seahurst?

I'm typing this as you've just called off again. Not coming over for Christmas and New Year. You've a lot on with Seth, but you know my views there. Sort your life out for you and for Alfie. I'll say no more about that here.

I glance up at the bedroom door. Did I hear Alfie out of bed? I listen for a moment. Rain pelting against the glass, and the window rattling against its frame. I look back to the screen.

I wanted to talk about Dad. It seemed easier to do that when you were here just in case I've got this whole thing wrong. Logic and common sense say I must have. But now you're not coming over, here goes.

Dad's research is in this file. I've covered pretty much the same ground over the last few weeks as he did just before he died. I'm thinking it's all a bit mad, to be honest, or I'm having some sort of psychotic episode. If I'm right, though, Dad never left us willingly. We've said so many times suicide doesn't fit with him. Just not his style. I've

highlighted the relevant sections in his research for you.
Read the rest anytime. It'll take you days!

I scroll past the emails between Dad and Maurice Broughton Jack and I read the other night. Plans of Seahurst fill the screen. Costings and drawings for the garage. Dad's timeline of the work starting, setting out what progress was being made. The few weeks before I came over for the last summer with Dad are detailed. Luke's highlighted some text.

'The excavation for the footings started and stopped today. Not virgin ground as we thought but remnants of an old courtyard.'

Dad would have been thrilled with the discovery. Maybe it's where Alfie gets his wishful thinking of buried treasure.

'We've found the usual broken pieces of earthenware and china. A small object I'm not too sure about. Ivory or bone possibly – research needed to identify. Opening up what we guess is an old well tomorrow. Its proximity to the borehole needs checking out.'

I glance up from the screen. Wind booms against the glass, stirring the curtains. The door to the bedroom is still ajar – no sound from Alfie.

'We've replaced the stone cover over the well today and decided to leave it as is. Can't bring myself to backfill. Structurally it should be okay.'

What did Dad mean – can't bring myself to backfill? He

must have known what state the well was in. He must have known what was down there too. It didn't take Adam and Iain long to discover the bones. The footings and garage floor were in place before I got over here for the summer. All work had stopped by the time I arrived. The well would have delayed his building for months if he'd let the authorities know what he'd uncovered. Luke's notes start again.

Do you remember Dad wasn't himself that summer? He started keeping the doors locked and just looked shattered most of the time. After we argued, Dad sent me back to Essex. I was so jealous of you up here all summer. Pissed me off for years! I wanted to ask you if there was weird stuff happening. Dripping taps, rank water in the shower and a feeling that never entirely goes away. You'll probably laugh. I can practically hear you having hysterics. Like someone else is here in the shadows. All that stuff has been going on lately, and I can't get to the bottom of it. I don't sleep at Seahurst as I have the most hideous nightmares. I've woken up on the bathroom floor twice with no idea how I got there. I'm not a sleepwalker, Evie. I can't rationally explain it. I'd love to speak to Jack, but Lou's right to worry about him. His breakdown after Juliet and then Dad dying was pretty bad. He closes up as soon as I turn a conversation anywhere near this.

I've tracked down Maurice Broughton. He's retired now but remembers Dad. He says they could never prove Sibilla existed or that there was any connection to Seahurst, but after Dad died, he continued to dig around. I'm hoping to visit him before the New year as he still lives in Norwich and look at what he's got. Sibilla and her family wouldn't have been held at the Abbey but somewhere close by. Maurice says the basement at Seahurst is likely to be as old as the Abbey, probably built around the same time. It's the best we'll get with it being so long ago.

I've asked the solicitor to email you if you're not in the UK. Don't fly over to check out Seahurst. Leave it to rot and fall into the sea. It won't be long before it does, anyway.

Tell Mum about all this for me. I know it's a tall order. She's not as bad as you think – it's important to me. I tried, but it didn't go down well. Maybe I am still trying to make suicide into something else.

As crazy as it all sounds, I think you'll get it, Evie. I can't see how Dad got to the point he'd walk over the cliff edge, but there has to be a link. There just has to be. And to be completely clear – if you're reading this, I've had an accident, or something weird has happened. You can show this to an inquest if you and Mum think it will help and won't be laughed out of court, but don't beat yourselves up as we have over Dad. I'm not suicidal. Can't wait to see you and meet Alfie. You're both important to me. I probably didn't say that to you, and I should have. You always were, and always will be, my annoying and much-loved baby sister.

Keep safe, be happy.
Love you always
Lx

I catch my lower lip hard between my teeth as I skim through the note again. Luke must have written this around mid-December. If he argued with Nicola on Christmas Day, he'd only been here a short time before I called him from Toronto. I guess the guesthouse was booked out for Christmas. The hotels in town would be too. I sit back in the chair and listen to the wind howl about the eaves. Precisely what did Adam and Iain see in the well? I hadn't pressed too hard with Alfie about, and to be honest, I didn't want to deal with that on top of everything else. I pick up Alfie's mobile and the screen lights. Just past midnight. Adam has work in the morning. Will's number is on here. It makes more sense to call Adam, but it's Will's voice I want to hear. I type a text.

'Are you awake?'

I glance up – the window catch rattling again. Alfie might be able to sleep through that, but I won't. I'll have to do something to fix it.

'Why? Is everything all right over there?'

I tap out a reply: 'Can I call you?'

I watch the screen. It lights with an incoming call.

'What's up?' It's late. Will's voice is low, but there's an edge to it. He must wonder what on earth's going on.

'Everything's fine. I just wanted to know what Adam thinks they found down the well. I've been reading some notes Luke left for me. I just thought . . .' What the hell did I think? I'm in the same spot as Luke now. Trying to explain something that sounds entirely irrational. 'What happened to Dad and to Luke . . . There might be some connection. With what was in the well.'

'What makes you think that? The well cover hadn't moved in years. You saw that.'

'Dad had it open, and Luke's read his notes about the garage build. Luke was convinced there's something weird going on at Seahurst.'

Silence draws out for a second or two. 'We don't even

know if the bones are human,' he says. 'They're more likely to be animal bones. Something that fell in the well years ago.'

'And if they're not?'

'Then they'll have to be removed and investigated however old they are. Why are you worrying about this now, Evie? It's past midnight.'

I explain about the laptop, the password and Dad's concerns about Sibilla. 'I know it's just a load of old wives' tales, but Dad and Luke clearly thought there's more to it.' My voice cracks as I speak the last few words. I suck in a breath and screw my eyes shut. I shouldn't have called him. Should have left all this until the morning.

'Do you want me to come over?'

I want to scream. *Yes. Come over right now! Look at all this stuff I've read through, and tell me what you think.*'

'Evie?'

'I'm fine.'

'You don't sound fine. You've had a rough few days one way and another. You need to switch that damned laptop off and get some sleep.'

'I'll be okay. We'll see you in the morning.'

I reassure him several times that I'll do as he says and go to bed straight away. If he comes over, I won't hold it all together. I know I won't. I end the call, switch off the laptop and gather Alfie's photos together. The one taken in my bedroom lies beside my empty glass. Alfie smiles at the camera. Over his shoulder, the dark shape looms at me. There are no features, but it feels like someone is staring, their eyes boring into mine. I scrabble amongst the photos and find the shot of Dad sitting with Jack. The darkness is far more than a fault in the film. I hadn't imagined that earlier. Someone is standing right behind Dad and Alfie, but I know no one was there. There are no features where the face should be. A blank space. No eyes that I can make out, but I sense them. I realise what I've been missing. They're not watching Dad or Alfie. They're looking straight at me.

CHAPTER THIRTY-THREE

I SHOVE BACK my chair. I'm not used to drinking gin so late at night, and the wonky floor does nothing to help. I won't look at the photos spread across the table anymore. The curtains shift, the gale pressing against the glass. I cross the room and open the bedroom door. The squeaking hinge doesn't seem to disturb Alfie, the mound of his duvet not moving. I walk silently to his bed, relieved he isn't sitting up awake, waiting for me, but he has had no mobile to game on tonight. I gently pull back the top of the cover and stare at a crisp, white pillow – no Alfie.

I yank the duvet further down the bed. Where the hell is he? I spin around to stare about the low-ceilinged room. There's nowhere to hide in here. Only the hem of the curtains moving.

'Alfie?'

There's an edginess in my voice. How could I not have heard him get out of bed when I was only next door? The bathroom door is ajar, the light on. I push it fully open. No one here. I cross the room and stop at the window; the fabric sucks back and forth in time with the moaning wind. I drag the curtains apart. The streetlamp outside pools yellow light across the tarmac to the narrow hedge, the marshes a dark space beyond. Betty is parked between two other cars below the window. Beyond them, walking towards the beach end of the road, is Alfie. I try to open the window, tugging at the stiff metal catch. It frees with a jerk. Wind and rain stream in as I lean out, my hand slipping on the wet sill.

'Alfie!'

He keeps walking. I shout again, several times, but the wind is roaring into my face, the sound of the storm loud in my ears. No way will he hear me. He steps beyond the streetlight, his black pyjamas blending into the night as he heads to the end of the road. I can barely see him. As hard as I try to fix my eyes on my son, he vanishes into the night.

I search back and forth along the empty street. Most of the houses are in total darkness, not a soul to be seen. My heart is racing, and for an instant, my mind, numb with panic.

I sprint through the sitting room, the wind banging the open window at my back. I run along the corridor, down the stairs, past the empty bar and reception to the heavy front door. I drag back the latch. Wind and rain suck in, slapping my face as I dash out into the street. I crouch against the wind and rain and stop beside Betty. I hold my hand up to shield my eyes and stare along the road. It's too dark to see beyond the streetlights – no sign of Alfie.

I start to run, aware my tatty old trainers have barely any tread left. I reach the end of the road and stare back along the street. Do I go and get help? Will is probably still awake. Jack, Adam and Lou are home. I turn back to the dark lane that leads up to the Abbey, the same path we've taken each day we've been here. Alfie will have gone this way; he knows no other route. I pull his mobile from the pocket of my sweatpants, the screen blurs with water. I turn my back to the wind and hit the last number dialled.

The ringtone cuts in as I run towards the narrow path. I pray Will is awake and doesn't turn his phone to silent when he sleeps. I drop my pace, barely able to make out the hedges, let alone the muddy track. My feet jolt with each step as the call rings and rings.

'Evie?'

'Alfie's got out of bed somehow . . .'

'What? What are you on about?' Will's voice sounds slow and dull. He must have been sleeping.

'I can't see him. He's up ahead somewhere, heading towards the Abbey.'

I hear voices in the background. Some sort of banging. Will saying something away from the phone. I squint against the rain, my top soaked and heavy, water drips from my hoody onto my face.

'Will! Can you come and help?' I scream out the words. 'Bring Jack's flashlight.'

'Evie, stay right where you are.'

'I have to go, Will,' I yell into the mobile, then cut the call. The phone still has a bit of charge. I switch on the torch. The track narrows, twists and turns, branches snagging at my hoody as I run. I came this way from Seahurst two days ago. There's another minute, maybe less, before the track ends and opens out. I should spot Alfie then. He can't be moving as fast as I am.

I climb onto the stile and hold the torch high. The thin light from the mobile makes the darkness seem vast. I know the Abbey grounds are here, but I can't see a thing. I grab hold of the slimy wet wood to steady myself, wind streaming rain at me, tearing my hoody back from my head.

'Alfie!' Lightning splits the sky open miles out to sea. For a second, the rising slope and Abbey ruins outline in front of me. 'Alfie!'

Sheet lightning flickers overhead behind furiously scudding cloud, the Abbey grounds flash in and out of view. I screw my eyes against the rain, but see nothing, only broken-down walls. The lightning comes again, no more than a second, but it's enough to make out the Arch. I can't make sense of what I'm seeing. I blink water from my eyelashes. The Arch, its back, broken, a single pillar standing alone against the writhing North Sea.

'Alfie!' The force of the gale stuffs my words down my throat. I jump down onto thick squelching mud and sprint up the slope, dodging between low walls, my trainers slithering beneath me. I strain to see any sign of Alfie. If he were sleepwalking, surely the cold would wake him? Why on earth would he come out in this? Sheet lightning backlights the sky, the old pillbox a hulking dark shape up ahead. I run towards it, holding the mobile in front of me. I skirt around it until I find the entrance and duck inside.

'Alfie!' The stench is so foul I taste it. I try not to breathe. Surely he wouldn't come in here? I hold the mobile at shoulder height and check the whole space, every dark corner looming at me as shadows bounce off filthy walls. I step back to the doorway and stare through the ruins up to the Arch as lightning brightens the sky. Beside the remaining pillar is a shadow, small beside the towering dark stones. 'Alfie!'

I run as hard as I can up the slope towards the ruins. My trainers find traction at last as I reach the flagstone path. Water gushes down it. The pillar is dark against the sky, a massive pile of rubble at its feet. Beyond the stones is the small outline. My son walks along the flagstones towards the post and wire fence.

'Alfie!' The wind is coming straight at me. There's no way I can shout loud enough for Alfie to hear, even if I wasn't already out of breath. Alfie's mobile vibrates in my hand, the screen flashing with Will's number. No time to answer it. They'll find us quickly with the flashlight.

I run to the pillar, my joggers heavy and wet, my feet slip-sliding with so much water in my running shoes. I pick my way over and past great chunks of stones. Up head, only two flagstones remain beyond the post and wire fence. The broken flag that hung over the beach is gone. The last stone now is whole, its lip hanging beyond the mud and tufted marram grass. Alfie has his back to me as he stops walking and stands on the last flagstone. I run to the fence.

'Alfie!' I feel the pounding waves through the soles of my shoes. Spray flies into the air in front of him. He's motionless now, facing out to sea.

'Alfie!' I step over the wire fence. He must hear me; we're no more than a couple of metres apart.

'ALFIE!' I dare not move away from the fence. Will's warning about the overhang rings in my ears. More than a metre of the cliff has gone tonight, and I've no idea if what's left will take my weight. I shove the mobile into the pocket of my joggers and grab hold of the post beside me. My heart thunders against my ribs just looking at how close to the cliff edge we are.

'Alfie – can you hear me, Alfie? Just turn around, slowly, walk back to me.'

My son doesn't respond. He stands so still, only the fabric of his clothing rippling across his body in the wind. Beyond him, the sky flares white as lightning rolls towards us above the clouds. The rain is torrential, eating at the cliffs.

'Alfie!' The crack in my voice is not just from running, from shouting myself hoarse, but from fear. I have no idea if he hears me. What choice do I have? I let go of the post and take a step forward. Thunder claps overhead, the sound vibrating through me in a great wave.

'Alfie. For God's sake, turn around.' In my heart, I know he won't move. Something is so wrong with my son. Two more steps and I will be close enough to reach out and touch his back, grab his hand. I close my eyes and take a step forward, my heart pounding so hard it's like the thunder is trapped inside me. 'Alfie.'

Grey sheets of rain are coming inland in waves, the rough grass beside the flagstones, sodden. I inch forward, unable to make myself take a step closer to the edge. Past where Alfie stands, I see the foaming surface of the sea. I look up at the sky. One more shuffle forwards, and I can reach him. Grab his hand and lead him back to the fence. I pray he won't pull us both over the edge.

'Alfie?' I try to sound calm, not to alarm him, as I reach out to touch his shoulder. A colossal wave hammers beneath us, water flying up and over the edge of the cliff. Saltwater stings my eyes, flooding into my nose and mouth. I gasp. The water is so cold. As my vision clears, the flagstone shifts beneath my feet. I grab Alfie's arm, but my fingers only curl into the palm of my own hand.

'Alfie?' He doesn't respond. What the hell happened? I reach out again. Even in this light, I should see the pale skin of his hands, his feet. The ring of flesh between the top of his pyjamas and his wet hair streaming in the wind. 'Alfie? Look at me, Alfie.'

The flagstone tilts. I freeze. Black dots swim across my vision, the ground rocking beneath my feet. I sink to my knees. Waves smash against the foot of the cliff, the earth shuddering beneath me.

'Alfie,' my voice is a whisper, but at last, he responds, his upper body twisting, his shoulders moving as he turns towards me. And a chill cuts through me – his face. There's nothing. No features, no wide smile or green eyes. A dark space where my son's face should be. I recoil, the flagstone rocking beneath me. And then there is nothing – only sea and wind and rain.

No Alfie. No one here. Only the overpowering stench folding around me.

'Evie!' The beam cuts through the air from behind me – a tunnel of light jiggering through the teeming rain. 'EVIE!'

All of me is shaking, my teeth chattering, nausea rising in my throat. The flagstone tilts forward, and for a moment I wonder what Dad and Luke thought when they were here. Did they stop at the edge? Did they know what they were about to do as they took one more step? I stare ahead, look down at the sea writhing below me. The water churns, tugging me forwards. How easy it is to fall. There is nothing left of my boy. No sign that Alfie was here. Was he here? The flagstone rocks backward as spray shoots up, flinging foam high into the air. The water seems to stop. The white droplets suspended in the stream of white light. Motionless. The world unplugged.

'Mom!' Alfie? 'Mom!' I stare at the waves, the battered and bruised sky. Thunder rumbles overhead, lightning forking the horizon.

'MOM!' He's screaming, terror in his voice. Where is he? Where is Alfie? 'Mom!' Sobbing, screaming. His voice is fractured, tossed around me in the wind. Impossible to catch hold of. Is Alfie below here, hanging onto the cliff face, not yet washed out to sea?

'Evie! Evie, move backwards. Slowly move backwards.' Will's voice. Calm, controlled. The flashlight bounces around me. A glimpse of wet grass. A patch of sky.

'Can you hear me, Evie?' Will sounding more urgent.

'MOM!'

The voices are behind me, calling to me and to each other.

Alfie is there? A wave swells towards the cliff, rushing as it grows. A massive wall of water collides with a thunderous crack against ancient soil. Spray spurts high above my head, beating down on me like a million jabbing cold fingers.

I try to move my head. Try to turn, to look back – a glimmer of white faces. A torch streaming light towards me. Will and Jack. The broken pillar pointing at the sky. Alfie.

The stone shifts beneath me, and the earth tilts. I scramble across the flags, my fingers clawing at the slimy rough stone. The fence is metres away. Will stands this side of the post, one hand outstretched, Jack, holding onto his other. Alfie wields the flashlight. It blinds me for an instant and I can't move. Only hear their voices and the wind roaring in my ears.

'Evie – keep moving this way.' I force myself forward, my fingers grabbing at tussocks of grass, the edges between flag-stones. Follow the sound of their voices, moving all the time towards the shivering beam of the flashlight.

'Mom!' Alfie, shrieking, clearer now.

'Evie, keep coming. Almost there.' Will. Someone has the back of my hoody and a hand clamped under my arm, forcing me forward, dragging me to my feet – Jack's voice loud against my ear. I step over the wire fence.

Alfie drops the flashlight. I'm kneeling in mud and water, my arms about him, his head pressed into my neck as his sobs vibrate against my chest.

'We need to keep moving.' Will, dragging Alfie to his feet. Jack pulling me up to stand beside him. 'The whole cliff is unstable.'

'Take the flashlight.' Jack hands the torch to Alfie. 'Lead the way, Alfie, my boy.'

Alfie is nodding and turns towards the pile of stones. Will strides ahead, passing the pillar, Alfie a few steps behind him.

The torch cuts a circle of white light on the ground in front of them.

'Let's get you home, Evie.' Jack's arm is about my shoulders, and I find I can't speak. It's all I can do to muster the energy to follow in Alfie's footsteps. The ground shudders with the force of the water pounding against the cliff-face. The moon glimmers between scudding clouds. I scrunch my eyes against the rain. Hear the scream leave my throat. It's hard to make it out. The pillar, swaying back and forth against the dark sky, chunks of stone breaking. Falling.

'ALFIE!'

Will turns back to stare at me as I tear towards my son. Alfie spins around, his face weirdly white in the glare of the flashlight. His head jerks to look up to the top of the pillar as I reach him. Huge stones topple and fall.

CHAPTER THIRTY-FOUR

THERE'S A SOUND I can't quite place. A murmuring, tinkling noise and a weight on my legs. My feet buzz with pins and needles. The discomfort woke me up. I try to shift them, but I can't. The room comes into focus as I hear scuffling sounds at the door to the hall. Molly peeps around the frame and ducks out of sight.

'She's awake, Mummy!' I hear her feet patter on the boards, the kitchen door banging - muffled voices. I try again to move my legs, and the weight shifts as I push myself up onto my elbow - pain sears through my head. I keep still and wait for it to stop.

Lou's sitting room; a Christmas tree laden with gaudy decorations and paper chains Molly made at school. Jack's fire has burned low, and I wonder what time it is? The curtains are closed behind me, but daylight pokes between the folds. I push back the mound of duvet and a thick blanket, suddenly too warm. Pain pulses behind my eyes, and I sink back down onto my elbow.

Last night. All of it crashes in on me. A dull pain throbs across my hip as I try to drag my foot free. The heap of covers shifts, and Alfie's dark head pops up at the other end of Lou's sofa. His eyes are bleary and he has a livid bruise down the left side of his face.

'Mom.' He crawls across the covers and settles himself against me, his head on my chest. He holds his hag stone in his hand. I lie back, my hand stroking his matted hair and listen to his breathing as he falls back into sleep. What happened last night? Alfie is safe. That's all that matters.

I must doze, too, as Molly stands in front of me holding a tray. Lou coming into the room, a mug in each hand. Alfie's not here.

'You're awake! We bought you some chicken soup. Mummy and me made it especially for you.'

I try to sit up. Alfie's hag stone is caught between the folds of the blanket.

'Where's Alfie?' I say, reaching for the stone.

'In the shower. He's still covered in mud from last night.' Lou perches on the end of the sofa as I sit up and let Molly settle the tray onto my lap. Soup and noodles have slopped out of the bowl and onto the tray. I wonder about suggesting a move into the kitchen, but my head is banging.

'He's all right, but what about you?' Lou looks at the hag stone in my hand. 'You got hit with falling debris. Alfie only smacked his face when you pushed him out of the way.'

'I don't remember much.' Nausea stirs in my stomach, my head thumping.

'Doctor Martin says you'll be okay. Any worries to take you to A&E. Good job he was here and could see you.' A fuzzy recollection of sitting on the sofa last night wrapped in blankets pushes its way back into my mind. Telling a man who I guess was Doctor Martin that I wasn't going to hospital. I was just fine. Lou natters on as Molly hands me the soup spoon. I smile at her and take a sip. Tepid and a bit salty, but actually just what I need.

'Do you like it?'

'It's delicious!' Molly beams at me, turns on her heel and rushes out of the room.

'Alfie's her next victim,' says Lou as she sips her drink. 'What the hell were you doing last night heading outside in that weather, let alone going up to the cliffs?'

'Like I said to Will, Alfie got out of bed . . .'

Lou is shaking her head in that way of hers when she disagrees with what's being said. Deep down in my gut, I know what I'm saying isn't real. What was it I followed onto the cliffs? The blank space, the unending darkness where a face should be . . .

'Alfie turned up here sobbing his heart out, hammering on the front door saying you'd opened the bedroom window at the pub and started shouting for him. He was terrified, poor kid. By the time he was awake and out of bed, you were up the road and out of sight.' Lou takes my hand in hers. I am shaking, my hand, clammy and cold. I can't get the blank face out of my mind. Don't know what to say. 'When the guys caught up with you, you were kneeling on the ground, looking over the cliff edge. Last night was one of the worst storms we've had here in ages.' Lou is watching me intently, waiting for a response. Everything she says is true, but I can't explain it. 'Alfie says there's something at Seahurst.' Lou's eyes hold mine. I can see she's not sure what to say. 'Shadows that watch you?' she tries. Once I feel a bit stronger, maybe I can explain. 'Adam called a few minutes ago to say Seahurst has been sealed off.'

'Did the storm do much damage?' Words finally splutter out of me.

Lou shakes her head. 'It's okay, but the well has to be excavated even though they think the bones are old.' She rubs my hand, and although her skin is soft and warm, I withdraw mine. Can't think.

'Dad's research says Middle Ages . . .' I say, folding my

arms across my chest as I stare back at her. 'A whole family thrown down there . . .'

'We read Marcus's research. Luke's message to you. I'm so sorry, Evie.'

The doorbell shrills, and I jolt the bowl and tray. I'm still strung out. Bone tired.

'Stay there, eat the soup. You're not over last night by a long way.'

Lou heads into the hall. Upstairs, feet thunder about. Alfie and Molly up to no good, no doubt. Lou's speaking to someone at the door. Normal life going on, but I feel weirdly detached from it all; an outsider looking in. Lou's voice gets louder again as she comes back down the hall, the front door slamming. She's talking to a woman, a discussion about tea or coffee. Jenna peeps around the door.

'Are you okay? What a dreadful thing to have happened.'

I manage to smile. My headache is beginning to recede, as long as I keep still. Jenna comes in and sits on the end of the sofa where Lou had been. She's casual today, tight blue jeans, the knee-high black boots and a loose-fitting grey roll-neck beneath a burnt-orange wool coat. Her shiny hair frames her perfectly made-up face. I resist the urge to run my fingers through my matted hair, sticky with sea salt and sand.

'William told me all about it. Thank goodness they got you back safely.'

I don't have any words to answer her. I look down and find the hag stone in the palm of my hand. 'I didn't realise you were here today.' I push the tray away.

'I wanted to pick up a few things and to talk to Louisa.' She looks at me as china clatters in the kitchen. I've only been out of action a few hours, but I get the feeling I'm out of the loop here.

'Didn't Louisa let you know?' Wrack my brains to recall anything relevant Lou might have told me. 'William and I split up a couple of days ago. I'm just picking up a few things I left here from Christmas.'

'Shit, I had no idea. I thought . . .'

Her smile stops me blathering on. 'It's okay. It's been coming for quite a while. With the proposal and all, it might not have seemed that way.' Better to say nothing, let her take it from here. 'Deep down, you know, don't you? That someone loves you less than you love them. Little things give it away. I was always first to suggest how we spend time together, look forward to things with an excitement William didn't have. Don't get me wrong, he's not a bad person, and there's nothing calculated in it, just . . .' She shrugs and smiles, and I can see why Will was attracted to her. 'To be honest, I think he was relieved when I said things were not working for me.' All I can do is stare at her, my mind still confused after last night. 'Anyway, there's someone at work. He's been around a long time. He's a good friend. There's a crowd of us at the uni, you know?' I nod. 'The usual work socials, Christmas party, quiz nights; we went kayaking last year, he organises all that.'

'And looks forward to you going?'

'It's better that way around, don't you think?' I watch her, the crinkle between her perfectly threaded brows deepening. 'Better than always living with the nagging doubt.' I shake my head, not understanding. 'That deep down you're not loved enough, if you know what I mean?'

Does she know about Seth? I suspect she probably does, but then that's a whole different situation.

'He's always talked about you, Evie. Always.' I gape at her, realise I am staring and should say something. 'It's okay, really it is. I always knew, like I said, deep down. It's why, when he said you were coming over to help Luke clear out Seahurst, I suggested we stay on after Christmas for New Year.'

'To meet me?' I say.

'To see how William was around you. As soon as we got here that night for dinner, I knew.'

'He's said nothing to me. Nothing has happened between us.'

She puts her hand over mine as she stands up. 'William's not like that, is he? He's not underhand. Like I said, he's a good guy.' She stops at the door and looks back at me. 'Superstition says they keep you safe and ward off the dead, but I expect you already know that.' She's looking at the stone in my hand. 'I hope you feel better very soon.'

I watch her walk from the room and hear the low buzz of conversation in the kitchen. I had no idea things weren't anything but perfect in her world. I feel sorry she won't be around. I'm not sure what I feel about Will. I turn the hag stone over in my hand. It's the one Alfie's been carrying around for the last few days.

'Can we stay here now until we go back to Canada?' I look up into Alfie's face. I hadn't heard him come in.

'I think that might be best, don't you?'

He nods and smiles. 'Jack's taking us crabbing after lunch.'

'Sounds like everything is fine then,' I say and smile.

FOUR MONTHS LATER

I SQUINT INTO the sunlight and let the salt wind stream through my hair. Around the curve of the bay, the power station shimmers in a mirage of white light. There one minute and gone the next. Alfie and Molly chase along the beach, running to catch up with Jack as he strides ahead. The jet lag passed quickly this time. Maybe staying in town, leaving the meals and cooking to the hotel staff make a difference. Certainly, we slept in late this morning.

'Come on, ginger nut, you'll get left behind!' Lou laughs as she slips her arm through mine. Adam and Will are deep in conversation as they pass us, Will pointing to the head of the bay.

'Less banter, Lou Goodrum,' I say, as we follow our little party. 'The beach is busy today.'

'A bank holiday weekend brings them all out, and the excitement down here makes it worse. Not that . . . I don't mean . . .' Lou's arm tenses against mine, and I glance at her. Her hair is sliding out of its scrunchie, long dark strands stream back from her face.

'It's fine, Lou. We would never go back to Seahurst.'

Water rushes over the toes of our boots, an empty bottle riding the wave getting stranded amongst the dead seaweed and flotsam. I pick it up and put it into the bag Lou holds.

'They get on so well, don't they? Despite the age gap,' she says.

'Adam and Will?'

'You know what I mean, Evie! Molly has been excited for weeks waiting for Alfie to get here.'

Alfie's been counting down the days to the end of term. The date of our flight ringed red on the wall calendar in the tiny apartment kitchen. Was Luke as excited to see me each summer all those years ago? I think he was, just too old to show it. I link arms again with Lou, and we follow the people making their way along the beach.

'You've always been a try-hard, Lou.'

'I'm an optimist!' she says, laughing.

'I'm so glad to see you look so well!' I squeeze her arm with mine. 'Adam seems to have a permanent grin plastered all over his face too.'

'I'll relax once we get the twenty-week scan done.' She stops as I scoop up a bottle top and drop it into the bag. 'It's been great having Dad around to help out. He's kept Molly entertained when I've been knackered.'

'You're better now?'

'Past that stage, thank God. It's helped Dad too. He's been so low again lately.' Further down the beach, Jack has stopped walking and stands looking up at the cliffs. The stump of the Arch is black against a crystal blue sky. Jack had been closed off at Luke's funeral and the days after, lost in his own thoughts, walking the cliff path for hours on his own. Only Alfie's pleas to accompany him night fishing seemed to penetrate the gloom.

'Dad feels responsible for what happened with Luke,' says Lou.

'Did he say that?'

She shakes her head. 'That's the trouble with Dad, he doesn't talk about stuff.'

'He's not to blame, how could he be?' I say. 'He'll feel better after the inquest is out of the way next week. I know I will.'

Lou is staring out to sea. She's far more worried about Jack than she's saying. The light is so bright and the wind cold, my eyes water.

'Marcus, and maybe Luke, spoke to Dad about what was happening at Seahurst. He feels he should have done something.'

'Like what? That's ridiculous, Lou.'

'There won't be anything different from the findings next week than for Marcus. I worry how Dad will cope with that.' Lou's voice is hesitant, her tone softer.

'We know what the hearing will find,' I say. 'It's enough to understand what really happened, even if we can't prove it in court. It's the best we're going to get.' She's watching my face as I speak. I smile at her. I've had weeks to turn all of this over in my mind. As Jack said, you could drive yourself crazy with what might have been. 'It's going to be okay, Lou. I'll talk to Jack.'

Lou holds my gaze for a moment. 'I think it would help.' She looks further along the beach and points up ahead to the Abbey. 'They lowered what's left of the Arch. If we walk back that way later, you'll see the pillar is fenced off now. That whole section is unstable. Will says the next decent storm will take the lot.' We walk in silence for a while, the wind whistling about our heads. Tracks of hard sand make it easier to walk as we leave the deep shingle behind us. 'Will has the day off to take Dad to Ipswich for the inquest. He said you can go with them if you don't want to take Betty that far.'

'I might do that. I don't fancy breaking down halfway there. Although I've arranged to meet Nicola for a coffee beforehand.'

'Things to sort out?'

'I need to let her have Luke's stuff that Jack put to one side when Seahurst got cleared. It'll be good to see her and talk about Luke.'

At first, it was impossible to speak about Luke without triggering a meltdown, but lately it's been much better. I've actually looked forward to Nicola's calls, and we've nattered for ages, way beyond just discussing the practical details for the funeral and inquest. Mum's been great, more help back in Canada than I would ever have thought. She can't understand about Luke, not the same way Nicola does, but she has finally spoken about Seahurst. The terrible sense of dread once the groundworks got started. Dad saying she was irrational. Hormonal and pregnant. Lou kicks at the water as it rushes past us up the beach.

'You must talk to Will while you're here.' I glance at her and realise this is where we've been heading all the time. Adam and Will stand beside Jack, watching us amble towards them. Molly squats beside her castle-shaped bucket as Alfie digs amongst the stones with her tiny pink spade.

'Speak to Will?' I say, as Alfie jumps to his feet.

'Mom!' He hurtles towards us, one hand raised, water spraying in all directions, sparkling in the bright light. 'Look!' He slows down as he nears us and opens his hand. 'Now the magic works for real!' he says, laughing.

'You can never have too much of it,' I say. Alfie runs back towards Molly, yelling for her to come and look at the hag stone.

'Speak to Will about Alfie,' Lou says. I don't immediately reply. Lou looks at me, and I search her expression for clues.

'Did Seth say something?'

'No.' She looks confused. 'It's bloody obvious just to look at Alfie . . .'

Since we returned to Canada, the truth I'd force myself to hide from for so long kept popping into my head. Buried so deep down, I hadn't dared to think about it for years. Almost didn't believe it myself any longer. But Seth's threat that he said something kept niggling away in my head. Had he spoken to Jack? It made it impossible to rebury it all. Not again. Not that I want to now anyway.

'Is he mad about it?' I say.

'Mad? No, he just wants to . . .' Lou shrugs. 'He wants to be involved, Evie. Why wouldn't he? Does Alfie know?' I shake my head – too big a secret to share even with our son. If he had ever let it slip to Seth . . . 'Why didn't you say at the time? Did you know before you left for Canada?'

'Not until I'd been back for a couple of weeks, and then I convinced myself it wasn't happening. By the time I couldn't ignore it any longer, I'd been with Seth for a while. He assumed for a long time, in his arrogant way, that it must be his.' I look at Lou as she stares back at me. 'I didn't put him right about that. As time went on, it became impossible to say anything. Mum, everyone, assumed it was Seth's. Will was at uni, getting on with his life. I didn't think I'd see him again.'

'Does Seth know?' Lou raises her eyebrows.

'He guessed a while back. When Alfie and I flew back to Canada after New Year, he was pretty unpleasant about it, and I guess he had every right to be. He said he'd told Jack when we were here. Said he'd tell Alfie. Turn him against me. I pointed out if he wanted Alfie, he'd have to support him financially. He's made no attempt to be in touch with Alfie or me since, other than through the lawyers sorting out the legal stuff for Maxwells.'

A crowd of people come into view as we walk around the

headland. They stand in front of a section of beach cordoned off below Seahurst. Dog walkers and runners, a few with cameras trained on the JCB currently moving a section of steel framework which was once part of the side of Dad's house. Even the newspapers are here. Jack has Molly on his shoulders, Alfie standing beside them.

Lou tugs at my arm and we stop a few feet back from the crowd. 'Just tell him, Evie. Will's not going to fly off the handle.'

'I know I have to say something. I need to find the right time to speak to Alfie as well. While we're here, away from everything, might be the time to do that.'

We walk to the back of the crowd of onlookers. 'What kept you?' says Adam smiling into Lou's face as he puts his arm around her shoulder.

'They removed the bones from the well about six weeks ago.' Will glances at me, and my stomach flips over at the thought of him knowing about Alfie. 'Once the university has done with them, they'll bury them properly. Jenna will let me know.' I nod as I watch the JCB slowly back away from Seahurst towards the track. 'They'll salvage as much as they can. Recycle metal and stone.'

'How long before the land goes?' I ask. Luke had worried so much about the cliffs eroding.

'It depends on what storms we get, the direction of the wind and the tide. Probably a year, maybe as much as five years. They can't risk all of that falling onto the beach.'

'It's not a problem for me, that's for sure,' I say, turning away. I walk past the crowd and continue around the curve of the bay. Although I would never want to go back there, I can't bear to watch it being torn down. I pull in a deep breath, push my hands into my pockets and find the hag stone. My fingers curl around it as I walk to where the waves spread white, popping foam across the sand.

'You okay?' Will stops just behind me.

'Fine.' I can't turn to look at him. My eyes are hot, my throat closing up. I hadn't expected it to affect me so much. Stupid. I should have seen it coming.

'We can walk a bit if you don't want to hang around here. The others will soon catch us up.' Will steps forward to stand beside me and puts his elbow out towards me. I thread my arm through his. We walk with the wind in our faces, gulls screaming and diving overhead.

'Lou says I've got to speak to you anyway.' Will is looking straight ahead as he speaks, towards where the cliffs slip lower, and the land flattens out to marsh and sky.

'Does she?' I say, a knot twisting in my chest. I'd assumed I'd have some time to think this through. Decide exactly what I need to say.

'She was nagging me to speak to you at New Year. You know how she can't wait two minutes.' I risk a glance at his profile, no clue what might be coming next. He's frowning against the wind and harsh light, looking down at stony sand. He could be thinking anything. 'But it didn't seem right then. Jenna had just broken off the engagement.' He glances at me, then back to the beach. I resist the temptation to say something, wait for Will to carry on. Unlike his sister, things take time with him. 'Jenna said she saw you when she picked up a few things?'

'Only briefly.'

'I felt a bit shit about it all, to be honest, and it didn't feel right talking to you right after that.' A seagull swoops low, its shadow undulating across the sand. It lands a few feet ahead of us on a mound of tangled string and flotsam. It pecks at the pile as a second bird lands beside it, jostling and flapping its wings. 'You needed time to get over your night adventure up on the cliffs.' Will glances at me, a smile curving his lips. 'And then you were back to Canada. You can imagine, though, Lou wasn't impressed with any of those excuses.'

'Patience isn't her thing.' I try to make my laugh sound light. I'm not sure I manage to.

'I said you needed to go back and sort things out in Canada first. You seemed pretty clear things with Seth were done, but I guess I needed to be sure.' His eyes hold mine and I find I can't look away. 'I said to Lou, you didn't need anything else right then. Now's different, right?' Will looks back at the beach as the gulls scream at each other. 'Lou says I got the wrong idea about us that last summer.'

The gulls abandon the tug-of-war over a rotting fish head and soar skywards as we near them.

'I think we both did. I was so sure your talk of university meant you didn't want me hanging around.' We walk in silence for a while, and I wonder what he is thinking. How did we get it so wrong?

'Have you made any plans?' I hear the uncertainty in his voice.

'Seth's keeping Maxwells, which is fine. I need a new project and always wanted something that focused on sustainability.'

'Surely you're not saying Seth is just about the money?' Will's laugh sounds like him for the first time.

'What can you mean?' I say, laughing. 'A place that's not solely vegan or vegetarian, but good food sustainably sourced and prepared. I think a small place here would do well, don't you?'

He's nodding. 'The tourists would go for something like that; locals too, I would think.'

Molly yells at Alfie, water spraying all around them as they run past us. I glance back along the beach. Lou holds Adam's hand as he chats to Jack. I smile at them, Jack raises his hand as he smiles back. Beyond them, I look at Seahurst for the last time. The side of the house is open to the elements; the kitchen so tiny from here, the sofas have long gone, just an empty space at the heart of the room, the metal banister winking in the sunlight as it curves out of sight into the lower ground floor. Dad had been so proud of his last big project.

'It looks like a doll's house,' I say, hearing the catch in my voice.

Will squeezes my hand as I squint against the bright light. The broken Arch rises from the cliff, and for a moment, a shadow lingers about its great stone feet, then there is nothing but old stones, cliffs and a wild, white sky.

THE END

ACKNOWLEDGMENTS

MY THANKS AND gratitude go to the following people. My parents and Aunt Bet for trips to the Suffolk coast when I was a child. Picnics on the heath and holidays in a beach hut kindled the earliest steps on my journey to Seahurst. Phil Johnson and Jon Blunket, *Seahurst's* first readers. I've asked you to reread drafts so many times. Thank you both. Andrew McDonnell for hosting our writing group when Covid lockdown rules allowed and for his encouragement when the novel was a bunch of half-formed ideas. My agent, Jo Williamson, for her faith in the story and my writing. Friends and writers Lynsey White and Jane Appleton, your opinions on all things writing are invaluable. None of it would be so much fun without you cheering me on. Thank you to Salt Publishing for turning my story into a book and to Chris and Jen Hamilton-Emery for all you do. Lastly, to my daughter Emily, for your brilliant ideas. *Seahurst* would have been a different story without them.